I, ANNA

ELSA LEWIN

This book is dedicated to
my sons Michael and Daniel
with love

A complete catalogue record for this book can be
obtained from the British Library on request

The right of Elsa Lewin to be identified as the author of this work has been
asserted by her in accordance with the Copyright,
Designs and Patents Act 1988

First published in 1984 by The Mysterious Press, New York

First published in 1990 by Serpent's Tail

First published in this edition in 2012 by Serpent's Tail
an imprint of Profile Books Ltd
3A Exmouth House
Pine Street
London EC1R 0JH
www.serpentstail.com

ISBN 978 1 84668 830 0
eISBN 978 1 84765 796 1

Printed and bound by CPI Group (UK) Ltd., Croydon CR0 4YY

10 9 8 7 6 5 4 3 2 1

MIX
Paper from
responsible sources
FSC® C020471

Prologue: One

There is something I'm trying to remember. It keeps slipping away, gliding in and out of my consciousness, like the moon tantalizing the clouds. It shows itself, glittering cruelly, beautiful and evil, and then slips furtively away, out of sight, leaving darkness and confusion. Leaving fear.

Maybe if there were someone to talk to . . .

It's Sunday.

I'm not sure I know why I'm talking into this tape recorder. It belongs to my daughter Emmy. Maybe I just want to talk to someone, and there is no one. I don't have any women friends anymore. Maybe I never did. It doesn't matter. You lose your friends when you lose your husband. Maybe you drop them yourself. Life becomes different.

But I need someone to talk to. I think something is happening to me. I don't know what it is. I don't know how it will end. I want someone to understand. I don't ask for forgiveness. I don't forgive myself. But I would like someone to understand.

If someone understands, it might be proof that I lived. That I mattered. I was a person in pain. And I mattered.

I, Anna.

1

Chapter One

Anna opened her eyes. Mean gray light intruded around the sides of the window shades. She closed her eyes tight. "Shit. I'm still alive. . . ."

She tried to concentrate on her two big problems.

One: She had to get out of bed.

Two: She had to decide what to do after that.

His name darted into her head. Suddenly. As though it had been lurking there all along, ready to pounce.

Simon.

It took all her strength . . . everything . . . to get herself out of bed.

The drapes were open in the living room. She went over to the window. It was going to rain. Some insane child had scribbled furiously in black crayon on the dirty sky. In the deserted street the wind hustled a piece of newspaper. It tumbled and flopped, struggling hopelessly.

She closed the drapes. Off-white, brocade, once elegant. She had brought them with her from the house. They didn't belong in this living room with Emily's sofa bed still open and rumpled.

The motor of the refrigerator stopped in the kitchen. When she heard it stop, she realized it had been going. She hadn't been aware of it until it stopped. There was no other sound in the room.

"The motor of the world has stopped," she thought. She said it aloud, to hear something, and realized she was talking to herself. It frightened her.

She peered out into the street from the side of the drape. The street was empty. Even the wind had left. There were only the brooding clouds.

Maybe the world was coming to an end. She laughed. The sound seemed to crack against the silence.

Nothing moved in the room. Nothing breathed.

"Maybe I'm dead." Maybe the auto accident two months ago had been successful and she was dead.

No. No such luck. There were dishes in the sink. Emily's dishes from last night. And a pair of Emmy's jeans and underpants and a sweater on the floor. Emmy's things.

"It would be just my luck to die and take my daughter's dirty laundry with me."

The stillness surrounded her—huge, dense, cutting her off from the world. She couldn't breathe. She listened for a sound: a car horn in the street, a faint screech of tires, footsteps in the hall. It was an old building. The walls were thick. The windows were closed. There was no sound.

Maybe she was buried. Buried like the pharaohs with their belongings. Did they bury the pharaohs with dirty dishes?

The silence gripped her, held her immobile. She thought about turning on the radio, and shuddered at the thought of the relentless cheer of the announcers, the bright, brisk voices reporting arson and murder and inflation and the next world war. Television. Maybe. She would have to climb over the sofa bed. For what?

She could do the dishes and make the bed. But that always made Emmy mad.

"Why do you have to make my bed? What difference does it make if it's made or not? Who comes to see it?"

"I see it. It's so messy. It's depressing."

"You're depressing! Hasn't that stupid shrink done anything for you!"

Ah yes . . . the stupid shrink. What had she done for her? Well, she had talked to Anna a lot. Made her the recipient of all the wisdom of a liberated thirty-year-old. Without benefit of bra. "You don't *want* to be your own person!" The poor girl's eyes had opened wide. Anna had worried that the contact lenses would pop out.

"My own person is married to the same man for thirty years. Forever. My own thing is growing old together. . . ." But Anna didn't say it. The shrink wouldn't have heard. The distance between them was too great.

It didn't matter. Anna wasn't seeing her anymore.

"I don't mind making the bed, Emmy."

"I mind!" Shouting. Emmy always seemed to be shouting lately. They used to get along so well, before.

The silence crept closer. It crept up to her ankles, to her knees, to her throat. She was drowning in it.

She stood motionless, her body rigid. If she stood still long enough, if she didn't move, could she turn to stone?

She'd make a gorgeous statue: Middle-aged lady with rumpled nightgown and unkempt hair.

The thing to do was to live AS IF. As if she had a reason to have breakfast, shower, get dressed. As if it mattered.

His name sneaked into her head. Again. Simon.

"God, what did I do wrong?"

Prologue: Two

It looked like rain all day. The sky was dark. In the rain the apartment closes in on me. A one-bedroom apartment with a sleep couch in the living room for Emmy and a narrow, windowless space for a kitchen area. I can't get used to living in an apartment.

By late afternoon there was no cleaning or laundry left to do. I didn't know when, or if, Emmy was going to come home. She isn't home much. She doesn't like the apartment, either. I guess she doesn't like me. She used to. She blames me.

The silence was oozing back. I looked in the Metropolitan Almanac and found a party. A Singles' Party.

It was drizzling slightly when I left the apartment, so I took my raincoat and umbrella. When I got to the bridge, it was raining so hard I couldn't see. The car kept skidding on the slippery grids. I fantasized that a huge truck lost control and smashed into me, and I hit my head on the windshield and my car skidded off the bridge into the river and I was killed. But I knew it wouldn't happen. I wasn't lucky.

I had trouble finding a place to park. I was wearing high-heeled, open-toed shoes and my feet got wet. My umbrella wasn't much good. It was a cheap, clear yellow plastic. The shaft, right below the handle, was split. I had to hold it by the metal, past the split, instead of by the handle, or it wobbled and flopped over. I was cold and I was afraid in the dark, wet streets in Manhattan. And I was nervous. I was always nervous at these singles' things, and angry at myself for going to them. I felt humiliated for being in this position. When I got to the party, I asked the man at the door if I could look in before I paid, but he said no, I couldn't do that. There were too many people in there, he said, and he couldn't have people running in and out without paying. So I knew right away it couldn't be much good, because if it were he wouldn't care if I looked in. Then I asked him what the ratio was and he said he didn't know. I said, "You're out here selling admissions!" He said he was too busy to see who was going in. I said, "You know if they're men or women, don't you?" and I laughed because I was embarrassed to sound angry, and I said flirtatiously, "I guess you can tell the difference between men and women."

He said, "Vive la différence," and laughed, and I made myself laugh too so I shouldn't seem like a bitter woman. No one likes a bitter woman. He said, "There's maybe . . . oh . . . four men to three women or three men to two women. Something like that. What difference does it make? It only takes one to be the right one for you."

Ask a stupid question and you'll get a lying answer, Anna. But it was raining and it was a long ride back and I had my makeup on. And what was there back in the empty apartment?

I paid my seven dollars and left my umbrella near some others in the hall and went in.

It was crowded. Smokey. A one-bedroom apartment. A nervous-looking woman was asking everyone to wipe their feet outside. Fat Louise was in the foyer. It was one of her parties. Louise ran a lot of parties. She lived in my town, the town I used to live in when I was married and had the house.

There were maybe eight men and about thirty women jammed into the living room. There was a bridge table against the wall with one plate of sliced cucumbers and some raw carrots and one dish of potato chips and a gallon bottle of cheap wine and a big bottle of ginger ale. No ice.

I took a paper cup of ginger ale so I could have something to hold on to while I looked around.

There was nothing much to see. It was the usual scene. No one I had actually met before, but I could have met them, and I knew I would meet them again: the men, mostly overweight, surveying the room, looking like they had toothache; the women looking lonely.

I went to the bathroom to comb my hair. It was a delaying tactic, before I had to face the party. The bathroom door was locked. I waited and then I knocked. I heard giggling from inside, and voices, and after a while a man and three women came out, hanging on to each other and giggling. They were high. The bathroom smelled from pot. I told myself the kids didn't have a monopoly on it, but I was shocked anyway. Weren't we really too old for this? All of it? What was I doing here? What was anyone doing here?

I combed my hair quickly and looked at myself in the mirror on the bathroom door. I wondered how I looked. I didn't really know. For twenty-eight years I had depended on Simon to tell me how I looked. Now I didn't know.

I was wearing fitted black slacks, a white body suit, a silver belt, and silver earrings. Nothing new. Nothing fashionable. But it showed off my figure, I suppose. I suppose my figure isn't bad. At least I'm not fat. Simon always hated fat. I have blue eyes and blonde hair. (I help out nature with my hair.) And wrinkles. I'm fifty.

I came back to the refreshment table and leaned against the back of a sofa and tried to look cheerful. Casual. Not anxious. Not desperate. Men don't like desperate women. Finally I went over to some man. I said, "Hi. Have you ever been here before?"

He was about twenty pounds overweight and had eyeglasses and crooked teeth. He was wearing a badly fitted checked polyester suit. Well, if he were handsome and rich and intelligent and charming, why would he have to come to one of these parties?

I asked him whether he was divorced or widowed. Widowed. He told me about his children, how smart they were, and he told me about his house. He told me all about himself and never asked a single question about me. It was mostly I was asking him questions and he was answering them, so he wasn't interested and I should have stopped before I did. Another woman kept cutting in to talk to him, too, but he wasn't interested in her, either. It's hard to start a conversation, and it's harder to stop. But finally I gave up and walked away.

Then two men came in. One of them was a tall, burly man without a tie. He was wearing a rumpled dark brown suit with a button missing. His face and his neck were sweaty, and he kept flapping his elbows as though he were trying to get some air under his jacket. His nylon shirt looked wet and pasted to his skin. His friend was short and chubby and had restless eyes and a pig face. I forget how we started to talk. I suppose I used that usual gambit of mine: "Have you ever been here before?" Something brilliant like that. I'm not good at small talk. They said they had just come from Tuxedo Junction on Long Island. I said I had never been to Tuxedo Junction or any other singles' bar, that I was too scared; and they said it was like any other bar, very crowded and people standing around looking each other over. Then I asked why were they there tonight—was something special going on? They said it was one of the stops on the way.

I guess they make lots of stops. What are they looking for? They're over fifty, both of them, one divorced, one never married. I guess what they're looking for isn't looking for them. The short one hardly talked at all. Mostly, he jiggled his leg as his eyes scanned the room, appraising. The big one said he was a teacher. I asked him what he teaches and he said art. I said that was interesting. I had wanted to be an artist before I got married. He had trouble hearing me. The room wasn't noisy. I guess he wasn't listening. He kept saying "What?" and pulling his eyes back from their searching, and I'd repeat my silly questions and he'd mumble his answer. I finally said, "I think I'll get something to eat. Excuse me."

Correct

There was a thin, bald man at the refreshment table. He said, "There's nothing to eat. Only some potato chips."

"They had some cucumbers before."

"This is a chintzy party," he said. "Other parties they have more to eat. They should have more for seven dollars than a couple of potato chips."

"They have all of us lovely women," I said.

"That Louise will kill the golden goose if she don't serve more than this," he said.

That about exhausted the topic. I moved off. Another woman came over and he complained to her. I noticed the art teacher was talking to a dark woman in a low-cut silk blouse. She had thick, shoulder-length, wavy black hair. A younger woman. Pretty. Expensive blouse. They were laughing. He didn't seem to have a hearing problem with her.

The place had emptied out a little. People had moved on. There were other parties. Dances. Another seven dollars, or ten, or more. I couldn't afford to go to more than one. And I'd probably meet the same people who had left this one. All of us running in circles.

Louise came over and asked me if I could drive her home. I said didn't she remember that I didn't live on her block anymore. I lived in Queens. She said it wasn't much out of the way. Ten minutes. And what was the rush to get home? "What's waiting for you there?"

It was really twenty minutes. Each way, there and back. But she was right; there was no rush. There was nothing waiting for me.

I said all right, only I wanted to leave very soon. I was tired. She said could I wait until 10:30. It was 9:30 then. I wasn't happy about it. I really wanted to leave that minute and I knew that if she said 10:30, she really meant 11:30 at the earliest because she always stayed till the end. It's her party. She gets people to let her use their homes and they get a percentage of the door.

A fat young woman, thirtyish, appeared and said, "Isn't this party boring?"

I said, "Yes."

She said, "It's really boring."

I was going to say yes again, but I thought about it and I said, "It's not boring. It's disappointing."

She bristled. "If you expect to meet a knight on a white horse at these things, you'll be disappointed."

"A horse of any color would look strange in this apartment," I said.

She glared at me. "It's nice if you enjoy your own jokes."

If I didn't, who would? There was a time when Simon thought I was funny. Why was I thinking about him so much today?

"It's all so meaningless," the girl said.

"That's life," I said gently, I thought, because I felt sorry for her.

She turned away angrily and stalked off. I watched her. She was turned out right; tight designer jeans, silk blouse, high-heeled step-ins, hoop earrings. But it didn't come off. Something was wrong. It was as though someone had dressed her in clothes that were the right size but didn't belong to her. A costume for a play in which she was miscast. Did I look like that?

I felt someone behind me reaching around and touching the underpart of my breasts, stealthily. I turned. It was Hy. I moved out of his reach. "Hello, Hy. How are you?"

"Fine. Great. How are you, Alice?"

I didn't correct him. He got the first initial right anyway. Inexplicably, I thought of the game the girls used to play with a ball when we were kids: "A"—my name is Anna and my sister's name is Alice and we come from Alabama and we sell apples. "B"—my name is Bertha and my sister's name is Betty and we come from Birmingham . . ." Was I getting hysterical? "How's your friend Sam?"

"He moved to Massachussetts. He got a good job."

Sam had said, "If this is a one-night stand, it's your fault, Anna."

Everything else is; why not that, too? How do you tell a man that you don't like the taste of his mouth?

"Say hello for me. Anna. Say Anna says hello."

But Hy was gone. It didn't matter. I would see him again. He appeared everywhere. He had this thing about breasts. He was always trying to feel them. You couldn't tell at first. He'd sit next to you, or stand close, too close, and talk, and move his hands, and they would touch you lightly, and then again. It was only after you shrank away and his hands followed that you realized. He was probably sixty years old. Older maybe. Distinguished looking. Silver hair. Stocky. Medium height. Well-dressed. He ran singles' functions for various charities. Expensive parties. Twenty-five dollars; thirty-five. I couldn't afford them.

The living room was fairly empty by then. Louise was talking to some women near the door, making no move to leave. I found a chair and sat down and thought again about going home. It wasn't an exciting thought. It was no more meaningful than not going home.

Then this man came in and sat in a chair across the room and lit a cigarette. He was smallish and very slim, and he wore tight-fitting designer jeans. His kinky salt-and-pepper hair was combed straight back and reached his shirt collar. He looked up from lighting his cigarette. His eyes were restless.

There was something familiar about him. I smiled at him. He smiled back. He had a puckish, childlike smile; the corners of his mouth turned up, making his mouth a crescent.

He got up and I slid over and made room for him in the chair with me. It was a big chair. There was plenty of room for both of us.

I had never met him before. I didn't know him. But he looked familiar. I told him he looked familiar. It wasn't just something to say.

"Yeah," he said with wonder, drawing out the word. "Yeah. You look familiar to me, too, man. . . ."

"It sounds like a line, doesn't it?" I laughed.

"No . . . no, man. . . ." He smiled. He kept the smile on his face for a long time, as though he were posing or waiting for something. I wondered if I had known him before he had the nose job. "I have to stop saying that," he said. "I have to stop saying man all the time."

"I didn't notice," I said.

"Yeah?"

"It's OK." I said.

I smiled and he smiled and I leaned back and looked at him and he looked at me and the smile began to hurt on my face. I said, "Have you ever been here before? I mean . . . these parties?"

"Oh, sometimes . . ."

His eyes slid away from me. Were we all ashamed of being here?

"Do you live in Manhattan?" I said.

"Oh yeah. Yeah. Manhattan. That's where it's at."

His eyes were back on my face again. They were slightly bloodshot. "Nice," he said. "You're nice, man. . . ."

"Thanks." I meant it.

"Do you have a nice apartment?" I asked.

"Great. I've got a fantastic view of the river. I'm only on the ninth floor. It's not the penthouse."

"It's easier if the elevator breaks down," I said.

"Yeah." He looked at me thoughtfully, speculatively. Then he smiled approval. I smiled back.

"I wish I could move to Manhattan. But it's too expensive."

"Not my place. It's rent-stabilized. $685 a month. But they're talking of going co-op. You know how much my apartment would be? $100,000. But I would get a discount because I live there. Sixty thou. I could sell it the next day for $100,000. Forty thou profit in a blink."

"But then where would you live?"

"Yeah," he breathed. "Yeah." His face lit up with his puckish smile. "And I don't have sixty thou." He lit another cigarette.

"*My son just moved in with me, that's the thing. I mean, it's a one-bedroom. But I couldn't tell him no.*"

"*Of course not,*" I said.

We were talking. We were really talking. A two-way conversation. He didn't look bored. I felt relief and gratitude. I was excited. I leaned back in the oversized chair. He sat with his legs curled under him, facing me. He was listening to me.

"*You're divorced,*" I said.

"*Yeah.*"

"*Long?*"

"*I got the divorce this year. We've been separated eight years. You?*"

"*Almost two years. Eight years is a long time to be alone.*"

"*I've had two relationships,*" he said.

"*Meaningful relationships?*" *He didn't hear me. Maybe I didn't say it.*

"*I only have relationships,*" he said. "*I don't screw around. I never screw around. I used to screw around when I was married.*"

I said, "Oh," sympathetically. I wondered what I was doing here. Why was I talking to his man?

"*I broke up my last relationship a few months ago. When I got the divorce.*"

"*She wanted to get married,*" I said.

"*Yeah.*" *He smiled.* "*But it was more than that. I mean, we had a lot of things going for us, and a lot of things we didn't. I mean . . . we're really different. But I like her. She's an artist. She's still my friend.*"

"*Are you friends with your wife, too?*"

"*Oh, I hate her. I mean . . . she's such a bitter person.*"

"*You got the children?*"

"*Oh no. My son decided to live with me a few months ago. He doesn't get along with his mother.*"

"*She doesn't understand him,*" I said. "*She's old-fashioned.*"

"*Yeah.*" *He smiled.* "*Yeah. . . .*" *His face lit up with his smile. His happy smile.*

I leaned my head back against the chair and closed my eyes. I thought about going home.

"Let's split," he said.

I hesitated. But he had gotten up. I got up too. "I promised to take someone home," I mumbled.

He didn't hear me.

"Where do you live?" he asked.

"Queens," I said. Then I said, "I used to have a house."

"I had a house," he said. "When I was married. My wife got it."

"You didn't fight her for it?"

"It was in her name. For business reasons. Anyway, I didn't want to change the kids' lives too much."

Ah, please accept the Father of Year Award. What was I doing with this man? He put on his coat. Brown leather. Designer jeans, tailor-fitted. Western shirt. Frye boots. Longish hair. No gold chain? Out of uniform, soldier! Two demerits!

I got my red poplin raincoat. I was uncomfortably aware that there was a line at the bottom where I had let down the hem.

The apartment was almost empty. Most people had packed up their disappointment and gone. There were only a few clumps of women left, talking to each other.

Louise was in the open hallway talking to two men who must have arrived late. I said, "Louise, I'll be back soon."

She didn't answer. I wasn't sure she had heard me. I thought she saw me, though, and she looked annoyed. I'm not sure. Maybe she didn't notice me. She seemed more interested in the two men. Maybe I was only feeling guilty and embarrassed. I wondered if I should be leaving with this man. I wondered if I would be back in time to take Louise home.

In the elevator, the man said, "Did you come by car?"

"Yes. Did you?"

"No. I have a car, but it's in the garage. It's a hassle to get it out. I cabbed it."

The elevator light was harsh. It made me feel exposed. I felt he could see every wrinkle. He seemed uncomfortable, too, and that made me feel better about him.

Outside, he said, "The rain stopped." It reminded me I had left my umbrella. I thought of not going back for it. I didn't want to inconvenience this man, a stranger, by asking him to wait for me. But I had lost so many umbrellas this year. And gloves. I could hear Emmy say, "If you're so hung up on how broke we are because Daddy doesn't give us any money, why don't you quit wasting money losing umbrellas and gloves and God knows what else." And husbands. She left that out. How come you couldn't hold on to your husband? She blames me, I know. I lost her father and spoiled her life. Daughters usually blame their mother.

I said I had to go back for my umbrella.

It was up on the third floor. It was easier and faster to walk up than to wait for the elevator. I walked. I noticed that Louise was still in the hallway.

I came back to the street, breathless and perspiring. I was surprised to see him waiting for me. I didn't know if I was pleased or disappointed.

The rain had stopped, but it was windy and cold. I stepped in an icy puddle. We walked fast, without touching, against a hooting wind. Why was I doing this? Why was I going with this man? We passed the car and had to turn around and go back to find it. "I get mixed up," I said. "I don't have this car long. I cracked up my other car a couple of months ago."

"That's heavy," he said. "That's real heavy. . . ."

I opened the passenger door and he got in. I walked around to the driver's seat. I wondered if he would reach over and open the door for me from inside. He didn't. I stepped in another puddle while I fiddled with the lock.

I could always drop him off at his apartment and say, "Hey, man, good night. See you around. . . ." and go on home. To what?

If I couldn't park easily, I'd do that. Leave.

There was a parking spot right in front of his building. It was like an omen.

The rain had started again. I took my umbrella. Inside the lobby, he waved to the doorman at his desk, and kept on walking. The doorman didn't look at me. The lobby was shabby, and so was the elevator. The carpet in the narrow upstairs hallway was worn and spotted. It looked like a carpet in a revolving doors motel. Had I missed the sign that said: WATER BED. COLOR TV. VACANCY?

The paint on his door was chipped. As he unlocked the two locks, he mumbled something about excusing the mess; since his woman wasn't coming anymore, the place was not right. I didn't know which woman, his second relationship or a cleaning woman. Maybe they were one and the same. Men are only interested in liberating women in bed. Everything else they want pegged at about 1890.

The door opened right onto his view of the river. It was only a view of the river. Nothing special. Water and lights and cars on the highway alongside it. Nicer than the courtyard my apartment looked out on, of course, but nothing special. Not like looking out of your window and seeing your own lawn, with a big old sycamore, and in the spring, forsythia and lilacs and azaleas and hyacinth. And in the summer, roses.

His son came out of a door on the right. He was wearing only jockey shorts. He was pudgy and his skin was very white. He looked like he ate too much junk food. When he saw me, he looked guilty, and said quickly, "I was just leaving, I'm almost ready," and raced back to the bedroom before I could say anything, before I could apologize for being there, and leave.

I put my umbrella in a corner near the door and moved to the window. It was raining hard again. I looked out at the cars racing purposefully through the wet, dark night. Cars always seemed to move purposefully from a distance, as though they were going someplace important. How many of the drivers were brain surgeons rushing to save someone's life? How many of them were scurrying off to cheat on their wives?

He had hung up our coats and he was very busy in the kitchen, mostly opening closets and drawers and closing them again. He asked me what I'd like to drink.

"An egg cream?" I mumbled hopefully.

"What?"

"You never lived in Brooklyn."

"Oh yeah . . . yeah . . . all my life, man. Till I split. Flatbush. Let's see, what've I got?" He seemed to have found the liquor cabinet, a low metal closet under a spotted toaster oven that looked like it was out of order.

"White wine," I said. I know the fashions.

"White wine," he mused. He stared into the cabinet. He seemed nervous, confused. Then he pulled out a bottle and fished in another closet and found a wineglass.

The wine tasted like vinegar. I thought I tasted dust, too. The stem and the stand of the glass felt grimy. He sat near me at the table with his own drink and asked solicitously if the wine was all right. Did I like it? I said it was fine.

I was touched by his concern. Why am I ashamed of it? I was grateful for his interest. It had been so long. . . .

He smiled, his lips turned up into a half-circle. He leaned toward me. Our knees touched. He plucked the name tag off my blouse as though it were a bug, and smiled brightly, pleased with himself.

I was suddenly embarrassed by the tag. "Anna," he said, and smiled again, as though he had performed a great trick.

He wasn't wearing a tag. I didn't know his name.

I didn't know his name. What was I doing here?

Oh, Anna, come off it. You know what you're doing here. You're being not alone. You're sitting with someone and your knees are touching; you feel someone else's flesh. A person is smiling at you, and his smile erases, for that moment, the pathetic aging lines around your mouth. You hear a human voice, not an electronic sound out of a box, addressing itself to you, to you personally, only to you.

You're feeling sorry for yourself is what you're doing, Anna, and it feels damn good.

19

I asked him his name and he said, "George," with surprise, as though he had told me before, and I laughed and said, "Oh yes," as though I had momentarily forgotten.

"How long were you married, George?"

"Twenty years. You?"

"Twenty-eight. And your wife got the children to raise by herself?"

"She got a lot of bread."

"She did?"

"I had it. I was pulling in seventy, eighty thou in those days." He smiled again. His face lit up as though he were turning on a light inside himself. "I had my own firm. I was an accountant." He waited; it was a dramatic pause. "An accountant! Would you believe it?"

"No. Never," I said. But I did. I believed it. Simon was an accountant.

He smiled again, proud of the surprise he thought he had sprung on me. "But now the girls are out of the house," he said. "Stevie is with me. I stopped paying her. She took me to court, the bitch."

I said, "She told the judge she had no skills. She had married straight out of high school, because she loved you so much. And you had children right away, and she kept house and had no way of earning a living."

"Yeah. . . ." he breathed. "I got a lawyer. It cost me. You wouldn't believe how much. I'm going to be paying him for years."

"But you won't be paying her," I said. "You won. The courts have changed. Women don't get it all anymore."

He smiled, looking very pleased with himself. I giggled. It was better than screaming.

His son came back into the room. He was wearing a tee shirt that had big black letters that said PHUCK. He can't spell, I thought, and suppressed another giggle. I suppose the wine was getting to me.

· *The boy walked past us to the kitchen. The back of his tee shirt had a picture of a cannabis plant. His body looked as if it were made of Play-Doh, and if you stuck your finger into it at any place, it would be mushy. Push-ups, not pot, that's what he needs. It made me feel better to think it.*

He was trying to avoid looking at us. He went into the kitchen and felt around in a closet and came out with a white plastic spray jar with a red top, the kind of thing one might use to spray clothes for ironing. He filled it with water and sprayed his hair. He had long, kinky black hair, thin and dirty-looking.

I asked what he was doing, mostly to make conversation. He said he was wetting his hair. I said, "What for?" and he said, "It makes it curly."

I said, "It's cold outside. If you go out with a wet head, you'll get sick," knowing it was none of my business. But he was a teenager. Sixteen or seventeen. And I was a worrier.

He didn't answer me. He put down the plastic jar and fluffed his hair with his fingers, and then he searched in the closet some more and took out a shoe box. He said, "George?" and held up two fingers. His father nodded, and the kid said, "Thanks," and left.

George followed him to the door and slammed it hard. "Something is wrong with the lock. It doesn't catch by itself," he said.

I felt guilty; the kid was leaving because of me. I asked, "Where's he going?"

He looked vague. "A friend . . ." he said. He had finished his drink. He tapped mine, and I said, "No, thank you." He went to the kitchen closet and came back with the shoe box. He put it on the table and opened it. There was a rectangular package wrapped in foil, about the size of a stick of margarine, inside. He picked it up and fingered it, probing, looking serious. Then he smiled, satisfied. "That's good shit," he said. "Clean. That's a lot of bread there."

"How much?"

"Two, maybe three bills. I mean, it's clean, man. . . ." He smiled again. "It could bring a lot of bread."

21

"Let 'em eat cake," I said.

He didn't hear me. He put the package back into the box. There was another, loosely closed foil package and a packet of Bambu. The bottom of the box had a sprinkling of tiny grayish-brown leaves. He pulled out two papers from the Bambu and opened the loosely wrapped foil. It contained the same tiny leaves as the bottom of the box. Carefully, meticulously, he sprinkled some leaves into the paper, rolled it, twisted the ends closed. I watched him. I had never seen this done up close before. I watched with fascination and fear and guilt. I felt as if there were a waterfall in my head, rushing and pounding . . . a terrifying roar. I'm fifty years old. It was the first time I had come close to the thing that every fifteen-year-old in America is encouraged to accept casually. A way of life. The Great Painkiller. I had seen teenagers turning on in the streets of Manhattan while bored policemen turned their eyes away.

I said, "Does your son know you have this?"

"Yeah. We share. He can always take it, so long as he lets me know. He took two joints when he left." He held up two fingers, the way the boy had, and smiled his puckish smile. "We're friends. That's why he can't live with his mother."

I traced a square in the air with my fingers and he smiled. "Yeah. . . ."

My hands began to shake. To hide it, I picked up the empty glasses and brought them to the sink and washed them and left them in the drain to dry. The sink and the drain were full of dishes. When I came back, he held out the lumpy joint. I hesitated, understanding how the kids must feel. If I didn't take it, I would get my coat and go home. To the silence.

I took it. The lingering taste of the dusty, grimy glass on my lips made me feel slightly nauseated. That, and the guilt. And revulsion. And curiosity.

My head began to hurt.

The roses in my garden had been so beautiful. I had devoted so many hours to them. When I lost the house, I dug up the roses and threw them out. It was like killing my children.

Simon said it was petty. "She is petty," he told Emily. "A bitch. Middle-class values."

Right, Simon. I have middle-class values. Even when I can't afford them.

I had tried to kill myself. In the car. What could be more middle-class than suicide?

George lit the joint. I took a deep breath, the way I had seen it done in the movies. All those explicit movies that the kids could learn from. And I waited. Nothing happened. I must be doing it wrong.

"George, you won't believe this, but I've never used pot before."

"No shit!"

I nodded.

"Wow, man!"

I was embarrassed, as though I were still a virgin. At fifty.

"Inhale deep," he said. "Swallow it. Hold it in. It's not like a cigarette."

Did I dare to tell him I didn't smoke cigarettes either?

I watched him inhale. Deep. Slow. Easy.

"It's all the way to your toes," I said.

He nodded, smiling his crescent smile.

I tried again, breathing in deep. Slow. Down the hatch. Alley-oop. This one is for the brave new world. You've come a long way, baby.

I waited, expecting to feel something. Expecting to float. No more worries. No more fears. No more Simon lurking in the shadows of my mind. I inhaled again, desperately. The man across from me smiled and nodded encouragement. George. His name was George. Sometimes I remember his name.

He got up suddenly and took a clarinet from the shelf that divided the kitchen area from the living room. He caressed the length of it. Black and silver. He wet his lips and put the mouthpiece into his mouth and raised it high, bending his knees. I watched, waiting for the golden sound. He blew. It made a short squeak.

He smiled. I wondered what he had heard.

"Do you like the music?" he asked. "Uh . . ." searching for my name.

"Anna," I said. Then I laughed, feeling light-headed. "No, call me . . . let me see . . . something Italian . . . something musical and happy. . . . Allegra. My name is Allegra."

"Oh wow, man . . ." He took a long pull on the joint and put the clarinet to his lips as if he were going to play it, then put it down and took another long pull.

I giggled. I wondered when he was going to inhale the clarinet and blow on the joint. He went over to the shelf again and searched through some records. "You gotta hear this, man! Jimmy Giuffre. The greatest horn, man. Greatest!"

He put the record on the turntable and stood listening, swaying with the music. He lifted the clarinet to his lips several times, as if to join in the music, his eyes closed, his knees bent, his head back, clarinet straight out. Erect. Then he smiled and lowered the instrument and breathed deep on his joint instead. I took another drag. I did that. Dragged the smoke in and held it there.

George put the clarinet down on the table and took off his shirt. His chest was hairless and very white. Boney. I got up and moved into his arms and started to dance. "You like to dance," he said, delighted.

"Do you?"

"Yeah. Oh yeah, man."

But he couldn't dance. We swayed together for a few minutes. Then I let go of him and danced away, alone. He watched me, admiring. He raised the clarinet to his lips and blew a small, croaking toot.

"Sing it, Giuffre . . . sing it, man. . . ." Only it wasn't Giuffre. There was no clarinet. It was Thelonius Monk playing "Blue Monk" with Art Blakey on the drums and Johnny Griffin on the tenor sax, and there was a trumpet and a bass. He didn't know a tenor sax from a clarinet. I didn't tell him. It didn't matter. I took another drag, and let my body move. I took off my silver belt and tossed it on the couch. The slacks were a problem.

The catch was broken and I had it closed with a safety pin. That took a little longer. My hands wanted to move and sway. Dance. Not mess with safety pins. I got the pin open and dropped it on the dusty round black glass table in front of the couches. They were wide-wale corduroy modular pieces set at right angles to each other. I tossed my slacks onto a couch, slithering around the table and back to George. We touched fingers. He held his new joint to my lips and I dragged again, and then again, hungrily, and floated away. In a far corner there was a bean bag chair, the size of a double bed, in purple leatherette. And across from that, on the other side of the window, a baby grand piano. The wood on the piano lid was splintered. There were no drapes or curtains on the window, only some plants, most of them dead. They hung from the ceiling in front of the window at irregular intervals and heights.

I pushed off my shoes. The rya rug was coarse and rough. I thought it would tear my panty hose. I put the shoes back on, still dancing. I felt attractive, sexy. High-heeled black sandals, man-made materials that looked like alligator. Black panty hose; tight white body suit. All man-made material.

"I am a man-made material," I said.

"Oh, wow . . ." he said, watching me, and took another drag.

He wriggled out of his jeans and put them on the back of one of the modular pieces, and swayed gracelessly, with the clarinet erect in his mouth.

"Charley . . ." he said. "Charley Mingus. Man, listen to that bass . . ."

I closed my eyes and listened to it, letting my body feel it. The sound wrapped itself around my body and held it, enfolded it, caressing, comforting. One hand unsnapped my body suit and lifted it over my head.

"Yeah . . ." George breathed. "Yeah . . ."

I unhooked my bra and tossed it away.

"You're beautiful," George said. "You're really beautiful, man . . ."

The music got hotter. Mingus's bass was joined by some horns and a piano and drums. Hot and hard and mean.

The music stopped, but I kept dancing. And then another record dropped and a piano made its statement: Someday he'll come along, the man I love. *And then Art Tatum's fingers surrounded the melody, embraced it, subduing, joining. But gently. Elegantly. Cool.*

. . . from which he'll never roam . . . I hummed.

George raised the volume. It was loud, very loud. "Sing it, old Art . . ." He raised the volume again. He rolled another joint and brought it to my lips.

"Now you're doing it," he said, and dragged on it, too.

I waited, wanting to feel high, to float. I wanted to feel bodiless. I wanted my mind to stop. Nothing happened. I didn't feel anything.

"It's a crock of shit," I said. "Like everything else. Like life."
I wanted to cry.

He had taken off his shorts, red bikini. His penis was medium-size and thin. It stood up by itself, dwarfed by the clarinet in his mouth. I thought of what Winston Churchill said, "If the measure of a man is the size of his penis, a gorilla is one hundred times the man I am."

And that was a crock of shit, too. Churchill and his cigar. Georgie here and his clarinet. He gave it another silly toot and started out of the room to the bedroom, and I followed him in my high heels and black panty hose.

The bed was unmade. I felt guilty. I was sure the boy had been sleeping there, and he had been awakened by my arrival to run out into the cold rainy night with a wet head. On the other hand, the bed looked as if it had never been made. The bed linen was a brown and black geometric print. I don't like loud printed bed linen. It isn't restful. I prefer solids. Or white.

This pot stuff was reaching me. I turned to George and put my arms around him and he kissed my lips. I clung to him and kissed him again and again.

He put his hands on my breasts and said, "You have great

tits," and kissed them. We sat on the bed and he kissed my mouth and my neck and my nipples and then we lay back on the bed. The linen felt sweaty. I tried not to breathe deeply. I hate the smell of dirty linen. I fought nausea.

He took my hand and guided it to his penis. I thought, "Well, to hell with you, Churchill. Bring on the gorilla." Because George's penis wasn't like Simon's. Simon's was thick and felt heavy in my hand. Chunky. I used to tell him that. He liked to hear it. He would preen. Not that I'm an expert on penes. Simon was the first. The only one for twenty-eight years.

George straddled my body on his knees. His penis dangled over my face. It curved up slightly, like the corners of his mouth. Crescent-moon mouth. Crescent-moon prick. He was smiling his silly, distant smile.

"Eat me," he said.

"I don't do that."

"But I like it," he said with astonishment.

"No." I felt guilty for disappointing him.

He moved down and lowered himself on me. The curve of his penis made it difficult for him to get inside me. I took his penis in my hand and guided it in. I was surprised to find I was so wet inside when I was feeling nothing. No interest, no desire. I only wanted to get it over with. I felt myself under him, gyrating gently, then faster, round and round and up and down, opening and closing the muscles of my vagina. I didn't want to disappoint him. I wanted to be a good lay. I didn't want him to be sorry he took me home and sent his son away for me.

One tries to please, man. . . .

"That's good," he breathed. "That's real good. You're really fucking me."

I opened my eyes and looked at his face with its silly, surprised, pasted-on smile. I didn't like him. I didn't like what he was saying to me.

But I was beginning to feel excitement. I said to myself, "You're here; you might as well enjoy it."

I pushed the upper part of his body away, so that his weight

27

was on his groin and he could get in deeper. I was very wet and I couldn't feel enough of his penis in me. He was sweating and I was afraid he couldn't hold out much longer. I was aroused a lot by then, so I pushed him out of me and rolled over onto my belly and guided him back inside me from behind and got one of his hands under me on my clitoris. I crossed my legs and moved up and down fast. It's my favorite position. I come most quickly that way. I was straining hard; I was almost there. Almost . . . I moved frantically. I could feel he was close to finishing. And then he groaned and pulled his hand out, off my clitoris. I felt him come. Then he rolled off me and lay on his back.

"You really fucked me," he said. "You started out slow, but you really fucked me."

I wished he wouldn't say that. The frustration inside me was terrible. I wanted desperately to finish. I thought of masturbating. I might have, if the room were dark and he weren't looking at me, but I was ashamed. Inhibited. He had failed me, and I was ashamed.

Then, of course, he asked, "Did you come?" I knew he would ask. He wasn't interested in me. It was his ego that was involved. If he were really interested or aware of me, he wouldn't have to ask.

"Yes," I said. I hate so to be asked that. It embarrasses me, as though I've let him down if I haven't had an orgasm for him; as though it were some failing of mine.

He lay on his back with his skinny penis shriveled like a cold broiled frank. He picked up the clarinet and put it in his mouth and blew a few sounds and took it out and laughed and put it back in his mouth, holding it high. He looked like he was sucking a monstrous penis. I got up and went to the bathroom. The frustration was almost unbearable. I had almost finished. Why couldn't I have finished faster? Why did I take so long? What was wrong with me?

I thought of lying down on the floor with a towel and finishing myself, but I couldn't bring myself to do it. The floor was too small to stretch out on, and too dirty. The towels smelled. I wondered when they had been washed last. And there would be roaches. I saw one in some dampness on the sink. A big one.

I washed myself and came back into the bedroom. I wondered again when the bed linen had been changed last. The brown and tan and black print could hide some stains, but not smells. Some woman must have bought it. One of his meaningful relationships. It looked like something a woman would have bought for a man if she were looking for a masculine print.

The pillow had a large wet stain. The clarinet was on it, resting majestically. I could get a good fuck out of that, I thought.

He was lying on his back, smoking a cigarette, and he looked at me when I came in.

"I'd better go," I said.

"Man, you really fucked me."

I wished I could say the same to him.

"Are we friends?" he asked anxiously. "Are you going to be my friend?"

"Yes."

He smiled as though a great worry had been removed from him.

"Come closer to me, uh . . ." he searched for my name. Allegra had vanished. "Anna," I said. "My name is Anna Nymous."

"Come closer to me, Anna."

The clarinet was enthroned on the pillow beside him. One hand rested lightly on his balls and he stroked them gently, lovingly, absently. The other hand held a cigarette. He dropped the cigarette stub into an ashtray that was filled with old butts, and grabbed me and pulled me down beside him on the bed. I put my arms around his skinny chest.

"I have to go," I said.

"I don't understand you. You won't suck me."

I didn't answer. I held him. Why couldn't he keep quiet and let me pretend? I felt so sad . . . so sad. I wanted to cry. I wanted someone to hold me.

He raised himself to a sitting position. His penis was hard again, turned in toward his belly. I glanced up at his face. It looked beatific, gentle. He lifted my head and put it on his thigh, near his penis. The hair around it was sticky. I could smell the stale semen. I could smell old juices that were festering there. The stink was overpowering. I was choking. I opened my mouth to breathe.

"I want you to eat me," he said.

"No." I shuddered.

"I like it," he said petulantly.

I moved to get up. He twisted my head and shoved his penis into my mouth. I struggled, gagging. He held my head, pressing it down hard. The sticky hair filled my nose.

"Suck, suck . . ." he crooned.

I gagged, trying to breathe, trying to break loose, trying to scream, feeling the penis harden as if to burst, feeling the throb, the stench, the horror. And then a gooey mucus filled my mouth, and still he held my head down in the slime and he breathed, "That's good, that's good; you're really eating me. . . ."

Desperate, enraged, I clenched my teeth through the filth into the flesh in my mouth and bit. I bit with all my strength.

I heard him scream. His hands began to beat at my head, tearing my hair. But still he held my head down into his groin. Frantically, I bit harder, tasting another hideous salty thick liquid, dimly aware of his screams through the hands beating wildly at my head. My hands felt blindly beside me. They closed on the clarinet. I lifted it and beat madly at his face and chest.

His hands loosened. His body flopped down. Rage took hold of me. Something deep inside me, something buried that burst loose. Exploded. I could feel nothing else. Gasping, retching, I sat up and beat at his face, pounding and hitting until my arms couldn't move anymore and I was exhausted. I crawled off the bed and stumbled into the bathroom. I was still holding the clarinet. It was bloody. I dropped it into the bathtub and stepped in beside it and turned on the shower. I washed my mouth. I washed it with soap and then with toothpaste and then rinsed it with mouthwash and did it all again. I used up all the mouthwash. I showered and washed my mouth again. I couldn't get rid of the hideous taste.

I didn't want to dry myself with a dirty towel. I found the linen closet next to the bathroom and pulled out a clean sheet and dried myself and wrapped myself in the sheet. With one end of it I picked up the dripping clarinet and dried it. I hoped it wasn't ruined.

I went back into the bedroom with the clarinet. I wanted to apologize to George. To explain how I felt.

His face was unrecognizable. Formless, bleeding pulp. It wasn't a recognizable face. It could have been anybody's. It could have been Simon's. I couldn't see anything else. There was too much blood around his groin to see anything.

I didn't feel anything at first. Then, slowly, I began to feel warm. Flushed. Feverish. My heart began to beat fast. I felt something more than joy. I felt release. Ecstasy. Exultation. I felt revenge.

I was happy.

"I hate you, Simon," I said. I said it again. "I hate you. I hate you, Simon."

Gently, I put the clarinet beside the man. I went into the other room. The record was still playing. Loud. Someday he'll come along . . . Cool. Elegant. It was so loud. And I hadn't been hearing it.

Carefully, I folded the sheet that I had dried myself with. I was feeling gay, light-headed. Weightless.

I thought I should lower the volume of the music, but I didn't know how. And I couldn't find the safety pin for my slacks. It didn't matter. The silver belt covered the waist.

The man at the desk downstairs was busy talking to a teenaged hooker. He didn't see me.

The rain had stopped. The air smelled washed and clean. I felt nice. Really good. I didn't know why I was crying.

It wasn't until I got home that I realized I had taken the bed sheet home with me, but I had left my umbrella.

I'd have to go back and return the sheet and get the umbrella. I can't afford to keep losing umbrellas.

Chapter Two

Freda Miller listened to the eleven o'clock news with her hot cocoa, as she had done nearly every night of her life. When Morris was alive, they had always listened to the eleven o'clock news together, with their cocoa, and then they had gone to bed. When Morris was alive, she used to fall asleep right away, his quiet, rhythmic breathing lulling her senses. When Morris was alive, this building she lived in was a whole different story.

Tonight she had just begun to feel herself drifting off, after tossing and turning, when that noise had started, that jazz next door. It jarred her awake.

The building never used to have people like that one next door. She and Morris had moved in when the building had been built, when the people who moved in wanted to be near Lincoln Center. They wanted to be close to music, to ballet, to *Culture*. Now it was changed. Everything was changed. She wasn't even sure she could afford to live here much longer, the way her pension was being eroded by inflation. The money from Morris' Social Security was so paltry. But where could she go? What

33

could she do? How many more things could she do
without? And alone. They had never had children.

So many things had changed. Once it had been a
wonderful building, and a wonderful street and a wonderful city. Once she had been young.

Morris was gone four years. She would never get used
to being without him.

The noise of the record next door went on and on. She
tried to relax, tried not to hear it, tried not to think or
worry. She tried to sleep.

The sound was turned up louder.

Freda groaned. She slid her body up slowly and dragged
her legs around and let them drop over the side of the bed.
She padded to the bathroom. Might as well urinate. She
was up five times a night to urinate anyway. The curse of
old women. Maybe she shouldn't drink the hot cocoa
before going to bed.

No. She wouldn't change that. How many changes
should she have to make in her life?

She got a tissue from the box on her night table and tore
it up and stuffed some pieces in her ears. Maybe that
would help. She lay down again.

It didn't help, of course. And the tissue in her ears was
annoying. She thought she heard other noises, too.
Screaming and banging. A wild, crazy party, probably.

Her bedroom wall was the living room wall next door.
She took the tissues out of her ears and banged hard on the
wall. Maybe they would hear it and lower the volume.

Nothing happened. She banged again, harder, mostly to
get rid of her rage. They wouldn't lower the volume.
They never did. She had had this trouble with them
before, but never for so long, or so late. She pounded
again, with her fists, her anger and frustration mounting,
and realized she was crying. Exhausted, she leaned her
head back against the wall.

"Morris, Morris, where are you?"

She sighed. Not that Morris would have been much help. She had always had to fight the battles for both of them. But at least there was someone to complain to. Or about.

The worst part of the noise was that it was the same record. Over and over, the same record. It was making her crazy. They probably fell asleep. Went into the bedroom and fell asleep and left the phonograph for her to suffer with.

She could go out into the hall and ring their bell and ask them to please lower the volume. But what if they refused? That wasn't the problem. She knew that wasn't the problem. If they refused, she would call the police. (Not that the police would bother coming because an old woman was disturbed by noise.)

The problem was that she would have to get dressed and put in her teeth. She wasn't a person who would go out into the hall in her bathrobe, without her teeth. And she would have to comb her hair, carefully, to cover the place where her hair had thinned so her pink scalp showed through. And she was tired. Her ankles swelled in the rain. They ached when she put her weight on them.

"Oh Morris, Morris . . . if you were alive, and you had a couple of hours, I could tell you all the things that hurt me." Not that he would listen. He never listened. He was always reading . . . a newspaper, a book, a magazine. She thanked God for one thing. His eyes never went on him. A little deaf, a little arthritic; the heart wasn't so good. But he had his eyes. God had been good to him. What good is it, Morris, to creep along like this, like me, for so long, with all my parts wearing out?

Freda looked at the clock with its small, round, red illuminated face and the numbers that glowed green in the dark. 1:45. Almost two o'clock.

She was so tired. So terribly tired. And her head ached. Well, this once, the only time she had ever done it in all the years she had lived here, she would put on her robe and go out into the hall and ring their bell next door and ask them politely. And let them dare. Let them dare refuse! She would call the police. She should call the police anyway, but after all, everybody deserved a chance. Why get someone in trouble with the police unnecessarily? And why get herself involved with police?

Her ankles ached as she set her feet down heavily on the floor and got her robe. Actually, it was Morris' robe. A good robe. Wool plaid. It had cost twenty dollars eighteen years ago. God only knew what it would cost now, a robe like that. It was worn a bit thin at the elbows and seat, but it was still good. And it was like having Morris around her. Now the teeth. After all, there had to be some standards. She rinsed her teeth at the sink and put them in.

As she stepped out into the hall, she saw a woman waiting for the elevator. A woman in a red raincoat. Freda stepped back quickly into her apartment. The one time, the one and only time she had ever stepped a foot out into the hall without being dressed, there had to be someone there! She simply was not going to be seen in Morris' old robe and with her hair uncombed. She rested back against the door and waited until she thought she heard the elevator door wheeze open.

She opened her door a crack and peeped out and saw the woman step into the elevator. She didn't see her face, only the back of her. Slim. Curly blonde hair. Red raincoat, with a line at the bottom where the hem had been let down. Freda knew all about letting down hems nowadays.

The elevator door slid shut. Freda waited, watching, until she heard the motor start and saw the numbers lighting above the door. Eight. Seven. Six.

She went out into the hall, and walking very straight, defying the throb in her ankles (arthritis, Morris), she marched herself up to the next apartment and rapped firmly on the door. The sound of the jazz could be heard clearly from behind the door, but it wasn't as loud as it was in her bedroom. The outer apartment walls were thicker than the walls between apartments. She rapped again, then rang the bell. She couldn't tell if the bell could be heard inside over the sound of the jazz. Some of the bells were broken. Management was very slow on repairs. The whole building had deteriorated. Like these halls. The shabby carpet. It was a disgrace. Probably it was because the owners wanted to turn the building into a co-op. What would she do then? She never could raise the kind of money they wanted. She had given up her good seat at the opera. She didn't go at all. She couldn't see from the balcony. She couldn't hear well, either. Probably this . . . riffraff that had moved in would be able to buy the co-op, and she would have to move. Where?

Her heart was pounding. She must stop thinking about frightening things. She must stop worrying. She put her finger on the bell and kept it there, pushing with all her strength, and then pulled her hand away suddenly and shoved it into the pocket of her robe. She didn't like to look at her hands. They were gnarled, snaked with thick blue veins and liver spots. Turning to go, she kicked furiously at the door. It moved. She stared at it. It was open. The music poured out like a flood. Tentatively, with embarrassment, she pushed it. It opened more.

She didn't mean to pry. She wasn't one of those old ladies with nothing better to do than spy on their neighbors. She wasn't even sure who lived here. A man alone, she thought, although sometimes she thought there was a woman there. But she looked into the room.

It was empty. On a shelf, to the left, against the wall of the kitchen was a phonograph. The speakers were up against her bedroom wall. Did she dare go further into the room and turn the thing off? This was someone else's home. A stranger's home.

She wasn't even sure she would know how to shut it. She wasn't wearing her glasses.

No one had heard her ring. Maybe no one was home. They might have turned on this noise and forgotten about it and left. Maybe it was that woman in the red coat.

"I'll only take a quick look, Morris . . ." And then, if no one was home, she would shut the machine herself. No one could blame her for that.

Standing on the threshold, she knocked again at the door. She felt as though she were being buried in an avalanche of sound. She didn't want the noise to disturb anyone else on the floor. She came into the apartment and closed the door behind her with the back of her hand.

"Hello," she called.

No one answered.

"Excuse me . . . hello. . . ." Very loud.

Slowly, still unsure what to do, she walked toward the bedroom. She stood still at the bedroom door.

She didn't know what she was seeing at first. She came closer, staring at the thing on the bed. Then she realized what she was looking at. The bloody mess that should have been a face. The gore below. She felt faint. Her body sagged against the doorjamb. Her stomach heaved. She was too horrified to scream. She turned and ran into her own apartment. Shaking and sobbing, she grabbed the phone.

"Operator . . ." she screamed. "Operator! . . ."

She stopped. She put down the phone.

What was she doing? What was she getting involved in? If she called the police, how could she explain what she was doing in the apartment? Why had she gone in there? They might even suspect her. She could hear a policeman say, "Did you kill him because he played that awful music late at night and didn't let you sleep?"

What business was it of hers, after all, what happened next door? That's what Morris would say. "What's it your business, Freda? Who knows what kind of person he was? Let someone else take care of it."

"Yes, Morris." She was going to do what she had done all her life. Mind her own business. She and Morris had always lived their own lives, minding their own business.

She had left the door to that dreadful apartment wide open. The hall was filled with the horrid sound. Someone else would complain. Sooner or later, someone else would go in there and find that . . . thing . . . on the bed.

She moved back into her bedroom, letting her feet drag, letting herself give in to the pain in her ankles. There was no one to hide it from.

Carefully, she hung up Morris' robe. It was no use to lie down again. She would never sleep. She lowered her body into the armchair by the window and stared out at the river. Where were all the cars going so fast, so late? The world goes on, Morris, without us. We don't even make a dent.

She rested her head back against the chair and closed her eyes, trying to erase that hideous sight on the bed next door. The memory would keep her awake.

Dimly, she heard sounds in the hall. Doors opening and slamming. Footsteps. A scream. Shouting. Commotion. The music stopped abruptly.

Someone was taking care of it.

"Morris, why did you have to die and leave me all alone in such a terrible, selfish world?"

"Freda, dumbbell, wouldn't I rather be with you? Never mind the noise outside. Go to sleep."

She did what he told her to do. She fell asleep.

Chapter Three

Bernie Bernstein didn't even try to sleep. He lay on his back in the narrow bed and felt the throb in his forehead where the doctor had stitched it. Nine stitches.

The kid is crazy, he thought. He's crazy. Throwing that fire engine at my head. He's twelve years old. Why the hell is he playing with a fire engine? Linda was going to have to face it. Sooner or later he would have to be institutionalized.

Outside, the rain had cried itself out. The wind flung itself against the window, crying dry tears. Bernie shifted his big body cautiously, afraid for an instant that he might fall off the bed. And that was another thing: the twin beds. Bernie had come home one night and found them there. Linda had thrown out their queen-size bed and bought the two twin beds and had them set up and covered with spreads and standing there as if they had been there the entire twenty-seven years of their marriage. It was a hell of a surprise. She hadn't consulted him at all. Hadn't even mentioned it, or that she had planned to do it. Not that it made any difference. They could be sleeping in different planets for all the good it did him. It had been two years, maybe even three, since she had done him a favor and let him make love to her. And she had lain like a limp rag doll, waiting impatiently for him to finish, then jumped immediately out of bed and run to the bathroom to wash. To wash the sex off her body. To wash him off her. It had been like that for years: he couldn't remember how many. But not in the beginning. In the beginning she had thrown her body at him, tearing at him, plucking and tasting. In the beginning, when she had thought that was going to give her a child.

Christ, she had been beautiful. All pale gold. Spun-gold hair, green-gold eyes. And dimples. Those wild, delicious dimples in a round face.

Her body was still beautiful. Her breasts were still plump and firm and high, her waist tiny, her hips round yet slim. But her face always looked like the nerves were drawn tight. Her face wasn't round anymore. She hardly ever smiled.

Why did he feel a sudden surge of guilt? It wasn't his fault about the children. It wasn't hers, either. It was one of those crazy twists of fate. They had had all the tests, gone to all the specialists, tried everything. There was nothing wrong with either of them. They had been told that countless times. With another mate, either of them would have had a dozen children. Sometime in their years together their lovemaking had become a desperate, cold, mechanical ritual to make a baby. Once he had dared to mention adoption. She wouldn't talk about it. "I was made to be a mother," she had screamed. "I have the hips for it, the breasts for it."

In the beginning, every month, he had held her in his arms while she wept, feeling every sob like an accusation. He would have climbed the air to get her a star. He couldn't give her a child. Guilty and frustrated, he didn't know when they had begun to pick at each other. All of a sudden they were always fighting.

And he loved her. He loved to watch her move her hands: thin, almost boney, pale, with beautifully shaped, short nails that she never polished. And she had this feeling for color. For clothes. She could tie a green patterned scarf around her neck and look like she was wearing emeralds.

He listened in the still, dark room and knew she wasn't sleeping. If he called her, would she answer him?

"Linda?"

No. Of course she wouldn't answer.

After they had been married fifteen years, still going through their baby-making ritual, rote, routine, hopeless, she had suddenly become pregnant. They had stopped talking about it. She had stopped crying, finally even stopped counting. She had thought she had a stomach virus when the first nausea came.

Their marriage was revived.

When they told him it was a boy, he had gone out immediately and bought two fishing rods. He had brought them to the hospital. Two fishing rods and a dozen long-stemmed roses. She had laughed. Was that the last time he had seen her really laugh?

She was still looking for a doctor who would tell her there was nothing wrong with Theodore. Theodore, for Bernie's father, the little tailor who loved the outdoors and had taken Bernie fishing whenever he could. The little tailor who had been so proud of his tall son. And died of TB from working in the sweatshops of New York when Bernie was seventeen. That had changed Bernie's aspirations from law to law enforcer. Theodore Sean. Sean, for her father, dead of cirrhosis of the liver. And for her brother Sean, whom she loved and hated. Theodore Sean Bernstein, the Crazy.

There had been something wrong with him from the beginning.

Bernie got out of his bed and walked over to hers. "Linda."

He stood looking down at her. Her eyes were closed, but her body was rigid. *Don't worry*, he thought. *I'm not going to touch you.*

"Linda, you could at least have asked me if I'm all right. How I feel. The doctor took nine stitches."

Why did he say that? It wasn't what he wanted to say. She looked so sad, so frightened, her body so stiff and tight it looked as if it might snap if she was touched. He wanted to comfort her. He wanted her to comfort him. He loved her so terribly.

"Linda, I know you're awake."

"He's angry at you," she said. "That's why he threw the fire engine. He knows you don't love him."

He didn't answer.

"You never pay any attention to him. You're always so wrapped up in your ball games and your newspapers and your hobbies and your job. Your goddamn job. You care more about the *force* than you do about him. You're never home."

"I can't do anything about my hours. You knew what a cop's life was like when you married me. Sean was a cop."

"You're not just a cop. An inspector can pick his hours."

"You know that isn't true."

"It doesn't matter. You don't pay any attention to him when you are home."

She was going to go on about that again. "I was trying to pay attention to him when he threw that truck."

"He knew you didn't want to play with him. He heard me tell you to."

"He missed my eye by an eighth of an inch. He could have blinded me."

"Accidents happen. Any child might have done that."

He sat down at the foot of her bed. She didn't make room for him. He tried to speak calmly. Rationally.

44

"Linda," he said, "we have to face the truth and find out the best way to deal with it. Theo is twelve years old. He may never . . . he may not ever be . . . competent. Yes, that's it. *Competent* to take care of himself."

She sat up, trembling. "You see, that's how you think of him! He knows it! Don't you realize he knows it!"

"Damn it, Linda, face facts! He's crazy! He was born crazy! Someday he's going to have to be institutionalized!"

Her body trembled violently. "There's nothing wrong with him! Nothing!" Her voice was strangled with rage. "What's wrong is you! If you weren't here making him feel there's something wrong with him, making him feel crazy, he wouldn't be crazy! He's better off without you."

"Oh, shit! Are we on that again?"

She got out of bed, careful not to let any bare flesh show, and put on her robe. "I want you to leave. I want you to get out of this house and leave us alone!"

His head ached. It wasn't only the stitches. "You weren't listening to me. You didn't hear me."

"I heard you. I listened. You're the one who doesn't listen. You're so busy being the good cop, the good Jew. Trying to prove to those micks and wops and now the spics and niggers that Bernstein can be as good a cop as they are."

"Better," he said.

"Big Bernie. Their token Jew officer."

"I earned it."

"I know. On my back and your son's. Always studying for the next exam. Always volunteering for the toughest neightborhood, the worst shift."

"So I could be away from you and your nagging and your bitterness."

"I suggest you be away from me for the whole rest of your life. Your son will be better off without you, Inspector Bernstein. You aren't really any more successful in your job than you are as a father. You could crucify yourself for the Department, and you'd still be that Jew bastard to them."

He had given her that piece of ammunition himself, twenty-five years ago. He had saved Feeley's life . . . his first partner . . . and taken a slug in the leg doing it. Feeley had said, "You're OK for a Jew, Bernstein."

She had wept for him then. Her tears had turned to bullets long ago. They still drew blood.

He nearly said, Is that what I am to you, too? A Jew bastard? How had they sunk to this? They had been so in love. . . .

"I'm sorry," she said suddenly. She turned away from him. "But I do want you to go. Tonight."

She had been so beautiful, so gay, so eager. Her laugh had been a fountain bubbling gold. He was terrified that he might cry.

"Linda, please stop this. Let's talk about Theo. We have to think about the future."

"That's exactly what I am thinking about."

Without thinking, he had moved to touch her. She jerked herself away from him. He felt it like a slap. His head throbbed horribly.

"You don't love me anymore," she said. "You think Theo doesn't feel that? You think he isn't affected by it? That's what's wrong with him."

"I wish it were true," he said. "I wish I didn't love you."

She shrugged. "You don't. You haven't for years and years. But you are obsessed with right and wrong, with being a good person. And good Jewish boys don't stop loving their wives. They don't get divorces."

"Neither do good Catholic girls."

"I didn't say I wanted a divorce. I just want to be rid of you."

"And good Jewish boys don't drink or beat their wives or fuck around like Catholic boys. Like Sean."

"He gave his wife children. Strong, healthy children," she said, her voice rising.

"Linda . . ."

"Oh, get out! Go away! Don't come back! You aren't any good to either of us!" she shouted fiercely, and ran out of the room. He heard the door to Theo's room close and then heard the lock click.

There was an extra bed in there. She would stay there all night. He knew that. She had done it often enough, more and more often in the past few months. Their fights were getting worse. He couldn't talk to her at all without its getting around to Theo and then a fight.

What about that Christ of hers? Why didn't he help? She had started going to church, taking Theo with her. But they had told her not to bring him anymore. He had kicked the seats and he sang out loud and yawned and shouted out obscenities. Finally he had bitten a woman on the breast. The woman had leaned toward him to reprimand him for being noisy and disrespectful. Linda had stopped going after that, but she had begun to wear a small gold cross. She wore it on a long, thin chain inside her blouse, probably to keep Bernie from seeing it. She hadn't been religious when they met.

The throbbing in his head was unbearable. Outside, the rain and the wind had stopped. The streets, in the lamplight, looked slick and shiny and pleasantly cool. The coolness was inviting.

To hell with her. Did she think he was made of stone? He dressed quickly. When he left the house, he slammed the door very loud.

Chapter Four

As soon as he got out into the air, Bernie felt better. The air felt washed and clean after the rain. The wind calmed him. He liked walking. He liked to move. He had always been proud of his long, muscular legs, his big shoulders. He was six-foot-four, broad and still lean. His size had always been a source of pleasure to him. It made him feel good. It gave him satisfaction to be the Jewish kid on the block that the gentile kids didn't mess with.

When he was a kid, he had had to pass the Italian block and the Irish block to get to school. But he had always been big, so he didn't get hassled much. When he did, he went for blood. "The Killer," they called him. And Big Bernie. Don't mess with Big Bernie. He didn't really like to fight. He never started it.

He had huge feet. Size thirteen and a half. He liked looking down at them. He felt good seeing his big shoes beside the bed in the morning. Linda used to like it, too. She thought it was sexy. Big feet, big prick. . . .

His size gave him protection, made him feel secure, powerful, gave him equality in a hostile gentile world.

Linda knew all that. He had confided it all to her, holding her in the nest of his arms after they had made love, in the days when they were making love, and she was soft and yielding, dreamily murmuring comforting sounds. Had she really been listening to him even then, when his bigness excited her, or was she merely waiting for the babies to start. All the secrets of his heart were now only weapons for her to use against him.

Was he doing that to her, too? He shouldn't have said that about Sean. Her feelings about her brother were so complex. She loved him so much and was so ashamed of him. "Shanty Irish!" she raged when he was slobbering drunk. "Dumb mick!" And wept. And adored the tall, curly-haired, improvident, lazy-natured brother. Sean would never be more than a cop on the beat.

He shouldn't have said that to her. He would tell her he was sorry. Try to talk to her. She was a good kid. She had never cheated on him. It would have been so easy, with his rotten hours. And it might have given her babies. . . .

She had really wanted so little. She had made no demands on him. She took good care of the house. She paid all the bills and handled all the money. There was nothing material she prized. She had even refused a diamond engagement ring. Even after the doctors had advised her to keep busy, forget about it, relax, and she had gone back to school and become a nurse, she had spent very little on herself. And she always looked so great. She had such a flair. He had been proud of her when she became a nurse. She was still taking courses to be a better nurse. He was still proud of her. It wasn't her fault that Theo was all the kind of kid she had been able to give him.

He had wanted children, too. Lots. Four, five, six. But not the way she did. It was all she had ever wanted. Big and strong, like you, she said. Theo was a damn shrimp. Tiny and skinny. He had these crazy eating shticks. For months at a time he would eat only well-done hamburger and apple juice. Three times a day. Nothing else. And then, suddenly, he would change. Once he ate only dry cereal, without milk, for a month. Now he was on American cheese and grape juice. Nothing else. Linda pleaded with him, played games, tried to bribe him, shouted and threatened and punished. Bernie learned to go out of the room, out of the house if he could, at mealtime.

Was Linda right? Maybe he had grown accustomed to being childless. He had grown to like having the extra room in the apartment to stretch out in or study in or watch TV and tinker with his clocks. He had learned to fix old clocks. It was his favorite hobby.

They had always had the extra room because they had taken a two-bedroom apartment as soon as they were married, even though they couldn't afford it. All their friends had taken studios or a one-bedroom, intending to wait before trying for a family, to save a little, to live a little. But Linda hadn't wanted to wait.

All their friends had two or three kids by now. Most of them were all grown, in college or married. He knew what it had done to Linda, making all those visits to the new mother, buying all those baby gifts, smiling. Always smiling. She had begun to cry alone, in the bathroom, at night, not wanting his comfort. They traveled on their vacations. He acquired another hobby; taking pictures. She stopped having company. She turned down invitations. She cleaned the house a lot. He turned more and more to his work.

Bernie sighed. He had walked around the block and was back at his building. He was standing irresolutely in the doorway, watching the wind hassling stray papers and leaves. There was no point in going back to the apartment. He wouldn't be able to sleep, and he would have to be up and out again at six to be at the precinct at seven. He'd be better off if he went to the precinct now. He could flop out on a cot in his office or in the dayroom until his tour started. He had done that before, a bunch of times.

In his car, he kept the windows down. The wind swept the cobwebs out of his head. He began to feel better. He thought of Linda locked up in the room with Theo and felt pity for her. His pity kept him from being angry. She was so small. Only five-foot-four. At most, maybe a hundred ten pounds. Fragile. Delicate features. Tiny wrists. Her frailty wounded him and drew her to him. He felt protective. And guilty. He couldn't give her what she wanted. He felt inadequate. He was mute before her frustration and rage.

He flipped on the car radio, searching for dance music. Something smooth. Music for dancing close. He loved to dance. Dancing was one of the things they had shared. He was aware of his bigness, his big feet that were so graceful, his big shoulders, his long, strong legs that moved smoothly, with assurance. He felt . . . masterful, leading Linda on the dance floor. She followed so perfectly. He had met her at a dance; some department thing. Sean had brought her. He smiled, remembering the waltz contest they won once on shipboard on the cruise they had taken. It was just before she became pregnant. He loved dancing with her. He loved letting her out at arm's length in a break and watching her snake back to him. He loved the moment she slid back into his arms. He loved the feel of her. What he loved . . . was . . . her. Christ, how he loved her. He wanted to touch her, to hold her. His hands felt empty. His groin ached.

When was the last time they had danced? Maybe he ought to try to get her to go dancing with him again. He thought he missed that more than sex.

He wondered, as he had many times, why he had remained faithful to her. It would have been so easy to cheat. Cops had a lot of opportunity, a lot of invitations, in fact: the hookers, the women in distress, the lure of the uniform. Cops had a rotten marriage record as a group. There were too many temptations on the beat. That, and the rotten hours, the boredom, the loneliness, the danger often.

But he knew, of course, why he had never yielded. It was because he was a Jew. He never let himself forget it. He carried the awareness with him as though he were wearing a yellow star on his chest. He was going to wear that star as though its honor were his responsibility.

When he had joined the force nearly thirty years ago, he was the only Jew in the precinct. There weren't a whole hell of a lot of Jews even now. And he was always aware of what they said about him. About the same things they said about the blacks and Hispanics now.

He had to show them. He had to be better than they were: bigger, more honorable, more conscientious, harder-working, smarter. He had to be the cop who never had his hand out, who never drank, who never tried out a whore before he pulled her in. It wasn't only himself he represented. It was all the Jews.

He had thought at first he was only going to be on the force for a short time. Save some money. Go to law school. But he found he liked being a cop. He believed in right and wrong. He believed in Justice. Lawyers played games with the law. A policeman represented it.

Linda had said, "What you like is being better than the goys."

OK Maybe. Well, he *was* better. Better than Sean, who still walked a beat.

Early on, his captain had said to him, "You're a good cop, Bernstein. Smart. You'd go farther if you changed your name."

He had answered, "What should I change it to, sir? Cohen or Levy?"

Better than the goyim. It had become a way of life.

Linda had once said, "St. Bernard. Your halo is blinding me."

"Halos are to catch the shit," he said. "They keep me clean."

"You are obsessed with Right and Wrong. Good and Evil."

He had never had another woman.

Linda said, with a bitter laugh, once, "I can't even have the comfort of becoming a drunk. You don't think I'd let you have the satisfaction of saying 'drunken Irish' to me."

"I'd never say it."

"You would think it."

She had her image to keep shiny, too.

He shut the radio and turned on his squawk box. It seemed to him to have an excited sound. He listened to it. There was a repeated 1010 . . . investigate DOA. On West End Avenue. It was in his precinct. He would be passing the block in a couple of minutes.

He might as well stop there and look in. If he got to his office early, he would only be in the way. Probably not be able to sleep, either. He wasn't tired anymore. It might be interesting to answer a call. He hadn't done that for a long time. He wondered what he still remembered about solving a crime.

Chapter Five

"Jesus!" Bernie rocked back on his heels as though he had been punched in the stomach. He sucked in air. He had been cloistered too long in an office. He had grown soft. He wasn't prepared for that hideous thing on the bloody bed. But he forced down the bile that leaped into his throat. He wasn't going to let himself be sick. Not with that ugly runt Darryl Johnson watching him, his black face shiny and unmoved as an ebony statue. Tough little bird, Johnson. Straight out of Harlem. Not big on honkies. Probably telling himself, "Scratch off one more white boy. One less can't hurt." Cold, hard-faced; kept to himself. But honest.

"You called for homicide and the ME?" Bernie said.

"Yes, sir," Johnson said expressionlessly.

Bernie nodded. He moved in closer to the bed. There was nothing left of the face, and the damn prick was almost off. He felt calmer now. Almost peaceful. The sight of the violence had calmed him. It was like a cathartic.

Ramirez, Johnson's partner, pushed past Bernie, rushing

out of the room to the bathroom. The sound of his vomiting filled the apartment over the gush of the toilet flushing repeatedly. Bernie focused his eyes on the bed, on the areas away from the body, more to cover the embarrassment of hearing Ramirez than for really finding anything. He stared at the clarinet. Some of the keys seemed to be broken off, but it wasn't bloody. Blood was splattered over everything else on the bed. All over that fancy bed linen. Ugly linen. He was aware that he wouldn't have noticed bed linen at home or anywhere else. But on a case, he saw differently. All his senses were more alert.

The clarinet could have been put there after the murder. He looked around the room.

Ramirez came back from the bathroom. Sweat stood out in tiny beads on his forehead. "Fucking fags," he said.

"Why do you say that?" Bernie asked.

Ramirez gestured toward the bed. He didn't look at it. "They go for that funny stuff with pricks."

"Some do," said Bernie.

Johnson was prowling around the room, using his handkerchief to open drawers and closets. Ambitious runt. It bugged Bernie that the department had lowered its standards on height. But Johnson was tough. He wouldn't be a pushover in a fight. Bernie looked around, not touching anything. The ashtrays were all overflowing. Ashes and butts and the tiny ends of roll-your-owns were all over the night table and the floor, but there were none with lipstick.

"There are two different sizes of men's clothes," Johnson said. He nodded toward a puddle of underwear on the floor. Tee shirts and jeans seemed to have been dropped anywhere . . . on the convertible chair and on a chest of drawers, but mostly on the floor. "No women's clothes in the closet."

Bernie moved into the living room. "Who made the complaint?"

"We don't know, Inspector. There was no one here when we arrived, but the door was open. The stereo power was on, like it is."

"No one wants to stick their neck out nowadays," said Ramirez.

Bernie glanced at the stereo. A button of light gleamed. He didn't touch it. There might be prints on the knob. Pity, he thought, the unit might burn out if they didn't shut it. And then thought how stupid that was. A man was dead. How could a machine matter?

"Why do the bastard fags do that kind of stuff?" Ramirez asked angrily, still embarrassed about his weak stomach.

Johnson said from the kitchen, "If there was a woman, she didn't do windows. Or much of anything else."

Bernie glanced into the room. The sink was filled with dishes. It wasn't possible to tell from how many people or how many days. He came out again and stood still in the middle of the room and let his eyes just look. Relax. Undirected. Let the evidence lead you; don't lead the evidence, he told himself. He began to feel the old excitement. Like the old days when he was a detective. He felt alive.

It was an ugly room. Uncared for. A place to flop. A picture askew on the wall. A painting hung up tastelessly. Odds and ends of furniture that looked left over from some other life or place or picked up at a Salvation Army store. Dust everywhere. A powdering of dust over the round, black cocktail table. There was a small object in the dust. A medium-sized safety pin. On the love seat near the table were a pair of Jordache jeans, a western-style shirt, red bikini undershorts. Maybe it *was* a fag murder.

"Any sign of forced entry?"

"No, sir. The door was open when we arrived. We walked right in," said Johnson.

"Did you talk to any of the neighbors? The doorman?"

"Not yet, sir. We were waiting for the detectives and the photographers and the ME."

Bernie glanced at the door. It was slightly ajar. He moved over to close it. The catch was not working well. It had to be pushed firmly. Beside the door, in a corner, was an umbrella. Cheap, yellow plastic. A woman's bubble-type umbrella. The shaft, directly under the handle, was split and bent. He knelt and looked at it without touching it. The floor under it was still damp. Someone had used the umbrella this night.

He smiled wryly and got up. It was possible that in the city of New York five thousand women had an umbrella like that one. What the hell did he think he was doing? This wasn't his job.

Once he had been a good street cop. And then a good detective. And captain. He had loved it. Now he was an inspector. Commanding officer of the precinct. He loved that, too.

All the same, this had taken his mind off his troubles for a while. He was grateful. He was grateful to that stiff in there.

He looked at his watch. He'd better get on to work. It was almost five o'clock. "I just happened to be passing by."

"Yes, sir." Johnson's face gave nothing away.

Bernie glanced again at the umbrella. He put his hand on the edge of the door. He didn't touch the knob. A shrill ringing from the bedroom stopped him. He stood still. Johnson and Ramirez looked at him. They all stared toward the bedroom where the sound came from. It came again. The phone.

Bernie moved quickly to the bedroom, taking out his handkerchief as he went. The other two followed him and stood in the doorway. With the handkerchief, Bernie lifted the receiver carefully. If he spoke first, it might scare off the person on the other side. He cleared his throat and coughed into the phone.

"George? . . ." It was a young voice.

"Mmmm," Bernie mumbled.

"Is it OK to come home now?"

Bernie had worked a part of the handkerchief over the phone to muffle his voice. "Why not?" he said.

"Well, you know you said . . . George? . . . Are you up? Hey, who is this? . . ."

"Who are you?"

"Shit, you're not George." The phone went dead.

Bernie hung up. Sometimes they thought they had reached a wrong number and they called again. He waited. The room was stuffy. He thought the thing on the bed had begun to stink.

Before the first ring had ended, he lifted the phone. The same voice said, "George?"

No point in trying to bluff it out. "This is Inspector Bernstein. Who are you?"

"Inspector Bernstein? Police?"

"Yes. Who are you?"

The phone went dead again.

Bernie put the phone down carefully. He nodded toward the bed. "This might be George," he said.

"It ain't anymore," said Ramirez.

Bernie nodded. Ain't anymore. When had he stopped being George? Was it when his face was destroyed? He might still have been breathing then. Was it at the moment when his cock had come off? Was he then not George anymore? When did life stop and a person cease to be? When had his own life stopped? Was he alive? Breathing and walking and all his parts intact. Unused, but intact. Was he alive?

59

He looked at his watch again. He hoped his face was as blank as Johnson's. A faceless face.

"Why haven't you sealed the place off?"

"We don't have a Crime Scene sign with us. Homicide will bring it," Johnson said. "We told them."

"Better seal it off right now. I don't like that broken door catch. The building will start waking up soon, and the curious will come out of the woodwork. I have a sign in my car. Come down with me, Ramirez, and I'll give it to you."

Ramirez followed him out, obviously glad to get out of the place even for a short time. The elevator came just as they went out of the door. They ran to get it. Ramirez didn't pull the door shut.

Chapter Six

The boy stood shivering in the street phone booth. The door had been ripped off. A wet wind whipped through the booth, lashing at him. In the dark, pre-dawn, the shapes of the city loomed like eerie enemies.

He wrapped his arms around his soft chest. His shirt, emblazoned with PHUCK, was drenched with his own sweat.

"Fucking cunt Shelley," he muttered. "Fucking damn cunt bitch." Four calls. He had to make four calls from George's pad to find some place to crash after George came home. Four calls to find where Shelley was. He didn't know nobody else he could call at that hour. He had no friends anymore. Since he left Brooklyn and school and his mother's house, he had no friends left. Those kids in Brooklyn he used to know, they never really were his friends. Nobody was his friend. Nobody gave one shit for him.

When he reaches Shelley, she goes, "You got some shit on you, man?"

"Yeah, man."

"How much?"

"It ain't a nickel bag."

So she says, "Well, sure, come on over. Why not, man?" He can hear laughing in the background, and music, like it's a party.

So he finally finds this fucking pad she tells him to come to, on this fucking street in this fucking place called NoHo. "NoHo," she goes, "like SoHo, only North, see." And the pad is, you know, like a loft building and it's dark and the door is locked. He rings the bell a million times and bangs on the door and nobody answers. He figures she lied to him and gave him a phoney address . . . sent him out on this wild-goose chase for a gag, to make a jerk out of him. Shelley could be like that. She's probably laughing her head off. Her and her friends.

He's freezing in his tee shirt, in the rain, without a sweatshirt or nothing, and his head is wet.

Why the fuck did George have to bring that old broad home? He had been feeling so nice . . . high and warm and nodding out, and then she was there with George, telling him he would catch a cold with a wet head, like his fucking mother.

Maybe he wrote the address down wrong. If he could find a telephone . . . But where could you find a telephone that fucking worked in this fucking city? It was a smart thing he took the phone number with him, anyway. He wasn't stupid. Even if he dropped out of school. He was flunking everything. Every fucking thing. He used to be smart in school when he was a little kid. He used to like it, even. When he was a real little kid. A long time ago. When George was his father, like. George didn't give a shit about him. Always counting how much hash was in the box, checking did his own son rip him off. He was his son, for Chris' sake, wasn't he? His own son, and he had to practically steal a little shit, say he took two when he took four. Never more than that at one time. He had to be careful. But he always took a little more than he said, and then stashed some away, like. Stashed the hash. He liked the sound of it. He said it out loud. Stashed the hash. For when he might need it. Like tonight. Or for some time when George maybe didn't have nothing. George never put nothing aside for him, for when the connection was cut off or something. He should of never come to stay with George.

But he couldn't stay with her, either . . . his mother. She was always on his case. He didn't even tell her he was flunking everything and he would have to fucking do the whole term again. He already did that scene. She called up George about it the first time, like George maybe gave a shit. Nobody gave a shit what happened to him.

What the fuck was he supposed to do? The things they wanted him to *learn* in school: the Civil War, for Chris' sake, and that play about a black family and they wanted to buy a house . . . like, who *cares*? And after they caught him nodding out in class a couple of times, this grade advisor tells him he has a high IQ and all and what's troubling him? *She's* troubling him is what. Fiddling with the papers on her desk, looking at the clock on the wall like she couldn't wait to get rid of him, with ten other kids waiting outside the office to see her. She didn't give a shit about him, either.

And what was he supposed to fucking do now?

He lit himself a joint and sucked at it a couple of times. Shit, maybe he should go back to George's now. Maybe the old broad was gone. Could he even find his way back? He didn't know where he was. He leaned against the building and finished the joint, using the clip in his pocket for the roach.

Feeling better, he put his finger on the bell and kept it there. He kept it there until his finger began to hurt, and then he put a different finger on it until that one hurt, too, and then kicked at the door.

He walked out on the curb and looked up at the building. A crack of light appeared at the bottom of a window, as though someone had lifted a shade a little bit. He ran out into the middle of the road where he could be seen, and waved his arms frantically, yelling, "Shelley . . . hey, Shelley . . . it's me, Stevie. . . ."

The curtain was lifted a few more inches, and a face appeared at the window. Stevie snatched a plastic bag out of his pocket and waved it. A hand signaled to him, and then the curtain was dropped. Stevie ran back hopefully to the building.

The door was opened cautiously. Someone tall and thin, in cowboy boots and black leather pants, was framed in green light from the hallway. An earring glittered in his left earlobe. A sleeveless, open vest of red sequins revealed a bare chest. His head was shaven, except for a two-inch tuft of hair, like a coxcomb, that ran from his forehead to the back of his neck.

"What do you want, man?"

"I wanna see Shelley."

"You the kid with the shit?"

"I ain't no kid."

The young man looked at him contemptuously. Something about him frightened Stevie. The skin of his face just covered the bones without anything extra. His eyes, in the strange green light, were cold. Mean.

"You bring the shit?"

"Yeah." Stevie aimed for the same tough, hard voice. But he sneezed, shivering in the cold. "Fucking rain," he said. He had no handkerchief. He sniffed back some mucus, brushing the back of his hand under his nose.

The young man stepped aside and Stevie pushed past him into the green light. An elevator with the same light was open on their left. They stepped in and the young man shoved a folding metal door across the opening and pressed the button. He didn't talk to Stevie. He stood with his back to him, one leg extended slightly, comfortable. Like it was his territory. He belonged here. Stevie didn't belong. He didn't belong anywhere.

The elevator shuddered and crept upward, clanging, a lumbering, ancient freight elevator. It seemed to be suffering. Stevie was afraid it might fall.

Nervously he said, "I'm Stevie. I'm Shelley's friend."

The tufted head nodded but didn't turn.

"Who are you?"

"Jo-Jo."

A sudden wild scream followed by a vicious burst of sound staggered Stevie. His heart began to pound. The sound continued rhythmically, punctuated by the howling, and then a male voice imitating singing, and Stevie realized it was a record. Punk rock. Stevie didn't like punk rock. The elevator groaned and stopped. Jo-Jo flung open the metal door and motioned Stevie to follow him. They stepped into the noise and into crazily shooting blasts of colored lights.

No wonder they hadn't heard the bell. Shit, he could just imagine what would happen if he fucking played his records this loud.

"Nice pad," he said. But there was no one to hear him. Jo-Jo had drifted away; he wouldn't have been able to hear him, anyway. Stevie felt dizzy and cold and all alone. Was there anything to fucking eat in this fucking place? He was all of a sudden starving. Someone touched his arm and held it. He turned and looked into the face of a very pretty girl. She was smiling at him warmly. She had this real nice smile. Shelley. From his class in school, when he was going to school. Smart, pretty Shelley, the cheerleader, with the shiny hair and long, shiny legs and shiny teeth and shiny skin. Shelley, who always had, in the pocket of her white sweater with the varsity letter, at least one of every pill and weed and dust and juice that is popped and

65

smoked and inhaled and burned and squirted and shot. She was talking to him.

"I can't hear you," he shouted.

She pulled him across the room to the stereo and lowered the sound, but she still rocked with the beat of the music, her long, shiny yellow hair swaying with her body. She was wearing a short, tight, sleeveless, red sequin vest like Jo-Jo's, open a lot at the top.

"I was ringing for an hour," he grumbled.

"I'm sorry," she purred. "The music . . ." she brushed her cheek against his shoulder and smiled at him. She had real nice teeth. "What'd you bring, Stevie?"

"Gold. Colombian gold," he said. "You got something to eat? I'm starving."

"I don't know," she said vaguely. "There might be something left . . ." She put out her hand. Her nails were painted black and had tiny silver stars on them.

He took a baggie out of his pocket, filled with the little leaves. She took it from him.

Jo-Jo appeared suddenly out of the lights. He put one arm around Shelley and pulled her close to him.

"What do we got, Fox?" he said.

She held up the bag.

He bared his teeth in a knifelike smile. "Not bad," he said. He reached around her with his other hand and took the bag.

"Hey . . ." Stevie said. "Wait a minute. That's mine . . ."

"You wanna share it, don't you, kid? That's what you're here for, ain't it?"

He moved off, his arm around Shelley. The lights struck their sequins and seemed to set them afire. Stevie rushed after them. Jo-Jo folded himself cross-legged on a pillow near a wall and Shelley curled herself beside him, leaning against him. The screaming record came on again. A few couples squirmed and twisted to the music, and a few others drifted toward Jo-Jo. A packet of Bambu appeared, and Jo-Jo rolled a joint swiftly and lit it. He passed it to Shelley, and folding the bag neatly, he put it into a pocket in his vest.

"Hey . . ." Stevie protested. "That's my bag. . . ."

Jo-Jo turned contemptuous eyes toward him. He said, "Give Fatso a drag, Fox."

Shelley held out the joint to Stevie, but he pushed her hand away. Shivering with fear and cold and rage, he said very loud, "I don't want no fuckin' drag. I want my bag back."

They didn't answer him. Shelley passed the joint to Jo-Jo. He took a long drag and then passed it to someone else. Some more people had sat down, forming a small, tight circle. The joint was passed around. A girl pushed past Stevie and sat on the floor in front of him, leaving him outside the circle. Stevie watched Jo-Jo reach inside the pocket of his sequin jacket and pull out the plastic bag . . . *his* plastic bag. He pushed into the circle, trembling, and grabbed it. Jo-Jo caught his wrists and bent his arm back, laughing.

"Foxy, your friend here don't got no manners. You gonna behave, Fats, or what?"

Shelley's head was on Jo-Jo's thigh. She opened her large, round blue eyes and smiled up at Stevie.

"Stevie, don't act like that. You said you needed a place to crash. Come on, sit down . . . here, by me. Let's all be happy . . ." Her words slurred together. She held a joint in her fingers. *His* joint, from *his* bag, for Chris' sake. . . .

He should be the one giving it out. It was all his, wasn't it? He had lifted it from his own father, hadn't he? He should be sitting in the center, and everybody should be looking at *him*, admiring *him*, paying attention to *him*, grateful to *him*, instead of that punker.

"Yeah, sit down, Fats," Jo-Jo said.

Stevie hated him. He wished he was dead. He wished he could kill him. He wished he was big and tall with big, broad shoulders and hard fists. He wished he had boots with spikes on the bottom so he could kick him, step on his face . . . instead of sneakers with a hole in the sole so his feet were wet.

And Shelley was lying there with her head in his lap, her yellow hair spilling all over like liquid gold. She patted the floor beside her. Jo-Jo put a joint to her lips and she breathed it in and held it, closing her eyes. *He* should be feeding her. Her head should be in *his* lap. Her hand, with the black and silver nails, patted the floor again, dreamily.

Shit, he might as well get some of it, too. What difference did it make? What difference did anything make?

He sat beside Shelley and took the joint she offered him. He kept it. He wasn't going to pass it around. Nobody asked for it back. They better not. Or else. Or else what, Stevie? He'd show them. He would show everybody. He was gonna *do* something someday. Maybe learn how to play that clarinet George had. And start a band and be a star. They would notice him then. They would love him. Everybody would love him.

He lay back on the floor. He was tired. Real tired. He was beginning to feel warmer. Nice. But the floor under his head was hard. He wished he had a lap to put his head on. He thought of Shelley, her long legs going up to her cunt. He bet it was nice in there. He bet if he got his prick in her pussy it would be real nice in there.

His eyes closed. The joint in his fingers felt hot. He sucked on it, holding it tight. They were OK. They fucking weren't bad. Even Jo-Jo, the Mohawk. He liked that. He said it aloud, "Mohawk the Shmohawk." He felt himself laughing. Feeling good. Feeling real nice. Floating, his arms and legs and all of him soaring, his head turning off . . . .

Someone was kicking him, screaming in his ear to wake up. He rolled away from the pain. It followed him, a hard, sharp, pointy thing. Someone grabbed his hair and pulled it, hard. He opened his eyes. This crazy Indian with mean eyes was yelling at him to get up. Were they going to scalp him? He rolled away from the Indian and scrambled up, cowering, terrified, his eyes straining in the dim light.

The Indian laughed. "He ain't dead. I told you, Fox. Wake up, Fats. You gotta split now, man."

"Split?" Where was he?

"Fox's old man works nights. He's gonna be home any minute. Move your ass! Scram!"

Stevie sneezed, shivering and blinking. The lights and the music were gone. All the windows were open. "Where is everybody?"

"Oh Jesus! *Move* it, man!" Jo-Jo shoved him, hard, to the door.

"I gotta take a leak . . ."

Jo-Jo pushed him into the elevator, stabbed at a button, and slammed the metal folding door.

Outside, dazed, Stevie walked. It was cold. He walked as fast as he could. Everything was gray. There was no color anywhere, and no people. Nothing moved; nothing made a sound. The sky was gray; the streets were gray; the thin drizzle was gray. The buildings, only a darker gray, leaned toward him, closing in. He began to run. He didn't know where he was running. When he saw a phone booth, he ran into it. The cord was ripped off. He ran out again, running until he was out of breath and his side hurt. Where was everybody? Was the world dead? Was there a bomb and the world was dead except for him? There was another phone booth, or was it the same one? Was he running in circles? He tried the phone. It was working. He called

George. Maybe the skinny old bitch would be gone and he could go back and get some sleep. Maybe George had something to eat. Some ice cream or chocolate milk. Maybe he could get George to spring for a taxi so he could get home without getting lost.

Fucking cunt Shelley, throwing him out.

He shivered in the phone booth. What was a cop doing in George's pad, answering George's phone? It must be a bust. They must have found George's stash. He couldn't go there now. Maybe they were even looking for him.

He stepped out of the booth, and the wind attacked his wet shirt. He sneezed. His nose was running. He was cold and wet and scared. He was trembling violently, and then he was vomiting. His head hurt.

All of a sudden he was crying. He was a fat, scared, cold, very unstoned sixteen-year-old boy.

He went back into the phone booth and dialed his mother in Brooklyn.

Chapter Seven

Anna hesitated in front of the door to her apartment. It was two o'clock in the morning, but she wasn't tired. She felt unaccountably exhilarated, filled with energy. From someplace in the distance she heard a faint thud and then voices; a sound that might have been a gunshot and a scream. She listened harder: It was a television, of course. She knew that there must be light behind some of the closed doors, people moving, the smell of coffee. Even sex. She thought she smelled sex.

And what was this wild patterned thing she was holding. Was it a neatly folded sheet? She didn't remember where she had picked it up.

And where had she left her umbrella?

It was too late to try to think about anything. And what was she going to tell Emmy? She had never come home this late. Emmy did. Even later. Often. Maybe if she was very quiet, if she moved in a whisper, she wouldn't wake Emmy up. It would be difficult. With the sofa bed open in the living room there was hardly room to walk around. In the dark she would bump into something.

71

Poor Emmy. She had no privacy. She used to have such a pretty room. It looked out over the garden. And really, basically, she had had her own bathroom. Simon and she hardly ever used that hall bathroom. They had their own bathroom in the master bedroom.

Emmy never talked about her room. She never talked about the house. Did she ever think about it? It wasn't a very big house, really. They could have had something much bigger. But she had never been demanding. Maybe she should have been. Maybe if Simon had felt compelled to make more money, to work harder, he wouldn't have had time . . . But they had seemed so contented in the house. It had six rooms; a dining room, living room, and huge kitchen downstairs. She loved a big kitchen. There was a screened porch off the kitchen. They had their meals there in the summer. She really missed that. They never put in the powder room downstairs that they had talked about. Upstairs there were three bedrooms. They had used the third bedroom for a den, with a color TV and a desk for Simon, and that wonderful leather chair and ottoman she had bought for him. He got that chair in the divorce. He said it was his. It was, but she had bought it for him. He loved sitting in that chair. It was real leather; it had that wonderful masculine smell of leather. She had thought he was happy with her, sitting in that chair, in their home. It would never have occurred to her that he would ever want to leave it. Leave her.

When had he started to want to leave? When had he started to wear tight pants and let his hair grow long? When had it begun that there was nothing she could do to please? What had she done wrong? She had tried so hard. . . .

Oh God, when would the pain go away? Would she never stop thinking about it? What was she doing in this narrow hall, in front of this heavy gray metal door with the little peephole like the door of a solitary confinement cell. The hall always had the faint odor of cabbage. Even with its pretensions of gentility, the gray-green carpet that didn't show dirt, the gray-green wallpaper, there was still the smell of cabbage. Like any low-class tenement.

Cooking cabbage should be outlawed in all apartment houses, she thought. She had always hated apartment houses. They waited a long time to have a child so they could save enough money to buy a house to raise the child in. Was that, too, a mistake?

What was it the shrink said so often? "You have to stop blaming yourself. It wasn't you." Mid-life crisis, she said. Jargon. Terms people invented. Excuses. So they could betray other people, destroy their lives without feeling guilty.

"Don't you want to be an Independent Person!" the young shrink cried, with shock. More jargon.

"I've always worked. I've always been an independent person. That's why I get no alimony. I would get alimony if I had stayed home all my life and played mah-jongg and spent my time polishing my nails and being helpless. Maybe he wouldn't have stopped loving me if I had been dependent and helpless."

Her mood was changed. The lovely exhilaration was gone. But she still wasn't tired. She was suddenly ravenous. Starving. She had to have something to eat. But if she went into the apartment and started messing around in the kitchen, it would wake Emmy.

There was an all-night diner down the street. She would go there and have something to eat and then come home.

Outside, in the cool, quiet street, she began to feel cheerful again. The click of her heels on the pavement seemed friendly and somehow young. The moon was teasing the clouds, peeping out, flirting, darting away. It made Anna think there was something she should remember. Or was it forget? She didn't know. She didn't remember. She found herself humming an old song she used to like: "Someday he'll come along, the man I love . . ."

She was still carrying the sheet with her. She put it on the seat beside her in the diner. She would have to return it and get her umbrella. That must have been what she had been trying to remember. Her umbrella. She had left it in the hall at the party. No. She had left the party. She hadn't taken Louise home, and now Louise wouldn't like her. She had put the umbrella in a corner near the door in that man's apartment.

She had a hamburger and french fries and chocolate cake with ice cream and two and a half cups of coffee. When she left the diner it was four in the morning. She still wasn't tired. On the way back to the apartment, she passed her car. Maybe she ought to drive back to Manhattan and get her umbrella. With all that coffee in her, she would never be able to sleep. Might as well do something useful. But what would she tell Emmy about staying out all night? Nothing. Simply nothing. It was no business of Emily's.

What if the man was asleep? Then she would ring the bell and wake him. Serve him right. Horrid man with his tight pants and long hair.

Feeling purposeful and defiant, feeling happy, she got into the car. At this hour, it shouldn't take her more than an hour to get there. Even less. She turned on the radio and found quiet music. It slipped gently into the empty spaces in her brain, blocking out thought.

It took Anna a full hour to get there because they were repairing the Long Island Expressway. They were always repairing the expressway, and it always remained the same. Huge puddles collected in the same places and potholes formed near all the fixed potholes.

It was five o'clock. She got a parking space right away, near the corner, only a few spaces away from the building entrance. She sat in the car for a few minutes; there was something in the back of her mind, something she had to remember.

Maybe she ought to start taking vitamins for her memory, the way Simon had started to do. Vitamin E. Or was it lecithin? She couldn't remember. The problem would be, of course, to remember to take it.

She got out of the car. Night was dying, she thought. The sky had a sickly gray pallor. Rain hung tensely in the air, like unshed tears. She felt her brisk, springy step was incongruous to the wet, thick air, but that made her smile. She felt unvanquished by the weather. The weather so often determined her mood. The weather and Emily and Simon and before that, her father . . . things over which she had no control. She had always tried to please them, to do what was suitable. Propitiating the gods. . . . Today she felt free of all of them. As though, for the first time, she controlled her own destiny.

She walked past the doorman in the lobby with her new, confident step, straight to the elevator. A wrinkled, white-haired man wearing rubbers and a rain cape and a plastic cover over his hat said good morning. He was carrying the Sunday *Times* and a brown paper bag.

Anna said good morning, too. She hoped the man wouldn't talk.

"Couldn't sleep," said the man. "Worst part of old age. You fall asleep in the theater, but you can't sleep in your bed."

"You're not old," Anna said.

"Of course I'm old," the man said testily.

"If you insist," said Anna. The man didn't hear her because the elevator had arrived and the door began to wheeze open. It was barely open when two men pushed out: a short, dark, Hispanic-looking policeman and a tall man, very big, in a rumpled suit.

"I suppose he's being arrested for something," the old man said clearly. "Burglary, probably. We have a lot of burglaries. A big, strong man like that, he ought to get a job. He ought to be ashamed of himself."

Anna blushed. She glanced back at the big man. Without breaking stride, he had turned around to look at them. He caught Anna's eye and grinned.

She felt herself blush again, and grinned back. He had a pleasant, friendly face.

"I don't think he's a burglar," Anna said, loud.

"You can't be too careful these days. You see this paper bag. Never go anywhere without it. I carry a brick in it. If anyone starts up with me, I'll swing it at him. If you're coming in the elevator, come along. It's slow enough as it is, without waiting for anyone."

Anna stepped in quickly just as the door had begun to slide shut.

"Floor?" said the man.

He pressed her number with his umbrella, then pressed his own. "Disgusting weather," he said.

"Yes. Isn't it wonderful," said Anna.

The man glared at her. "My windows were so wet I thought it was raining. I took my umbrella in case the doorman forgot to get my paper and I would have to go out for it. Not much good, the doormen. I think they're in with the crooks."

"It's nice you didn't lose your umbrella," Anna said.

"Never lost anything in my life. If it was up to me," said the man, "I would say 'Rain, and get it over with!'"

"If I could, I'd let it be up to you," Anna said kindly.

The man stared at her angrily again. "You think I couldn't do better than whoever it is who takes care of the weather. You bet I could!"

The elevator stopped. "Nine," said the man.

"Thank you."

As Anna stepped out, the man said, "Whoever heard of a newspaper costing a dollar. A dollar! I used to feed my family for a week for a dollar."

"You have a very good memory," said Anna.
"I have all my marbles," said the man.
"And a brick, too," said Anna.
The door slid closed. The elevator started up.

A dark green Chevy, four years old, pulled up and parked alongside the hydrant directly in front of the building, although there were at least two other parking spaces nearby. The car had MD plates. A tall, gray-haired man with glasses, carrying a black doctor's bag and a covered styrofoam cup, got out and looked around. Bernie waved to him. He came toward Bernie quickly. Bernie got the police sign that said CRIME SCENE KEEP OUT out of his trunk and handed it to Ramirez.

"Get it on the door right away."
"Yes, sir." He turned to go.
"Ramirez."
"Yes, sir?"
"How long you been on the force?"
"Three months, sir."
"I never puked," Bernie said. "I had nightmares. Woke up in a sweat, scared shitless. Still do. Better to puke. Get that fucking sign on the door before there is an invasion of the curious. You stand guard outside the door. Good, law-abiding citizens will take hair off the victim's head for souvenirs if they can get it. Homicide detectives ought to be getting here soon. In the meantime, as soon as you get the sign up, tell Johnson to get a list of all the tenants and their apartment numbers. Everyone. Check anyone who goes in and out of the building. Elevators and stairs. Get ID's. Find out who was the tenant in 9E. Maybe get a line on him from the doorman. Doormen know a lot sometimes. And start ringing doorbells. Ask questions. Find out all about last night in 9E. Start with the people next door. They have to have heard something."

Bernie watched Ramirez trot back into the building. He

hoped his lie had helped. The only thing that ever gave him nightmares was his son.

An ambulance, its siren screaming, tore down the street and pulled into the circular driveway in front of the house. Two men in white were out of the ambulance almost before it stopped. They opened the back and wheeled out a stretcher.

"9E," Bernie called to them.

They ran into the building.

"You'd better drink the coffee now, Doc," said Bernie to the man in gray. "You won't have the stomach for it upstairs."

"That so? What have we got up there, Bernstein?"

"Bloody pulp where the face should be. Prick off, or mostly off."

The medical examiner's gray face looked slightly grayer. He pushed his glasses up higher on his nose. They were always slipping down. Then he took the cover off his cup and took a long swallow. He held the cup out to Bernie, who took a small sip and coughed and looked into the cup. "That's scotch!"

"Yep. Coffee's bad for you. Caffeine." He took the cup back and took another long belt, covered the cup carefully, and looking very dignified, walked a perfectly straight line into the building.

A man had come out of a dirty tan sedan across the street and was headed for Bernie. A burly man in a nondescript raincoat. He had brownish hair, light eyes, ruddy skin. *Detective* might have been printed across his forehead in neon letters. He moved fast without seeming to hurry.

"A dillar, a dollar, a ten o'clock scholar," said Bernie. "Nice of you to show up, Donlon."

"Overworked and underpaid, Inspector. Citizens want faster service, they ought to hire more detectives."

"In the meantime, the perpetrator could have come back three times and removed all the evidence."

Donlon shrugged. "Over eighteen hundred homicides in New York City last year. Can't win 'em all. People keep killing each other; we can only do what we can do. I just came from a beauty. Body in a hotel room without hands, feet, or a head. What will they think of next?"

"I can tell you . . ." Bernie stopped. Three cars pulled up fast. They had large signs that said PRESS on their windshields. "Press," said Bernie out of the corner of his mouth.

Donlon nodded. His face seemed to close. As if on cue, the two men turned and walked very fast into the building.

When Anna got off the elevator, she waited for the door to close. She watched the numbers going up: 10, 11, 12, 14, 15. Slowly. A cranky old elevator. She turned to the apartment doors. They all looked alike. Greasy-looking, chipped brown metal.

Last night they had gotten out of the elevator and turned right and walked past a few doors. She wasn't sure how many. She stopped in front of a door. The name under the bell read "Miller."

Had he told her his last name? She didn't remember. What was his first name?

She rang the bell. There was a shuffling sound, and then an eye was staring at her from the peephole. She stared back at it. It disappeared. Then the peephole opened again and the eye blinked and a woman's voice said, "Who is it?"

Anna said, "Excuse me. I didn't mean to disturb you. I wonder if you can help me . . ."

"I don't want any. There is no soliciting here." The peephole snapped shut. Anna thought she could hear footsteps moving away.

"I'm not selling anything."

There was no answer.

Wrong door. She moved to the next one and rang the bell. She didn't hear anything. The bell didn't seem to be working. She raised her hand to knock and noticed that the door was slightly ajar. That silly joke Emmy used to like when she was a little girl came into her head: "When is a door not a door"—"When it's ajar." Why did she think of that now? She remembered that the man's door didn't close properly. Something was wrong with the lock, he said. She could see his face, suddenly, with his silly smile, but she had forgotten his name again. Had she left the door open when she left? Tentatively, softly, she poked at it with her finger. It slid in a few inches. She could see a piece of a brown couch and a black glass table. On the back of the couch was a strip of red. The bikini undershorts. He must still be sleeping. No point in waking him. Softly, with one finger, she pushed the door open a few more inches. The umbrella was where she had left it, in the corner near the door.

The elevator was starting down. She could hear it cranking in the shaft. If she didn't catch it, she would have a long wait.

Swiftly she reached her hand in and grabbed the umbrella. It took less than a second. She held it tight. She was glad she had it.

She rushed to press the elevator button. Behind her she heard a man call, "Ramirez?" and heard a door open. The elevator stopped and the door crept open. She stepped in quickly. She was glad it was empty. The elevator started down wearily. She felt suddenly impatient to be away. Home.

It stopped one time. A man got on. He looked half-asleep and grumpy, and went directly to a corner and leaned back and closed his eyes, catching a few more seconds of sleep. She was glad he didn't talk to her.

When they finally reached the lobby, there were a lot of

people waiting for the elevator. The short, dark policeman was there, holding a sign. He was in such a hurry, he pushed in rudely, without waiting for her to get out. There were two men in white. And the big, attractive man. He was busy talking to another big man in a raincoat. She thought he noticed her. She thought he noticed everything around him. She caught a flicker of recognition on his face, and she would have smiled at him, but he didn't smile first. She didn't want to seem to be flirting. He was a very attractive man. Very masculine. She never met men like that at those silly Singles' Things. Men like that didn't have to go to them. The good ones are taken or dead.

She wondered why there were so many people around suddenly. Something must have happened. There were more police, and through the big glass outer doors she could see an ambulance, its lights flashing.

She glanced back at the elevator. The doors were closing. She thought the big man was staring at her. It even seemed, for an instant, that he was going to get out, maybe come over to her.

Oh yes, Anna. You will soon see men under your bed. Strong, handsome, charming men, and they will fall madly in love with you at first sight.

Maybe Emily is right. You ought to go back to your shrink. That braless wonder.

Outside, the mist had become a slow, tentative rain. Anna opened her umbrella. She thought what a good idea it was to have gone back right away to get it instead of waiting until later in the day. Peering out through the yellow plastic made her feel it was sunny. That was why she had chosen this yellow, so it would seem like a bright, sunny day even when it was raining. She could use a sunny day.

She walked slowly to her car. She wasn't in a hurry to get home now.

* * *

Bernie saw her. The woman in the red raincoat. She was holding a yellow, plastic umbrella. It was the woman he had seen at the elevator with the old man. He was startled when he saw the umbrella, but then he felt foolish and thought there must be a million of those in the street today, one on every other block. Still, something about it bothered him. He watched her. She had great legs. He really went for good legs. Linda had great legs.

Ah, Linda. His head had sneaked that in very nicely.

He wrenched his thoughts back to the case. Actually, it was still early. Not even 5:30 A.M. He had plenty of time before he was due in. He had thought he would duck out of the elevator at the third floor, walk down the stairs and out the delivery entrance to evade the reporters. But he decided to go back to the apartment. Lend a hand. Look around some more.

Chapter Eight

"What umbrella?"

The question sent Bernie tearing out into the hall to the elevator. He caught it as the doors were closing and jabbed his finger on the "L" button and kept it there as if that would make it go faster. Damn elevator crept down as if it were afraid of falling. When it shuddered to a stop on 4 to let a young woman in with a laundry basket, he ran out to the stairs, tearing down the four flights, getting to the lobby before the elevator did, and dashed outside into the middle of the street. Why hadn't he stopped her? He had wanted to. Almost did. He could have talked to her.

And said what? "You're under arrest for having a yellow plastic umbrella." It might not even be *the* yellow plastic umbrella. The shaft on that one was broken. And even that would have proved nothing.

He could have said something. Said, "Hi." Go from there. What was he, a dumb rookie, a puker?

She might know something. Anything. She might have been in the apartment last night. She might have been a

83

witness. She might be able to give them a lead. She might even be the killer.

He stood in the middle of the road and stared down the broad street, looking on both sides. What the hell was the matter with him? The woman could be anywhere, blocks away in any direction, or in a bus or subway or in a car of her own, alone or with someone else, or in any building or restaurant or store. And what was he chasing her for? She had a yellow plastic umbrella like the one in the apartment. An umbrella that no one else had seen.

For the first time he noticed the rain. It was coming down hard. Rain was dripping down his neck, inside his collar. He was drenched. He turned. And then he saw her. She was in her car, at the corner, only a short distance away, stopped at a red light. He started toward the car. The light changed. Her car began to move. He got the license number.

The press was coming toward him. He got to his car quickly and drove off. A few blocks away he stopped and wrote the number in his pad. Then he called the precinct. It took them less than five minutes to get the information. They hit it directly into the computer in Albany. He wrote it in the notebook: Anna Welles. And her address.

He'd check it out. Himself. Quietly. He didn't want to cause the woman unnecessary grief. It could be a mistake. Probably was. She looked like a nice person. She had a pleasant, intelligent face. Sensitive. And he knew she had a sense of humor. She was a trifle nervous, maybe. Somewhat like . . . OK . . . say it out loud. "Somewhat like Linda." Faded, maybe. Sad. Vulnerable.

He'd check it. Something about the case excited him. Involved him.

Chapter Nine

It wasn't night anymore. But it wasn't morning either. It was that breathless time. Suspenseful. Emily Dickinson had written about it. "Will there really be a morning . . ."

They had named their daughter for Emily Dickinson. Why was she remembering that now? Tired. Out of control. Lucky there was no traffic at this hour. Simon had loved her then. He had! Why did he say he hadn't? Why did he have to take that away from her, too? That was the cruelest thing. As if she had never been loved. To have forgotten how he had always wanted to touch her . . . her hand, her neck. He couldn't walk without holding some part of her. Why had he forgotten that? Said it was only youth. Sex. Ignorance.

Guilt, said the shrink. It would make him feel too guilty. He had to deny. . . .

And why did he have to be so mean at the end? So critical and cruel and impatient, always sarcastic, never wanting her opinion, belittling her, putting her down, cataloging her faults, destroying her self-confidence so she couldn't even fight back. He didn't have to do that.

And why did he suddenly buy her that lovely opal ring she had only casually admired?

Guilt guilt guilt. . . .

Not enough guilt. He counted the ring in adding up her assets for the divorce.

It was raining again. The windshield wiper didn't help.

No, stupid, it isn't raining. It's tears. You're crying again. That's how you cracked up the car last time.

No, it was deliberate last time. A person has the right to decide when she's had enough.

Cut it out, Anna. Stop feeling sorry for yourself. Look at the statistics on marriage and divorce.

Statistics don't help me. They help *him*. Make him feel less guilty. So many men are doing it, it must be OK.

Women are doing it, too. That's called Equal Opportunity, no doubt. Singles' Dances. Singles' Parties. Singles' Bars. Singles' Raps. You've come a long way, baby. Let's fuck.

Simon's wife is thirty-two. I saw her once at the theatre with him. They had orchestra seats. She was wearing a beige silk top with spaghetti straps. Her nipples teased the shimmering fabric. Nipples are IN, baby. There is nothing in the world so lovely as full, upright, young breasts, Simon. Who could blame you? Out with the old, in with the new. By the time she's fifty and you will have forgotten how you felt about her in the beginning, it won't matter. Nothing will matter. I don't matter now. Not to anyone.

Sternly: You must matter to yourself.

Right. When they bury me, they'll put it on my tombstone.

SHE MATTERED TO HERSELF

Turn off, head. No more thinking.

What was that thought niggling at her head, gnawing at her?

Forget it.

Why couldn't a head be like a faucet? Turn it on, turn it off. Mine would drip.

Emily likes her father's new wife. She's a nice person, Emily said. Pleasant and reasonable. Naturally. She's happy. And she never nags at Emily. She doesn't care enough to nag or worry. Emily has two mothers: the old pain in the ass and the pretty, new one. That was really the cruelest part. The truly unbearable part. He had given away to some other woman a part of her child, the child whom she had borne, who had come out of her body. He had made some other woman her daughter's mother. He had no right to do that. A younger, prettier stranger. And Emily liked her. Maybe even liked her better. Anna couldn't fight it. She withdrew. Gave up. She lost Emily, too, because she didn't dare to feel so close to Emily as she had before. Was it true when Emily said in anger, "You don't love me anymore"?

I love you, Emily. I love you more. You're all I have. I am afraid to love you too much for fear of becoming too dependent on you or making you feel responsible for me. For fear of losing you, too.

Tired.

Scream. Go ahead. Scream. There's no one in the car with you.

And then there was no place close to her building to park. She had to park blocks and blocks away.

Concentrate on walking, on the click of her heels in the still dawn, on the slowly waking sky, on holding the umbrella in the wind. After she got some sleep, she would remember the thing that was chipping away at her head. She hoped it wouldn't mean another trip to Manhattan.

She had been out all night. What was she going to tell

Emmy? I hope she isn't worried, poor kid. I'm too tired to make explanations.

Emily wasn't home. Since the divorce Emily often stayed out late. She didn't call or explain.

OK. I won't ask for explanations. I won't worry or make demands. I'll be casual and reasonable, like Mrs. thirty-two-year-old new wife. How much did that bit of beige silk cost, Simon, while I count nickels and dimes and take down hems and use broken umbrellas? I have to get Emily through college. Simon doesn't. The court said he didn't have to, not after Emily was eighteen. Emily, too, will leave me. Children do that. They should.

Scream. No one will hear you. No one is home. Or shut your head and go to sleep. Put up a sign: MIND CLOSED UNTIL FURTHER NOTICE. No thinking allowed. No worrying. I'll go straight to sleep. I'll only brush my teeth.

Her mouth tasted terrible.

The last thing Anna remembered before falling asleep was that she had left that folded-up sheet in the car. Always forgetting something.

Chapter Ten

Every morning of her marriage, before Anna opened her eyes, she felt beside her for Simon. She liked feeling him there. She liked touching him. At night, when she woke up, she always felt for him. She touched him, and it calmed her and she could fall asleep again.

She still did it. Every morning her hand reached out and then her eyes flew open in a panic.

He wasn't there. It wasn't a bad dream. He wasn't there.

But today Anna was out of bed and in her robe before she realized she hadn't felt across the bed for Simon. She had awakened and gotten straight out of bed. Something had wiped him out of her mind. Whatever it was, she was grateful.

It was almost noon. She never got up so late. She must have come in very late. Where had she been? Another great singles' function, no doubt. She tried to forget them right away, not always so successfully. What had she done last night?

She couldn't think before coffee.

She opened the door to the living room quietly. Her

daughter was still asleep on the convertible couch. Her jeans and tee shirt lay where she had dropped them on the floor. Anna tiptoed around them through the room to the kitchen. She had paid the super to put a door between the living room and the kitchen. It was only an accordian door and it didn't close tightly, but it was better than nothing. She tried not to make much noise. She put on the coffee and heated a couple of rolls in the toaster oven. The windowless room was stuffy and hot. She set the table for herself, and for Emmy, too, with place mats and napkins, and poured milk for her coffee into a pretty creamer. It made her feel good to set the table nicely. She wasn't going to be one of those dreary singles who ate her dinner straight out of a can.

The accordian door was pushed open and Emmy stuck her head in.

"Good morning." Anna tried to sound cheerful. It didn't work.

Emily came in and slumped into a chair. This wasn't her carefree Emmy who used to chatter and giggle, always bubbling, this girl with the bloodshot eyes and disheveled hair. Anna poured coffee for her.

"Why don't you ask if I want it first?" Emmy said irritably.

Anna flushed. "I'm sorry, dear. I always think everyone is like me and is desperate for that first mouthful of coffee." She picked it up. "I'll pour it back."

"Oh, don't *bother!*" Emmy snatched it from her angrily. The coffee spilled over and burned both their hands. "Oh shit, let me have it!" Emmy put it down hard on the table. "You always make such a big deal of everything!"

"Did you burn yourself?"

"Forget it; just drop it, can't you!"

Anna ran cold water on her own burned fingers. She did it mostly to keep her back to her daughter until she felt calmer. Then she refilled her own cup. Emmy stirred her coffee. She didn't drink it. "Did you meet Prince Charming of the Denture Set last night?"

Anna didn't answer. Should she tell her daughter again that there was nothing shameful or degrading in going to singles' functions? How was she going to convince Emmy of that when she didn't believe it herself? She finished her coffee in one gulp and got up. "Will you have more coffee or should I pull out the plug?"

"I don't know. It doesn't matter." Emily's voice sounded suddenly depressed. "No. I guess not." She got up and carried the dishes to the sink and washed them. Her shoulders were hunched. She looked defeated.

"Are you all right, Emily?"

Emily didn't answer. She finished the dishes and wiped her hands on her pajamas. She didn't turn around. "I went to a party at Betsy's last night," she said, obviously choosing her words carefully. "Everybody was there. All my old friends."

"You were afraid they wouldn't want to know you."

"They haven't called me in a long time."

"Telephones work both ways, Emmy."

"Laura's parents are separated. And Eric's parents are divorced."

"It's an epidemic."

"It doesn't hit everybody," said Emmy.

"Neither did the bubonic plague."

"What would be the point of calling Betsy, or anyone? I can't do the things they do anymore. Could I invite them here?"

"Of course. It's not your house, it's you, they want to know."

"Oh shit! Eric isn't going to have to leave his school and go to a stupid city college the way I did."

"City colleges aren't stupid. They're more demanding than the Ivy League schools. Who's going to pay for Eric's school?"

"His father. And his mother got the house, too."

Their house had been in both their names, hers and Simon's. The lawyers agreed the house should be sold and the money divided equally, even though they would never have been able to buy the house or to maintain it, at first, if Anna hadn't worked. And even though Simon's current income was almost triple hers. After the mortgages had been paid off, there was enough left in Anna's share for her lawyer's fee and the move to the apartment and the tuition for Emmy's first year of college. She had no savings of her own, though she had worked all the years of their marriage. She had trusted her husband.

Statistics.

Emmy knew all that. She probably knew the statistics.

"Maybe Eric's mother was smart enough to get a good lawyer," Emmy said. "Maybe she didn't fall apart like a dropped egg."

"You could have taken a loan and stayed on at Skidmore."

"You're on that again. Loans have to be paid back. With what does a liberal arts graduate pay back loans?"

"I'm sure Laura has loans. She did even before the separation."

"I've told you and told you, Laura is a brain. She's a physics major and she got scholarships and she'll have no trouble getting a great job when she graduates. Besides, she's so beautiful, some man will be happy to pay it all back for her."

"If she's really a brain, she's too smart to count on that."

"There are some women who know how to get what they want from men."

"Yes," Anna said. "I know. I was not a success as a woman."

"I didn't mean that. I really didn't, Mom. . . ."

Anna got up.

Emmy turned suddenly and faced her mother. Her face

was losing its fight against tears. "They're all going to Florida for the spring recess next week."

Anna waited.

"They asked me to come along."

"You know I don't have the money, Emmy."

"It would only be a loan."

"I don't have it to lend you."

"You could borrow from your pension."

"I borrowed from my pension for the car. I haven't paid it back yet."

"If you hadn't cracked up the car, we wouldn't be in so much trouble."

Anna didn't answer.

"You could borrow from a bank. They'd lend you money. I'd pay it back out of my job. Every week."

"Emmy, you aren't able to cover the expenses you agreed on from your job."

"I can work more hours."

"You're barely passing everything with the hours you're working now."

"So I'm not bright."

"I didn't say that. Your grades used to be excellent. It's a bad time for you. For us."

Emily pushed past her mother and ran out of the kitchen. She flung herself down on the open convertible bed and sobbed. Anna watched her helplessly. She didn't know how to comfort her.

"I know how you feel, Emmy."

"You don't! You don't give a damn about me! You don't love me! You never did!"

"That isn't true. I do love you, Emmy."

"All you care about is finding yourself a new husband!"

"I'm sorry, Emmy. I'm sorry you feel that way. I've done everything I could. More than I could."

"I *have* to go to Florida! How can I have friends if I can't do what they do?"

"I wish I could help you."

"Oh, let me alone!"

Anna said what she had promised herself she would never, never say: She said, "Ask your father for the money."

Hating herself, she went quickly through the living room to her bedroom. Emily shouted after her:

"You're crazy! Only crazy people try to kill themselves. You ought to be put away! Locked up! I don't blame him for leaving you!"

Anna closed the bedroom door. Trembling, she leaned against the wall. *I don't blame him for leaving you!*

The words echoed over and over in her ears. It was like her most frequent nightmares, her most persistent fear. She stood alone in the center of a circle of jeering women . . . her friends who were still married and the women she knew and strangers, and behind them, scornful men, all pointing a mocking finger at her and chanting: *I don't blame him for leaving you! I don't blame him for leaving you!*

She forced herself into the shower and dressed quickly. The trick was not to linger, to keep moving, to keep busy, not to think. She stripped her bed and gathered the laundry to do in the basement laundry room. When she came out into the living room with the laundry basket, Emily was sitting on the rumpled bed, her feet dangling over the side. She was staring disconsolately at nothing.

"Strip your bed, please, Emily. I'm going to do the laundry. Shall I defrost something for dinner? Will you be home?"

"I don't know. What difference does it make? What difference does anything make?"

Not much anymore, Anna thought. But when she had gotten up this morning, she had felt free of Simon. For the first time, for a brief moment, she had felt as if he didn't exist anymore. . . .

Emily put her bed linen into the basket. "I already asked him," she said. "I asked Dad for the money. Last night. He said he didn't have it, either. He has a whole new life now. Nobody has room for me."

Poor Emily. Conceived in love. What have we done to you? Anna sighed. "I'll see, Emmy. Maybe I can manage it."

Maybe she could wear her winter coat for another year. The collar and cuffs were wearing out, but she could get some fabric, a plaid or velvet, and make new cuffs and a collar. The rest of the coat was really not too bad, especially if there was no monkeying around with hem lengths this year.

"Don't worry about it, Emmy. You'll be able to go." She went out with the laundry.

While the laundry was in the machine, Anna got her car and picked up a few things at the local deli for lunch. Virginia ham and German potato salad, foods Emmy liked. She wondered again where she had gotten that ugly sheet she found in the car, but she was more concerned with Emily. How was she going to get the money for her? She was worried about Emmy. She wished they could talk. Was there anyone Emmy could talk to? Not her old friends, she knew. Emmy would be too proud. Maybe they would talk today. She would ask Emmy to stay home for dinner. But Anna had tried that before. She never could say the right thing. Everything she said nowadays seemed to anger her daughter. It was not a good time in a girl's life to lose her father. She had been seventeen. An adolescent girl needed her father. Anna had tried to tell that to Simon. Simon had said to Emmy, "I'm going to be happy. I think you should be glad for me." European-fit shirt open to his belly button, gold chain around his neck, thick sideburns. Or had the sideburns been earlier? Or later? He colored his hair, too. Played tennis to keep slim.

Anna used to make him blueberry pancakes on Sunday mornings, and they would sit in the den or on the porch and read the *Times*. She used to love Sundays. Then he began to come home later and later from tennis. He said the court next to them was empty and it was offered to them. Anna had been glad for him, glad he was enjoying himself.

When Anna came back with the groceries and the finished laundry, the sofa bed was closed and the apartment smelled of ammonia and furniture polish. Emily was dressed in a skirt and sweater, and she was sitting at the table with the *Times* and a pencil. Startled, Anna wondered if she should tell Emily how nice she looked with her hair brushed and neat with a blue hair band that matched her sweater. She didn't remember when she had last seen her not wearing jeans. She wondered if she were to say, "You look nice, Emmy," if her daughter would tear off the skirt and pull on a pair of rumpled jeans for spite. She knew she should have been pleased by the change, but it worried her. She felt uneasy.

"You should get a new raincoat, Mother."

Anna didn't answer. She took off the coat and hung it in the closet. "Everything looks so nice. Thank you for cleaning up."

"I live here, too."

"You should be studying. It's more important that you study."

"Grandpa once told me you wanted to be an artist."

"Grandpa is dead."

"I know Grandpa is dead," Emily said angrily. "It's so hard to talk to you, Mother."

"I'm sorry." She was glad he had died before Simon had left her.

"Is it true you wanted to be a painter?"

"No. I have a small ability. A skill, really. I draw nicely.

Good enough to illustrate the PTA bulletin. I enjoyed doing that."

She started to fold the laundry. Emily got up to help.

"Where did you get this sheet?"

She had taken it out of the car and laundered it. Might as well return it clean, when she could remember where she had gotten it. "It's a long story. I have to return it."

"You used to make the best costumes for the school plays. I was always very proud of that."

"That's about the extent of my talent."

"You always put yourself down."

Anna laughed. "I've read those articles, Emmy. 'I Gave Up My Art For My Husband, That Rat, And Now He's Left Me, I Have Found Fulfillment In My Work.' I didn't give up my art. I was as proud as you were of the costumes. I never wanted any more art than that."

"A woman should have more than a husband and children."

"What woman?" Anna said. "To each her own. My failure shouldn't make you cynical about marriage."

"You didn't fail by yourself. He had to have something to do with the failure, too. A woman should have something to fall back on."

"Maybe they'll start selling love insurance. Like life insurance. If love dies, you collect."

"The insurance companies would go broke. Love always dies. Besides, anybody would rather have the money."

"No," said Anna. And was instantly embarrassed. She said, too cheerfully, "Shall we have lunch?"

Emmy went into the kitchen while Anna put the folded linen away. She put the mystery sheet on the lower shelf of her night table. She couldn't shake the sense of foreboding.

When she came into the kitchen, Emmy said, "Daddy and Rosemary are going on a cruise."

Anna didn't say anything. Why did that hurt so much?

She hadn't been able to get Simon to go farther than New Jersey.

"That's why he can't lend me the money for Florida. He says."

"I told you I'd lend it to you, Emmy."

"No, Mommy." Her voice was very firm.

Again that stab of fear.

Emily had arranged the ham and cheese and potato salad on a platter, decorating it with some olives and strips of pickles, and she had put the rolls in a basket. There were daffodils in a blue vase on the table. Emmy must have bought them when she went out for the paper.

"That really looks lovely, Emmy."

"You haven't said I look lovely."

"I was afraid to. I thought you might fish out some dirty jeans to change into immediately."

"Am I that rotten?" Tears sprang into Emily's eyes. She turned away. "I'm sorry."

Anna's head pounded. "You're not rotten. Not at all. You've always been a wonderful girl. It's . . . it's a stage. Teenagers go through these things. Rebellion. Besides, it's a bad time for you. For us. Even Daddy."

"Oh, fuck Daddy!"

"Emily!"

"What were you going to do *without* to lend me money for Florida? Do you know how guilty that makes me feel? You and your let-down hems and your shiny-in-the-seat slacks?"

"You wanted me to lend you the money! You asked for it!"

"I know. I'm sorry. Listen, Mother, I don't want to fight with you. I want to talk to you." She poured them both a cup of tea and straightened her shoulders. "I've decided to leave school."

"Emily, I told you I'd give you the money."

"I know. I knew you would."

"I will. I promise you. I understand. You're young. You'll never be young again. I want you to have as much out of life as you can."

"What about your life?"

"That's not your responsibility and it's not your problem. I had my chance."

"I want to get a job. I'm nineteen. I want to have money of my own. An apartment of my own."

"I know you have no privacy. I offered you the bedroom."

"Stop offering me things!" Emily shouted. Then she started to cry. "I'm sorry. I'm sorry about this morning. I'm sorry about every morning. I've felt so . . . torn apart. . . ."

"All right, all right. It's no reason to leave school. Emily, don't do this. You always wanted to go to college. It's not something I only wanted for you."

Emily tried to smile. "People are starving all over the world. There's a button some nut will push that will end the world. What difference does it make if I go to college?"

"It will make a difference to you. To your life."

"Which life? All that belonged to a different life. Different lives have different dreams. Anyway," she said briskly, "I've been trying on clothes to look for a job with. Do I look OK?"

"Yes. Lovely. Emily, listen, you're upset. Go to Florida with your friends. Have fun. You haven't had any fun for a long time. You'll feel better about things when you get back."

"No. I'd feel worse."

"At least finish the term."

Emily shook her head. "I have to do it while I can. I've been thinking about it for a long time. Today I looked through the paper and I cut out some possibilities."

"What kind of job can you get? You have no skills."

"Waitress. Factory. Anything. I can brush up on my

typing later." She got up. "I'd better save these clothes for tomorrow. Mommy . . . what I want you to understand . . . it's not your fault."

"No?" Anna said bitterly. "Whose fault is it?"

"No one's. The world. The times. Life. Does it have to be someone's fault!" She was suddenly shouting. "What are you crying for?"

Anna stood up sharply. "I'm going to call your father. I've never called him before. I've never once asked him for help. But I'm going to call him now."

Emily stood in the doorway. "He isn't interested. My life is changed, Mother. Different. I have to do different things with it. I have to face facts. You ought to face facts, too. He's never coming back. Never."

"But I know that."

Emily was crying now, tears Anna had never seen before. "He really doesn't want us."

Anna held her. "No darling, it's *me* he doesn't want. You'll always be his daughter."

Emily shook her head, sobbing. "She's pregnant. Rosemary's going to have a baby. He's fifty-six years old; he should be a grandfather, and he's going to be a father. He said"— Anna didn't know if Emily was crying or laughing—"he would let me b-baby . . . babysit for them. . . ."

Anna held her, rocked her, comforting, trying desperately not to cry herself. For an instant yesterday . . . was it yesterday . . . she had felt free of him. As though he were dead. She remembered that. When had it happened? How?

Emily moved out of her mother's arms and dried her eyes. "Mother, please let me do what I want to do, without making me feel I've disappointed you, without making me feel guilty."

"All right," Anna said. "Anything." She wanted to say try to be happy, but she no longer believed in happiness.

She no longer believed in anything. She had had a world and it had crumbled. Vanished. She was abandoned in a void. There was nothing she even hoped for now.

"Mother, I'm moving out."

"All right."

"I met two girls at a party last month. They need a roommate. They said they'd carry me until I got a job."

Emily must have been thinking about it for a long time.

"All right."

The silence had come back into the room. Cold. Dead. She felt its icy breath. It reached for her.

"I'm not abandoning you, Mother. I'll see you. We'll talk. You'll come to dinner."

"All right."

"Don't do this to me!" Emily shouted. "Say something!"

"I'm sorry . . . I'm sorry, Emily. I was thinking of something else. Of course you have to do what you think best. It's your life. You're grown up. If it doesn't work out, you can do something else. Go back to school. You'll always be welcome with me."

"You have to start a life of your own."

"If I can help in any way, let me know. I won't offer. I know an offer seems to be interference . . ." She was talking too much now, and too fast. It didn't keep the silence from coming for her. "When are you planning to move?"

"I'd like to move as soon as possible. Today. I spoke to my friends while you were out. If I get settled there today, I can look for a job early in the morning. The apartment is in Manhattan."

"Oh . . . then you'd better pack. Can I help?"

"I don't need . . ." she started impatiently, and then stopped herself and smiled. "Sure, of course you can help. Can I take a couple of sheets and pillow cases and some towels? They don't have enough."

"Of course. Take anything you want."

"I won't be able to take everything at once. I'll come back for the rest. I'll see you."

"Of course."

Emily looked happy. It had been so long since she had looked happy. She chattered about the girls she was moving in with and the jobs she was going to apply for tomorrow. "I'll let you know as soon as I get something. I'll talk to you tomorrow night."

Anna smiled and nodded and folded and packed. The silence lay waiting. It was everywhere. Patient. Inexorable.

The suitcases were packed and zippered and ready. Emily said, teasing, "You won't have any jeans and underwear on the floor anymore, or any unmade bed in the living room."

"I'll miss it," Anna said.

"When I come to visit you, I'll make a mess for you," Emily said. "The girls are kind of neat. The place is small."

They both laughed.

"Thanks for your help, Mother. You always were a wonderful packer. I remember when I used to go to camp, how much stuff you could cram into a suitcase."

The spectre of Simon returned, laughing at her when she cried after they had seen a carefree Emily off to camp for the first time. He had bought her a hot fudge sundae with nuts and whipped cream to make her feel better. "How will it make me feel better to be fat?" she had laughed. Then they had gone home and torn their clothes off and gotten into bed. It was like a second honeymoon.

"I wrote the address and phone number in your book."

"Good. I can drive you there, if you like."

"No. I want to start by myself. Doing for myself. Please understand. . . ."

"All right," said Anna. "It's all right."

Emily hugged her for a long moment.

"Go. Scram out of here before I cry," Anna said. "And good luck."

"I love you, Mother," said Emily.

And she was gone.

Anna turned back into the apartment and faced the silence.

And the memory that was forcing itself into her consciousness.

Chapter Eleven

The case invaded Bernie's head. He didn't try to fight it. Something about it excited him. He wondered if he was just looking for something to attach his mind to.

He had gone over the thing several times with Johnson and Ramirez. They hadn't noticed any umbrella. They hadn't looked in that area of the apartment yet. Had Ramirez closed the door? He thought he had. Well, he wasn't sure. He had gone out in a hurry to catch the elevator.

Had anyone come to the door?

No. Or maybe, yes. Johnson had thought he heard someone at the door. When he went to look, there was no one there.

Was the door open when Johnson went to it? He glanced at Ramirez. He didn't want to get his partner in trouble. A partner was a vital person in a policeman's life. But yes, the door was open.

Was anyone in the hall?

Yes. A woman got into the elevator. He wasn't sure what she was wearing. It might have been red. A red coat.

The elevator was right there and she was getting in. He didn't notice any umbrella.

Did he mean she didn't have one?

No. He meant he didn't notice.

Could she have had an umbrella? Would it be possible? They'd throw the case out of court on a question like that.

Was the door open enough for someone to reach into the corner from outside and take an umbrella standing there? Any five-dollar lawyer could murder him on that one.

They were wondering if he was nuts. He knew it. After all, what umbrella?

It wasn't even a case he had to become involved in. He could have left it completely to homicide. He got a call from Captain Feeley, of homicide.

"What's with the umbrella bit, Inspector? You sure you saw it? I mean, you know . . . sometimes a person thinks he saw something, and actually he was remembering it from some other place."

"No shit? That really happen, Feeley?"

"I know I don't have to tell you."

"You're right. You don't," he said. He didn't say, "I'm the CO. Your superior." They had known each other too long for that. Feeley had been his first partner.

"Hey, come on, Bernie . . . you been pretty touchy lately, you know."

"I didn't know." He didn't. He hoped it wasn't true. He didn't admire people who dumped their personal garbage in the office.

"My guys figure it to be a straight faggot knock off. With maybe a drug twist. There was a lot of stuff there."

"If it's faggot, it's not straight."

"Funny, Inspector. The hamper had two sizes of men's clothes. No females'."

"So it was a faggot's umbrella. They use umbrellas, too. All you have to do is find it."

"What umbrella? Besides, you saw the sliced-off pickle. Who else does that?"

"I don't know. But fags don't have exclusive rights in perpetuity to that shtick. Also, it wasn't sliced. The ME says it was teeth."

"You really are interested."

"It only took a phone call."

"Why?"

"That was the easiest way to get it."

"You'll get the academy award for best comedian in the department, sir. Why are you interested is what I mean."

"It happened in my precinct. I happened to be passing. I happened to hear the 1010. I happened to have time. I decided to drop in. I do that sometimes. It keeps my people on the ball to know I could appear anywhere, anytime." He hung up. But he understood. Every department has to protect itself. Feeley felt threatened. And Feeley was his friend.

"So forget it, Bernstein," he told himself. "Pick some other case to think about."

Alone in his office, Bernie became aware of noise outside. Loud voices and raucous laughter. Women's voices. The hooker roundup. There had been a lot of lather in the newspapers recently about sin city. The mayor had dusted off the usual mayoral statement about cleaning up the town. The message had been passed down to the precincts. "Pick 'em up." Damn nuisance. The girls were out again in a couple of hours; they would only have to work longer or roll more johns to make up their quota for their pimps.

Noisy bunch they had this time. They were giving him a headache. He went out to see what was going on.

There was a group of eight, maybe ten, mostly young girls, in skin-tight electric-colored pants. It was still too cool for the short shorts season, though some of them had abandoned their jackets and wore only their skimpy tops. They had all been there before, except one, a very young blonde kid, probably fifteen, in a tight, low-cut blouse with long sleeves. Undoubtedly, needle tracks under those sleeves.

He walked up to them. "Shut up, all of you!" he said angrily. "You're giving me a headache."

The young blonde sidled up close, close enough for him to see her red-rimmed, bloodshot eyes and the dilated pupils. She was tall and very thin, with slender hips and large breasts, and her hair made him think of wheat fields, though he had never seen a wheat field.

"I got the best cure for headaches," she said, her speech slightly slurred. She put her arms around his neck, pressing her body against his. "I could cure whatever you got, Gran'pa," she murmured, and blew into his ear.

To his horror, he felt a painful rise in his groin. His face flamed. He shoved her away so hard she lost her balance and fell. "Book her," he said, turning away fast to hide the bulge in his pants. "Keep her on ice till we find out where she belongs. And the rest of you, keep it down." He strode back to his office and slammed the door.

One of the black girls laughed. "Didn't nobody warn you not to mess with the ol' rabbi, child?"

"Come on, Minnesota, upsy-daisy. Get up. Your mama wants you." That was one of the young officers.

"No, she don't." The girl's voice, sullen. "And you could've paid me before you pulled me in."

"Hell, you aren't going to pull that old shit on me," the officer laughed.

"It ain't shit."

"You just met the old man. You think I would do that with him the CO? Kid, you *belong* back on the farm. This is the cleanest precinct you're ever gonna find anywhere."

Bernie went into his inner office where he couldn't hear them, and closed the door. He needed to be quiet, to sit down and think. His body was trembling. The girl, with her strong, young body, the smell of sex and cheap perfume, had reached him. He felt a mingled shame and rage. Rage at Linda. He was still young, still vigorous, still strong. He wasn't made of stone. He would have to talk to her. She would have to understand. She was still his wife.

Chapter Twelve

When the phone rang in the darkened bedroom, Janet Stone thought it was the alarm clock. She stuck an arm through the blankets and stabbed at the clock without opening her eyes. She would lie there another ten minutes, getting used to being awake, gathering herself together. The ringing didn't stop. It hit her suddenly that it wasn't the alarm, but the phone. At this hour, it had to be one of the kids in trouble. She shot out of bed and seized the phone.

"Hello!"

"Mom . . ."

When she heard Stevie's voice, she knew right away that something had to be terribly wrong. He never called her. "What's happened? What's wrong?" she cried.

Stevie felt a familiar rage. Right away it had to be something wrong. That's how she was. Fuckin' pain in the ass.

"Who said something was wrong?"

"Do you know what time it is? Why are you calling at this hour?"

"So I'll hang up if you don't want to talk to me."

"Stevie, of course I want to talk to you! But it's five o'clock in the morning. Where are you?"

"I don't know."

"What do you mean, you don't know? Aren't you with your father?"

"I'm in a street phone." He sneezed. His nose was running. He felt terribly cold.

"What are you doing in a street phone at this hour? You should be sleeping."

She was worse than the fuckin' cops, for Chris' sake. Maybe he should go back to George's. The cops could be gone by now. But he had no bread. And what if the fuzz was still there. What if it was *him* they wanted!

He was crying again.

"Stevie, listen, don't hang up. Go outside and see if you can read a street sign. Wait. Give me your number first. Can you do that?"

"Yeah."

"OK. Read me the number."

He read it to her. She said it back to him.

"All right, hang up, now. I'll call you right back. Don't go away, Stevie."

Damn George. She never should have let Stevie go and live with him. She never should have listened to that damn social worker. She should have forced Stevie to stay with her. The court would have forced him. Just let that social worker open her mouth now. She dialed frantically. The phone was lifted on the first ring. "Steven?"

"Yeah."

"Thank God. All right, now don't hang up. Go out and find out where you are. Look at the street signs. Come back and tell me."

He had to go to the next corner to find a street sign. His body felt like he was made of ice when he got back and told her where he was.

"I'll come get you. Wait for me."

"Do you know where it is?"

"I'll find it. Don't go away."

"How long will it take?"

"Not long. Half an hour. The traffic's not bad at this hour. Could you get home on your own?"

"I have no bread," he said sullenly. "And there ain't no taxis around here."

He shouldn't have called her. He didn't want to go home. Do your homework; make your bed; practice the fuckin' fiddle. And always criticizing George. He wanted to stay with George. Who could have blew the whistle on George? Maybe that old broad was a narc. George was always coming home with these fuckin' broads. You'd think one of them would at least do the dishes for them, for Chris' sake.

"Stevie, are you there?"

"I'm very cold."

"I'll bring your jacket that you left here. And some chocolates. Wait in the phone booth, just in case something happens and I have to call you back."

She was always expecting something to happen. That's how she lived her life. "Just in case . . ." And what the fuck was he supposed to do while he was waiting for her?

Janet Stone determined to be very careful. The social worker had always said, "*Don't* criticize his father to him. *Don't* force him to defend his father or make choices. *Don't*, above all, *don't* make the boy feel guilty for not calling you or for anything else he may have done or not done. *Don't* tell him his eyes are bloodshot. *Don't* ask him questions. Let him tell you what he wants to tell you. If you make him an offer, *don't* insist he accept. *Don't* argue. *Accept* him. Remember, you love him. ACCEPT him."

OK. She would try it that way. She would try it *any*

way. But she wasn't going to let him get away from her again.

She didn't say anything when she found him huddled on the floor of the phone booth. She gave him the jacket and the chocolate in the car, and the thermos of hot tea she had made while she was throwing on her clothes. She turned the heater up high. She didn't protest when he turned the radio on loud, to rock. *"Don't let yourself be provoked. He'll try to provoke you."*

When they got home, she asked him if he wanted a hot bath and he said no. She didn't insist. His face looked flushed and feverish. After he went upstairs, she heard the water running in the tub. He came down in his pajamas and robe and she said, "Would you like some breakfast?"

"I can get it myself," he said. "I'm not a baby, you know."

She closed her lips tight and went out of the room. She heard the refrigerator and closets open and close and dishes and silver bang. When she heard him grumble that there was no sugar-coated cereal, she went upstairs and made her bed and cleaned the bathroom. When he came up, he looked into her room.

"Ain't you going to work today?"

"It's Sunday."

"Oh. Yeah. Lucky thing you don't work today."

"I would have come for you anyhow, Stevie."

Wrong thing to say. She saw him freeze. "I'm only visiting," he said. He turned away angrily and went to his room and slammed the door.

She wanted to know what had happened. But the last person in the world she wanted to talk to was George. That bastard. She would have to wait until Stevie chose to tell her. The important thing was, Stevie was home and she wasn't going to let him leave again.

An hour later she opened his door softly and looked in. He was sleeping, breathing heavily through his mouth.

Her eyes filled. She remembered when he was a baby, how she used to tiptoe into his room and watch him sleeping. Her son. His sisters used to accuse her of loving him best because he was a boy. Round and sweet. This is my son, Dr. Steven Stone . . .

Oh God . . . my son, the pot head.

My husband, the son of a bitch.

She closed the door. OK, social worker, a day at a time. I got through yesterday; I'll get through today. I'll make it. I'm strong. And you're going to make it, too, Stevie. You're home with me.

She went back to the kitchen and washed and dried the dishes and put them away. She would make lasagne tonight. Stevie loved her lasagne. And a string bean casserole with onions and mushrooms in cream sauce and salad with sour cream dressing and chocolate pudding pie with real whipped cream. She would put him back on a diet tomorrow. He had gotten fat again. Eating junk food with his father. Today she would feed him everything he liked. Slow. She had to go slow.

Stevie was still sleeping late in the afternoon. The sauce for the lasagne was bubbling on the stove and the string bean casserole was on the counter ready to go into the oven when the doorbell rang. She peered out of the diamond-shaped window in the door before opening it, as she always did.

There were two policemen at the door; a black man, tough; the other one looked Hispanic.

"Please, God . . . let it not be for Stevie. . . ."

She took a deep breath and opened the door.

"Mrs. Stone?"

She had to think. She had to stall a minute. "May I see your identification, please?"

Politely they gave her their ID's. She looked at them carefully, without seeing anything, stalling for time to calm herself. Fear, pounding through her head, fogged her eyes.

"Thank you. A woman alone can't be too careful," she said. She had to be calm. She couldn't let them see her hands shake. She handed back the IDs.

"Yes, ma'am. Are you Mrs. Stone?"

Still she hesitated. It made her uncomfortable now to say yes to that. Someday she was going to change her name. When the children were grown and it couldn't matter to them anymore. Why should she say she was Mrs. Stone when she wasn't Mrs. Stone anymore?

"Yes," she said finally. "That's my name."

"Mrs. Stone, there seems to have been a problem at your husband's apartment."

"Ex-husband."

She stepped out onto the front porch and closed the door. If this was going to be something about George, she didn't want Stevie to hear it or be involved. "What kind of problem?"

They looked uncomfortable. "A body was found in his room, in his bed. A man's body. We need to make an identification."

"I'll give you a picture. You can check it out yourself."

"It isn't that simple, ma'am. The body is hard to identify. Can you tell us if Mr. Stone had any identifying marks. Birthmarks or scars. Anything distinctive."

"There is nothing distinctive about Mr. Stone," she said drily.

"Do you know who his dentist was? He could be identified by his teeth. Caps or bridges . . ."

"I can tell you who he used to go to. In Brooklyn. I don't know who his dentist is now. Why can't you recognize him by looking at his face?"

"There appears to have been some kind of . . . accident."

"What kind of accident?"

"It's possible Mr. Stone was murdered. If it *is* Mr. Stone."

She forced her face to show nothing, but she shivered. "I'm cold out here," she said. "I'm sorry I can't ask you in; I just washed the floor. I can't help you. I'm sorry."

"Would you be able to recognize his body? The torso. The rest would be covered."

"It's been eight years. Ten, really, since I saw Mr. Stone's body. I don't think I can help you." She felt calmer now.

"Would you try?"

"Do I have to?"

"No."

"I don't want to see him."

"Can you tell us who he was living with?"

"No. I don't know anything about him. I haven't seen him personally, or heard from him, in years. Any business we had was through lawyers. I understand he has . . . changed . . . a great deal since we . . . since I saw him."

"You don't know who might have been sharing his apartment? A man?"

"No. No, I don't. Some lowlife like himself, I would guess. I have had no contact with him at all. I'm sorry I can't help you. It's very cold." Shivering, she turned to the door.

"I suppose you didn't like him much," the black policeman said.

She turned back to him. "We were divorced," she said coldly. "Did you come to arrest me for that?"

"No, ma'am. We didn't come to arrest anyone."

"Then, good afternoon," she said. She went quickly into the house. She leaned back against the door, shaking violently. She couldn't stop. She was afraid they would hear her teeth chattering across the street.

She turned around and peeped out of the glass in the

door and she saw the two policemen drive off. She was sure the whole block had seen them, too. Damn George. Damn damn damn him.

Still shivering, she sat down at the kitchen table to think. She didn't want to know what happened. She only knew she had to get Stevie away from there. Out of the city. Out of the state. Away. Away from whatever trouble he was in. It was all his father's fault. She didn't want the police asking him questions.

Chapter Thirteen

Driving was the hardest time, Bernie thought. He couldn't control his thoughts when he was driving; they crowded in on him. The radio didn't help. It was full of this morning's murders. The reporters were having a field day. He felt like a prisoner in the car, held captive by his own head, tormented by it. The rain didn't help, either. It was like a dark, wet curtain that enclosed him, isolated him from the outside world.

The incident with the young hooker had unhinged him. He had been too long without a woman, without Linda. Tonight he would do something about it. He had been patient long enough. Too long.

He went over and over in his head what he would say to her. Revising it. Planning. Rehearsing. They ought to go away together. Take a vacation. Just the two of them. Be alone. Without Theo. They never went anywhere without Theo. They never went *anywhere*. They could go for a couple of days. Relax. Laugh. Love. "I love you, Linda. I need you . . ." He would hold her in his arms, kiss her. . . .

She had to need him. There was no other man. He was sure of that.

He stopped at a florist and bought her flowers. Long-stemmed roses. Expensive. He didn't care. He was excited. He hadn't bought Linda flowers for a long time. He used to bring her flowers every Friday night, as his father had for his mother, to usher in the Sabbath. He would do it again. Things were going to change. He could barely wait to get home.

When he got there, he dashed from the car, oblivious of the rain. Things were going to be better. He knew it. He knew he could convince her at least to try. Just try. She had to. Once she had loved him.

He was too excited to wait for the elevator. He ran up the three flights to their apartment, his keys ready in his hand.

The key didn't fit in the lock. He shoved hard. It only went in part of the way. He had trouble getting it out. Damn! He must have taken the office keys.

But they weren't the office keys. He looked at them carefully. The keys had never jammed before. He tried the upper lock. That didn't go in at all.

Was he on the wrong floor? At the wrong apartment? No. It said 3D. The name slot read "Bernstein." The locks gleamed like new on the dark metal door.

They were new. The locks had been changed. He wasn't sure he understood what had happened.

He put his finger on the bell and kept it there. He could hear the ring inside, a steady, harsh sound. Nothing else. No sound of feet inside, coming to answer the bell.

She was there. He was sure she was there. He believed he could hear her breathing behind the door. She was always home at this hour. She would be home with Theo. He pounded on the door and shouted, "Linda!"

The door next to his opened. A teenage girl poked her head out. "Hi, Inspector Bernstein." Coyly.

He took his hand off the bell and struggled to control his voice. "Hi. Hi, Patty."

"Mrs. Bernstein asked me to give you this letter. She said she had to go out for a while with Theo."

He made a painful attempt to smile. "Thanks, Patty."

She was watching him, waiting for him to open the letter. Pain-in-the-ass kid had a crush on him.

"Thanks," he said again.

"Oh . . . yeah. You're welcome." She pulled her head back in, blinking and smiling, and finally shut the door.

His hands were shaking. He made a mess of the envelope. The note inside was brief.

> I have changed the locks. I have thought about this for a long time. Theo will be better off without you. I packed one suitcase for you. It is with the super. Call when you are ready to take the rest of your things. This is really the best way for everybody. There is $300 left in the bank for you. I took everything else and put it in Theo's name and I am the executrix. You know Theo will need the money.

He read the note and reread it. He didn't know what to do. He felt totally impotent. His brain and his body were paralyzed.

Down the hall a door opened and a woman came toward him. She passed him and smiled and went on to the elevator. Bernie smiled too. He knew everyone on the floor. He and Linda had lived there all their married lives.

Was this how a marriage ended? With a note, not even signed. Not even addressed to him. No "Dear Bernie . . . your loving wife, Linda . . ."

"Shall I hold the elevator?"

"What?"

"Shall I hold the elevator for you, Inspector? Are you going down?" The woman was holding the elevator door.

"No. No, thanks. Thanks anyway, Mrs. Gardner."

He was absolutely convinced Linda was in the apartment. Probably locked in Theo's room with him, reading to him, helping him with his homework, or giving him his bath. He was twelve years old, and she was still bathing him.

He could pound on the door until she answered. Pound on it and ring the bell. Make a scene. She would hate that. It would upset her terribly. She was so concerned with what "people" thought. Neighbors. Friends. Strangers.

How about what I think, Linda? What I feel?

If he pounded on the door, would she call the police? He smiled bitterly. The police was here.

He could get a locksmith and say he'd lost the keys. Get the door open. And then what? Do what Sean would do? Her precious Sean. Blacken her eyes and break her nose and knock out a couple of teeth. And then what? Pick her up, all one hundred seven pounds of her, and throw her on the bed and tear her clothes off. . . .

And then what, Bernie Bernstein, good Jewish boy? Then what?

He was very tired. He hadn't slept much the night before. His head was pounding again where the doctor had taken the stitches. He had had to answer a lot of questions all day about those stitches, tell a lot of lies. Bernie didn't like to lie.

He couldn't stand in the hall all night. He got his suitcase from the super.

"Going on a trip, Inspector?"

"Mmmm . . ." nodding, trying to smile.

"I understand. Secret police work."

Bernie smiled some more.

He put the suitcase into the trunk of his car. He was still holding the bouquet of flowers, and he threw them into the trunk, too. He got into the driver's seat and he was paralyzed again. He was wet and cold and alone. What did he do now? Where could he go?

He had no real friends. Over the years Linda had cut them off from friends. He didn't remember the last time they had invited anyone in, except Sean and his wife, or gone out with anyone except to visit Sean on an occasional Sunday afternoon. He had no family to turn to. His mother was in a home for senior citizens. Sometimes she recognized him; most times she didn't know who he was. His two sisters lived in California.

He sat in his car for a long time, not really thinking, not really feeling. Numb. The wind hurled furious fistfuls of rain against the windshield.

Suddenly he felt all alone, and afraid. He hadn't ever really been afraid before, even when he had been in physical danger. He wasn't even sure what he was afraid of.

And he was cold and wet. He sneezed.

"Gesundheit, Inspector," he said. "Just what you need now, a cold. Get yourself a hotel and a hot bath and then . . ."

Then?

Chapter Fourteen

The bellboy said, "Thank you, sir. If there is anything else I can get for you, don't hesitate . . ." He lingered briefly, then went out and shut the door.

Bernie was alone.

Nothing moved in the somber room. Dark wood, dark bed cover, dark drapes. He strode to the window and opened the drapes. The window looked out on a courtyard. Square and dark and empty, with all the windows shut and shrouded, it was like a deep tomb. Even the wind seemed to have died there, and the rain fell listlessly. He closed the drapes and turned back into the room. He felt utterly desolate, abandoned in this gloomy and unfamiliar place. Six feet four inches, two hundred pounds of firm, hard flesh, and he felt abandoned, like a lost kid. The feeling humiliated him. He was an attractive man, he knew that. If Linda didn't want him, that was her loss. He was a man with love to give.

He shivered in his wet clothes. Big-city cop. Streetwise. Up from the ranks to inspector. The things he had seen and dealt with along the way . . . and this was the first time he had ever actually had a room alone in a hotel in the city. He had been embarrassed, registering alone. Like some homeless stumblebum, with no place to hide from the rain. No wife to open the door to him with a smile, with love. Oh yes, and chicken soup, Bernstein. Don't leave out the chicken soup. . . .

He sneezed. Move your ass before you catch a cold.

He opened the suitcase. Linda had packed beautifully, as she always did. He knew he would have everything he'd need. He found undershorts and a robe, got out of his wet clothes, and headed for a hot shower.

He stayed in the shower for a long time. With the hot water pouring down on him, he could concentrate on getting warm, on loosening the tight wires in his limbs.

When he got out of the shower, he turned on all the lights and the television. It didn't help, but he left it on, anyway. The television was a voice, at least. It distracted him, even if he didn't listen to it. It kept him from thinking. He didn't want to think yet. He started to unpack, admiring the neat way Linda had prepared her send-off: underwear slipped into the fold of the trousers so they wouldn't crease, socks tucked into empty spaces, shoes in plastic bags. Even a new toothbrush. How long had she been planning this?

He let the suitcase close. It was suddenly too painful to unpack. Unpacking would make the whole thing real. It would be accepting it.

He looked at his watch. Five o'clock. What you need, Bernstein, is something to eat. Not that he was hungry. But it would be something to do. He didn't want to go out again into the rain. He called room service.

The same bellhop brought his dinner. A young man, scrawny and tough. A street kid. He had seized the suitcase before Bernie could stop him and carried it up. Bernie never liked anyone to carry his suitcase. He was always bigger than any bellhop. The young man lingered again at the door after Bernie had tipped him. "Would you like anything else, sir?"

"This looks OK." Bernie said.

"Besides food." The young man looked at him directly, openly.

Bernie hoped he didn't look as uncomfortable as he felt. What are you, Bernstein, some poetic, virginal adolescent? "What have you got?"

"Blonde, brunette, or redhead," said the bellhop. "White, black, or yellow."

"How do you know I'm not a cop?"

"Are you?"

"Do I look like a cop?"

He shrugged. "You look tired and lonely." He waited.

"No blondes," Bernie heard himself say hoarsely, angry and sad.

"In about an hour, sir?"

Bernie nodded. He turned up the TV and stared at it because there was nothing else to do, and ate some of the food he had ordered because there was nothing else to do, and brushed his teeth with the new toothbrush because there was nothing else to do. And waited. In the desolate room with the flickering light from the TV. He heard a laugh once, and was startled. It came from the television. He was astonished that people were still chattering and laughing. He got up and turned off the sound and lay down again. He wondered suddenly about the girl. Would he really be able to do that?

He had never been with a whore. He heard Linda's voice: "Bernie Bernstein, good Jewish boy," mocking.

Well, fuck you, Linda.

He was ready for the girl when she arrived, a plump, big-breasted girl, with long, bushy orange hair. She said, "You're a real big mother, ain't you!"

"All over," he said. "Let's not talk."

127

"Anything you want, honeyman," she said. "But I get paid first. Fifty dollars."

"The kid said twenty-five."

"Thirty-five," she said.

"Thirty." You're stalling, Bernstein.

"No." Firmly. "Thirty-five."

He got up and got his money out of his wallet. He counted out thirty-five dollars and gave it to her and put the rest back into his wallet. She put the money in her purse. Then she reached behind her and unzipped her dress and stepped out of it and put it neatly on a chair, on top of her purse. Her large, pendulous breasts swung freely as she moved. She wore only green flowered bikini underpants. She took those off and moved over to the bed on her spike heels.

"You want something special, honeyman?"

"Just shut up," he said. He turned off all the lights. When he came back to the bed, she was lying on her back with her legs apart and her knees up. Her thighs were fat and very white. For one terrible moment he thought he wasn't going to be able to go through with it. But she rolled over onto her side and took his penis in her soft, plump hands and fondled it. She knew her business. "Fill mama's pussy with your big rod, honeyman," she said. He pushed her onto her stomach. He didn't want to see her face. And got on top of her.

For a moment, for one long, intense, delirious moment, he loved her; he loved this soft, yielding flesh that opened up to him, responded to him. He heard himself groan and shudder and sigh. . . .

Afterwards he lay on his stomach beside her with his arm across her breast, drifting toward sleep. He heard her say softly, "You're great, honeyman. . . ."

He didn't answer. He breathed deeply, rhythmically, as though he were asleep, wishing suddenly, desperately, that she would vanish.

"Sleepin', honeyman?"

He didn't answer. He was glad he had paid her first. Maybe she would go away, and he would sleep. Softly, too gently, she slid out from under his arm, and then lay still. He could feel the tension in her body, waiting tension. "Honeyman . . ." she whispered. He was suddenly wide-awake, alert, but he didn't answer. He didn't move.

He heard her get up. He opened his eyes. She had put on her shoes and was moving noiselessly over the carpeted floor to the chair with her dress. She put the dress on and glanced hastily back toward Bernie. In the shadowy light, he knew she couldn't see his eyes, half-open, watching her. She could only see that he hadn't moved. She opened her purse and felt around and took out something and held it in her closed hand. Glancing again at Bernie's motionless body, she moved soundlessly toward his trousers. She had his open wallet in her hand when he moved. He leaped off the bed and rushed at her. She whirled, dropping the wallet. He heard a click and saw the blade in her hand, thrust straight at his belly. He dropped into a crouch, grabbing at her knees with one hand, pulling them toward him, and pushing her backward with the other hand. She fell on her back, knocking down the chair, but she didn't drop the knife. She rolled over swiftly, away from him, and got up onto her knees, with the knife in front of her, aimed at his groin.

"Move," she said. "Make one move and I'll cut your fuckin' balls off." Slowly, warily, her eyes never wavering from him, she got up and circled away from him toward the door. The knife was steady in her hand. She got to the door and reached behind her. She turned the lock to open it. The bolt sounded like a shot in the silent room.

He could have let her leave.

But rage flooded his body. And shame, for having

gotten himself in this position. And something else. Hatred. For Linda. It ripped through him like a bullet.

He sprang at the girl, grabbing her wrist with his huge hands, and twisted. She gasped, and the knife dropped from her hand. She kicked at his naked groin with her knee. His hands closed around her neck; he pounded her head against the wall. She struggled, trying to scream. No sound came out. Her eyes began to bulge and her tongue hung out; he didn't see. He couldn't hear. A pounding like a storm roared in his ears, deafening him.

Her nails raked his face. He felt nothing. Her arms dropped limply to her sides; her body hung heavily. Something wet dropped off his forehead into his eyes. He took one hand off her throat to wipe his eyes. He looked at his hand. It was red. Sticky and wet. Like blood. And suddenly the pounding stopped. He loosened his hold on the girl. She slumped to the floor, gasping and coughing.

He stood staring at her stupidly. He smelled vomit and urine. Her dress was wet with both, and with blood. His wrist was bleeding, and his face.

The girl staggered to her feet. Trembling violently, she sidled away from him, to the door. He stepped back from her. Killer Bernstein, the kids used to call him. He didn't like to fight, but when he did, he went for blood. . . .

He might have killed this girl, this poor, stupid, pathetic girl.

She had gotten to the door and opened it.

"Miss . . ." he said hoarsely.

She didn't look back. He bent down and got his wallet and took out the bills and shoved them toward her, but she was out of the door. He opened it wider. "Here, take it . . . please . . ." he called, and threw the bills out into the hall after her and locked the door. He leaned back against the cold wood, trembling.

He became aware of the flickering, changing gray-white

light in front of him. The television. It had been on all the time, without sound. The only light in the room. There was a picture of an ambulance in front of a large building, and two men wheeling out a covered stretcher. It looked familiar. Had he killed the girl? Were they wheeling out her body? He moved over and turned on the sound. ". . . grisly murder early this morning . . . unidentified male . . . mutilated body . . ."

Had that been this morning? Only this morning? It seemed years ago, a life ago.

Work. That had always kept him going. He would get some sleep and go to work. Maybe on that case. It interested him.

And of course, he'd have to find some other hotel.

But he couldn't sleep. Twice he picked up the phone to call Linda, but he put it down. If Linda wanted to talk to him, she knew his number at the precinct.

Finally he got up and washed his face and shaved. There were two deep, ugly scratches in his forehead. One of them kept opening and bleeding into his eyebrow. And there were three long scratches on his cheeks.

"You're gorgeous, Bernstein. That's all you needed to go with the stitches in your forehead.

He took out his notebook. The wistful umbrella lady, with the shy smile. She lived in Queens. He knew the area slightly. Tall buildings on a trafficky street, where people paid high rents for a big lobby with an ugly chandelier and tiny apartments. They thought the streets were safer than Manhattan.

At 8:00 P.M., dressed in beautifully coordinated beige tweed sports coat and cocoa brown slacks, courtesy of Linda's planning, Bernie was in the big outer lobby of Anna's building. He pressed the button in the building intercom that said "A & E Welles." He pressed several times. He was about to give up and put the phone back

131

when he heard an answering buzz, then a voice coming weakly through crackling static: "Yes? Hello? Emmy? Who is it?"

"United Parcel. Arthur Welles live here?"

"Arthur? No. The A is for Anna. Anna Welles."

"Oh. Sorry to trouble you."

He hung up and went out to his car that was double-parked three cars back from the entrance to the building where he had a perfect view of anyone coming in or out.

Chapter Fifteen

Huddled in a corner of the couch, clutching her body, her feet pulled up under her, off the floor, Anna heard the rasping sound faintly, muffled, as though it were forcing its way through cotton. It plowed through to her consciousness, startling her back to awareness. She couldn't remember where she was or where she had been. Had she been asleep?

She heard the buzz again. It seemed to rout the silence, as a rooster crowing at dawn routs the ghosts and terrors of the night, scattering them. But they didn't go away. They weren't destroyed. They hid, like the silence, waiting. Waiting to return.

When the buzzing stopped, the silence would steal back.

The sound came again, harsh, persistent. She recognized it suddenly. It was the intercom. Maybe it was Emmy, coming back.

She lowered her legs quickly onto the floor, and nearly fell. Her legs were stiff; she couldn't feel them. She must have been sitting on them for hours. Pins and needles shot through her feet. And something fell out of her lap. But

she must get to the intercom before Emmy went away.
She held on to the wall and dragged herself to the foyer.

"Yes? Hello? Emmy? Who is it?"

It was only some strange man wanting an Arthur. She
hung up the phone. She didn't turn back to the room.
Would the silence steal back now? Had it ever left?

Defiantly she clicked on the light in the foyer and the
kitchen and then the living room, blinking at the sudden
glare. But the silence wasn't afraid of light. It wasn't even
afraid of noise.

She rubbed her legs and feet hard and caught sight of the
microphone from Emmy's tape recorder on the floor. That
must have been what dropped when she got up. She
picked it up and put it, and the tape recorder, on a shelf in
the living room. What was she doing with the tape
recorder? She didn't know. She put away the clothes that
Emmy had decided not to take and had left on the couch.

When had Emmy left? Was it today? Sunday? Was it still
Sunday?

She had to keep moving. Keep busy, run away.

There was the regular Sunday Singles' Rap and Dance in
that church on Long Island. That was relatively cheap.
Four dollars. She seldom went out two nights in a row. It
was too expensive. But tonight was different. Tonight she
had to get away. She had once counted how many ways
there were to commit suicide in an ordinary house. She
had stopped counting after ten. Maybe the eleventh way
would be appealing.

She would do without something this week and go out
tonight. She would manage. When they had first been
married and Simon was still going to school, she had
managed. Simon had thought she was a great little
manager. Great little do-withouter was what she was.

*"What were you going to do without to lend me the money for
Florida?"*

She covered her ears with her hands. So many ghosts

. . . so many ghosts . . . She couldn't block out the ghosts. Don't look back, Anna; remember what happened to Lot's wife for looking back. Changed to a pillar of salt. It wasn't salt. It was tears. And where was Lot when all that was going on? Why didn't he protect her? At least speak up to God for her? Probably glad to get rid of her. Engineered the whole thing with his lawyers and hers. Had a thirty-two-year-old waiting in the wings.

Tears didn't help. Laughing didn't help. The silence was creeping back. She had to get out of here. Fast.

Her mouth tasted terrible. She brushed her teeth and used a lot of mouthwash and then showered quickly.

Emily had said, ". . . shiny-in-the-seat slacks . . ." So what to wear? There wasn't a great deal in her closet to choose from. There was really only the lavender silk. That was the newest thing she had. A fantastic bargain at a church bazaar. She had been saving it. For what? For *him*, of course. The knight on a white horse. With her luck, the horse would shit in the lobby and she'd lose her lease.

Wear it. Use it. Live it up. You could be dead tomorrow (with a little luck). And poor Emily would be saddled with big funeral expenses. I want to be cremated and I want my ashes dropped on a cruise ship in the Caribbean. It's the only way I'll ever get there.

She had a pretty scarf, only ten years old, that looked nice with the lavender silk.

By 8:30, in her red raincoat, and carrying her yellow plastic umbrella, she walked briskly out of the lobby into the misty rain and headed toward her car. She didn't notice the dark sedan that followed her.

Chapter Sixteen

Jake Harris looked at the photographs on the desk of Detective Captain Kevin Feeley and lit a cigarette. It was an excuse to turn his eyes away from the photos. He already had a cigarette burning in an ashtray in front of him.

The ME, sipping from his paper cup, held up an enlarged photo of the severed penis. "I have a great headline for you, Jake," he said. "'Do You Know This Prick?'"

"You missed your calling, Doc," said Jake.

"Right. My mother wanted me to be a newspaperman, but I couldn't stand the smell of whiskey." He raised his cup in a long swallow, and went out.

"Great weekend we've had in shitty city," Jake said. "A headless corpse, a prickless corpse, a young girl ODs and flies out a fifth-floor window."

"The girl wasn't in this precinct," said Feeley.

"Right," said Jake. "It doesn't count. Got anything for me that's fit to print?"

Feeley shook his head. "Nothing on the one without the

head. The other one . . . probably the clarinet was used on the face. It's in the lab now. There are no fingerprints on record for the victim. We're not sure who he was. We're doing the usual: samples of hair from the bed. Semen. Pot. Tobacco. Popcorn."

"Popcorn?"

"It was a well used bed. And of course we're questioning everyone in the building: neighbors, doormen, super. Something will turn up. You know, by now. It's never anything glamorous. Just slow digging."

"You really got no ID?"

"Well . . . tentative. A George Stone. Don't use it yet, Jake."

"Ok. The talk is homosexual."

"Maybe. There was some other male in the apartment. You guys are really milking that."

"The public is bored with your regular everyday mugging of old ladies. They want something jazzier."

"Great. Then they start imitating. There's going to be a whole rash of penises bitten off pretty soon."

"Not after you guys get the killer."

"We're working on it; we're working on it," Feeley said irritably.

Chapter Seventeen

Janet Stone hated ironing. But she knew the only way she could control her nervousness until Stevie woke up was to keep busy. She had a full basket of ironing to catch up with. The only way she could iron was to turn on the TV, something she would not otherwise have done in the daytime. Which was why she happened to catch the report of the gruesome murder. She saw a stretcher wheeled into an ambulance surrounded by a small crowd. She recognized the building in the background. The pounding of the blood in her head was so loud she could hardly hear. "Possible homosexual link . . . possibly drug-related . . . large cache of marijuana and some cocaine and heroin . . . seek young man believed to be last roommate . . ." A shudder ran through her. There had been blood on Stevie's tee shirt. They were looking for him. There was no doubt in her mind. She had known that she would have to get him away from New York. Now she knew she would have to do it in a hurry. Immediately. She wasn't going to ask him any questions.

The announcer went on to the Middle East crisis and

inflation. Janet pulled out the iron plug. She sat down. She had to think.

When the police had told her George might be dead, it hadn't fully registered. She was so removed from him. Now that he wasn't even sending her money, it was as though the last thread to him had been severed. She had only felt she must somehow keep the information from Stevie. Get him away.

Now it was more urgent to get him away.

She couldn't imagine what had happened to George. She didn't care. How often had she wished him dead? And now she didn't care. It didn't matter. She wasn't even curious about how he died. She only wanted to protect her son. Whatever happened, whatever was wrong with Stevie, was George's fault. Yet she realized she didn't even hate him anymore. He was a part of her life that was finished. She hadn't been able to start a satisfactory new life. After the divorce, it had taken all her energy to get a job, to go on, to keep the family together. She had felt, at first, crippled; she had tried to go on with her old life, her old friends, her old activities, and it had been like a man walking on one leg pretending he had two. But she had grown accustomed to that, too, after a while. She had settled into a life without a husband, never trying to find another. One Singles' Dance had been enough to decide that. Besides, who was going to be interested in a middle-aged woman with three children and a house she could barely maintain on a bookkeeper's salary and sporadic alimony payments? It was becoming more and more difficult. Now that the girls were out and partly on their own, she had even begun to think of selling the house. She didn't know why she clung to it. It was the last vestige of some dream of normal life, a dream of husband and family, barbecues in the backyard, everyone together in the family room, reading the papers, watching TV, arguing, laughing, playing Scrabble or Monopoly; grandchildren splashing in a plastic pool in the yard with Grandma and Grandpa. The dream had ended long ago. She had finally awakened. She was going to sell the house. Maybe some other woman would have better luck in it. Besides, she needed the money.

She wasn't going to ask Stevie any questions because she didn't want to know the answers. She had to concentrate on getting him away from the police.

First she had to make sure he didn't get to the TV. She knew he would turn it on as soon as he woke up. That or the radio. By then the body might be identified. She knew it was George, dead on that stretcher, as though she had seen the body. Separated him from his penis, had they? Good. She hoped they had cut it off with a dull knife. She should have done it to him the first time she found out about the other women. Impotent with her, he said. Her fault, he said. He was using it up on other women, instead.

Forget him. Forget George. Concentrate on Stevie. She had to make sure he didn't get the news.

She went down to the basement and loosened all the fuses in the fuse box. She would tell him they were temporarily out of power, some kind of shortage that couldn't be fixed until tomorrow. They would be gone by tomorrow.

Her parents lived in Florida. She and Stevie could stay with them. But Stevie wouldn't want to be with them. George had turned him against them. Maybe they could visit Disney World. He would like that. She would say it was her vacation and they were going to visit Disney World. She would get tickets tonight. She would say, "I didn't mention it to you because you were so tired, Stevie. Also, I didn't want you to feel you were imposing on me. But it's my vacation. I already had a ticket. I was able to get another one for you. For Disney World. You always said you'd like to see Disney World."

She didn't want him to hear her on the phone if he woke

up now. And in the meantime, she didn't want him calling George's apartment. Who knows? The police might be able to trace the call. There was a phone in the kitchen and one in her bedroom, and an extension in the laundry room. Stevie didn't know about that one. It was new. And he would never go down there, anyway. She ran down the basement steps and took the phone off the hook, and just to be sure, she emptied a basket of laundry on top of it. With the phone off the hook, he couldn't make any calls or receive any.

She left a note on the kitchen table for him in case he woke up. "Power off. Phone out of order. Went to the drugstore to call repair service. Love, Mother." No. She erased *love*. He wouldn't like that. Even *Mother*. But damned if she would sign it "Janet." He called his father George. George didn't like being a father. She left it unsigned.

She put on her coat quickly and ran out to her car to call her parents and the airlines.

Chapter Eighteen

Freda Miller was determined. Absolutely. After all, hadn't she discussed it all thoroughly with Morris? Never mind he was dead. She knew he was dead; she wasn't crazy. But when you were married to a person forty-seven years . . . forty-seven years you had dinner with him every night and breakfast with him every morning, and sometimes even lunch . . . and don't forget hot chocolate every night for forty-seven years. Even in the summer, because Morris believed that when it was hot, a hot drink cooled you off better than a cold drink. After forty-seven years she didn't have to talk to him to know what he would say. And what he said was, "Butt out, Freda. Mind your own business." He always said it.

She was not going to tell the police anything. They could give her the third degree; she was not going to be involved. So she was prepared for them when her bell rang.

Her hair was freshly washed and combed carefully to cover her scalp, and her teeth were in; she wore her corset and stockings and shoes. Penurious, but proud. No one was going to say that Freda Miller ever answered her door like a sloven. She had even put on a dab of rouge and some powder. No one would be able to tell how little she had slept last night. What was it her mother used to say? "A little powder and a lot of paint make a lady what she ain't."

She moved slowly to answer the door. Let them ring twice: She was too old to hurry.

She opened the peephole. "Whatever it is, I don't want any," she said.

"Police, ma'am. Please open the door."

She opened the door, but kept the chain on. She saw a burly man in a raincoat that looked like he had slept in it. "May I see your identification?"

He handed it to her through the crack in the door. She examined it carefully, holding it up close to her eyes. Andrew Donlon. Irish. It could be a fake ID. He could be Italian. Mafia. That could be a Mafia killing next door. The news story on the radio mentioned drugs. She handed back the ID and opened the door a few more inches, but she still didn't remove the chain.

He said politely, patiently, "We'd like to ask you a few questions about last night, ma'am. Can you tell us what you heard?"

"Heard? I heard nothing."

"Isn't your bedroom wall up against the living room next door?"

"I don't know. I haven't been next door. I'm not a person who runs around coffee-klatching and snooping in her neighbor's kitchen."

"I realize that, ma'am." His mother had been right. He should have become a gym teacher, like his brother. "Would you mind letting me have a look at your apartment?"

Freda drew herself up. "Does it matter if I mind?" she said bitterly. She opened the chain and let him in. She walked behind him. He walked right into the bedroom and tapped the wall. She was very glad she had made her bed with the bedspread.

"Pretty thin, ma'am. You could hear if someone sneezed in there."

"My hearing isn't all that good," she said. "Besides, I took a sleeping pill last night."

"They work for you? You're lucky, ma'am. My mother, some nights she doesn't fall asleep till four, five in the morning. Nothing helps." Some nights his old lady snored so loud his father went down to the basement to sleep.

"Has she tried a little hot milk before she goes to bed?"

"Hot milk? I don't know. I'll tell her. Thank you very much." Hot brandy would be more like it for his mother. "Nice apartment. You keep it real nice. Have you lived here long?"

"Since it opened. Twenty-six years."

"Is that right? That's beautiful. That's really beautiful, ma'am. I suppose you know everybody."

"I don't know anyone," she said stiffly.

Shit. He had lost her again. "I'm surprised to hear that. You seem like such a pleasant person. Easy to get along with."

"When Morris was alive . . . Morris was my husband . . . we had each other. We didn't need anyone else."

"That's beautiful, ma'am. That's really beautiful. How long has he been . . . gone?"

"Five years."

"Long time. One never gets used to it."

"No," she said, stiff again.

He couldn't get a handle on her. Maybe it wasn't too late. He could still go back to school and become a gym teacher.

"It's hard to talk about, I know. My father, God rest his soul . . ." (And God rest mine if he ever hears I killed

145

him off like this, and him a great ox of a man who could still knock my head off with one blow.) "It's hard on my mom. . . ."

"How long has he been gone?"

"Three years." He crossed himself.

Freda didn't seem to hear at first. "It's a lie, what they say about time, you know," she said finally. "Time doesn't cure anything. It gets harder every year." She turned sharply away from him. "Is there anything else you would like to see?"

"No, ma'am. Not right now." He followed her back to the door. "Lots of changes in this area in twenty-six years," he said, very softly.

"Yes."

Nothing wrong with her hearing. She had her hand on the door.

He said, more softly, pleading, "It would be a great help if you could tell me anything. Anything at all. A man was killed, you see."

"I know," she said.

"You do?"

"I heard it on the radio."

"Could you tell us who lived next door? You might have seen him on the way to the incinerator, or run into him in the elevator."

"I saw him once or twice."

"What did he look like?"

"Gray hair, too long. Tight blue jeans. Ridiculous person. We never used to have people like that in the building."

"What was the other man like?"

"I didn't see any other man."

"There appears to have been two men living there."

"Only for a month or so. Not a man, actually. A boy. He called the man George. He was pudgy. Looked like he needed a bath. And he wore an obscene tee shirt."

"Obscene, ma'am? In what way?"

"It had a word printed on the back."

"Could you . . . spell it for me, ma'am?"

"P-H-" she said. Her face colored. "P-H- . . . instead of F . . ."

"That's disgusting," said Donlon. "You didn't happen to hear his name?"

"No. I only heard George because he shouted it in the hall. He said, 'I'm holding the . . . the' . . . that word . . . 'elevator, George. Where the' . . . you know, that word again ' . . . are you?'"

"Was he in the apartment last night?"

"I don't know anything about last night."

"You didn't hear any noise? Music? A party? A fight?"

"No."

"Did you see anyone come in or leave the apartment?"

"No. I told you. I took a sleeping pill and went to sleep."

"Some of the people on the floor heard loud music."

"Talk to them," she said.

He wasn't going to get anything more out of her. Not today. It was easier to crack a Mafia hit man than these old ladies. He'd have to try again later.

"Thank you, ma'am. I hope I haven't disturbed you too much."

She didn't answer.

"I'll tell my mother about the hot milk."

She nodded. Clammed up again. Well, there were four hundred other tenants in the building. Maybe one of them knew something.

"We may have to talk to you again. You understand. . . ."

"I don't know anything about last night. I mind my own business," she said.

Chapter Nineteen

A couple of times it occurred to Bernie that Anna Welles knew he was following her, because of the way she was driving. First off, she got herself onto the Long Island Expressway going to the city, and at the very first exit, she got out and went back to the expressway going the other way, out to Long Island. At the entrance, she drove right on, without stopping to see if the road was clear, only inches in front of a car whose driver put his hand on the horn and waved a furious fist at her. Then she drove at about twenty miles an hour, holding up traffic for miles back. Cars passing her turned to look and blew their horns. She seemed oblivious. A truck came in ahead of her, going slower than she was, and she suddenly, without signaling, switched into the next lane very fast and then continued to drive as if she had suddenly awakened. Again, without signaling, she darted into the right lane and out at an exit. Bernie, following her, had to swerve sharply and almost crashed into a truck behind her. When she got to the first red light, she kept going, and then, at a stop sign, she stopped for so long that in an automatic gesture, Bernie, right behind her, honked his horn. He was making no effort to hide. She looked back in surprise, and then started to move immediately, without looking to right or left, and narrowly missed being hit by another car. Bernie had to wait for several cars to go by before he could catch up with her. He realized she wasn't trying to shake him. She wasn't any more aware of him than of anyone else on the road. Either she was the world's craziest driver or she was a lady in a fog. Wherever it was she was going, he began to have serious doubts that she would ever get there in one piece and to have serious fears for his own survival if he hung in too close to her. Several times he wondered if she was trying to kill herself, and if she knew she was. Then they crawled through a crowded surburban main drag that he thought she was probably familiar with, because she seemed to anticipate the lights and to slow down ahead of time, and then past that street to a winding, tree-lined road where the houses were set back a quarter of an acre as though by ordinance. She was driving slowly again, dragging her feet, he thought. He stayed further behind now, even letting a car get between them a couple of times.

When she turned left into the parking field of a church, he continued on for a few yards and then U-turned and doubled back slowly. He saw her park in the crowded lot and he stopped some distance away and cut his motor.

Had she traveled all this distance to pray? It should be to St. Christopher, the patron saint of travelers, who had spared her life. He'd go in himself and light a candle. This being a cop was not a safe job.

Anna didn't get out of her car right away. He thought of her as Anna. He didn't know why. Something in her reached out to him. He found himself grinning. Maybe it was sharing danger with her, and relief that they had both survived that drive.

Another car pulled into the lot and two women got out.

They wore low-cut dresses and high heels and the kind of makeup that went with strong perfume. He saw Anna look after them. When they had passed, she put her head back against the seat of the car. After five minutes, slowly, she sat up, combed her hair, put on lipstick. Still hesitant, she got out of the car. She straightened her shoulders and walked briskly to the entrance. He noted that she wasn't carrying her umbrella.

He waited only until she had turned the corner of the building before following her. Two other women came out of cars and caught up to him. He hung back, behind them.

"Thank God, it stopped raining. My hair frizzes."

"I wonder what'll turn up tonight."

"Don't expect too much. That way you won't be disappointed."

"Are you kidding! After those creeps at the Temple last night, nothing could be disappointing."

"You think so? You should've been at the Parents Without Partners Rap on Friday. I was almost ready to go back to Irving."

They both laughed. They were youngish women, not past thirty. This was one of those singles' things he had heard and read about. He shuddered, thinking of Linda. Is this what she would be up against if anything happened to him? And then he remembered: Linda had locked *him* out.

He paid four dollars to a woman sitting at a table in the hallway, who asked him if he wanted to be on the mailing list. He searched the list looking for her name. He saw it. She had started to write "An-," and then had crossed it out and had written "Allegra." Allegra Welles, and her address and phone number. He wrote "Kevin Feeley," and Feeley's address. He enjoyed that. Feeley's wife called the precinct a dozen times a day on some pretext or other, checking up on him. It drove Feeley wild. Bernie wished he could be

151

there to hear her when the mailings came from Sunday
Singles' Rap and Dance.

The hallway was outside the church rec room. From
inside he could hear dance music. He felt the beat. It was a
good band. He went in. The room was crowded. Probably two hundred people. Some dancing, some standing
around talking or watching. There were people at tables
around the room.

He watched the people dancing. He couldn't see Anna.
For an instant he was afraid he had lost her, that she might
have led him here and then slipped away, that she had
known she was being followed.

Then she came through the door. She must have hung
her coat outside.

He liked her dress. Lavender silk with a fitted top and
full skirt. A nice dress for dancing. And she had a pretty
scarf tied around her neck. He liked that. Linda did that a
lot.

Linda. How was his darling Linda? Did she think about
him at all? Worry?

Anna wasn't looking in his direction. She had come in
and stopped and looked around, tentatively. Shyly. He
thought he saw her sigh and then move into the room.

Christ, he had altogether forgotten how to ask a woman
to dance. And what was he thinking of? He hadn't come to
dance. What was he doing here? He watched Anna move
to the bar. He started after her.

"Hi, Bernie."

He turned guiltily. It was a tall girl in a silk blouse with a
lot of open buttons. Gold hoop earrings gleamed against
her dark hair. He didn't know her.

He said, "Hi . . . uh . . ." and looked for her name
tag.

"It ruins the material." She raised her arm and showed
him her wrist. The tag was on it. "Shelley," it said.

"Really Shirley," she said. "But if you say Shirley, I scream and vanish in a puff of smoke."

"Don't do that," he said nervously.

"OK, Bernie. Do you cha-cha?"

"I used to."

"Let's try."

"Sure. Thanks."

"I haven't seen you around anyplace. Are you new on the scene?"

"What scene?"

"This. The meet market."

"Oh. Yes. I'm new."

She took his hand and led him out on the floor. She was tall in her heels, almost as tall as he was. He wasn't accustomed to dancing with such a tall woman. He was accustomed to dancing with his wife, who knew all his moves. He danced badly, and was embarrassed. He kept glancing around the room, to look for Anna, and stepped on Shelley's foot. When the dance was over, he said, "Thanks for the dance," quickly, and went off to the bar.

She was standing near the bar with a glass of white wine, looking out over the dance floor.

He came over and said, "Hi, Allegra."

She looked surprised. He pointed to her name tag and she smiled. He really liked her smile.

"I'm Bernie."

"You look familiar," she said. "Have you ever been here before?"

He shook his head. "You?"

"Yes," she said. She looked at him again. "You really do look familiar."

"I have that kind of face."

"It's a very nice face," she said. She blushed. "I must be drunk."

"I hope you don't have to be drunk to think I have a nice face."

153

"Oh no," she said quickly and blushed again, and he laughed.

The music started again. It came from tapes, set up on the stage. A fox-trot. He could probably manage that without destroying her feet. "Dance?" he said.

She nodded and put her wineglass and purse on a table nearby. He took her hand and threaded through the crowd already on the dance floor. He put his arms around her. She fit nicely. He was instantly aware that he liked the feel of her. Their thighs were touching; she followed him as though they had danced together for years. They didn't talk. The fox-trot led into a lindy, and then back to a fox-trot. When the set ended, he waited on the dance floor and held her hand. He said, "You're five-foot-four and you weigh one hundred and ten pounds."

"One hundred nine. Blue eyes, blonde . . . with a little help. I can't tell if you're divorced or widowed. I can almost always tell."

"How can you tell?"

"I don't know. But I always can. Except you."

"Separated," he said. "You?"

"Divorced," she said. "Two years. I have one daughter. I live in Queens. I'm a librarian in a public library. Now you know all the statistics."

"I live in Manhattan. Do you ever go to Manhattan?"

"Of course. I went to a party in Manhattan last night."

"Really? Where?"

"In someone's house on West End Avenue. Do you know Louise King?"

"Louise King," he said, to remember it. "No."

"She runs singles' parties. She ran this one. I guess you haven't been single long."

"No," he said.

"It's an awful word, isn't it? *Single.* I hate it." She smiled. "That's a hustle."

"What is?"

"The music."

"I'm afraid I don't know it."

"I'll teach it to you. You can't be a successful single without the hustle." She led him over to a corner of the room away from the dance floor. "It's very simple. It's all to a count of six . . ."

He enjoyed it. He learned it fast, and she taught him two simple breaks. They danced by themselves in their corner and laughed when they got out of step. They went on dancing after the music stopped. Then the announcer said, "It's Latin Time. Rumba." But they didn't go back to the dance floor. They stayed in their little space. A man passed by close to them, holding two glasses of wine, and Bernie pulled her close, out of the man's way, and she stayed that way, close to him. He felt, if he closed his eyes, it could be Linda he was holding. The old Linda. . . .

"I suspect your husband is an idiot," he said.

"There's a thirty-two-year-old who doesn't think so. You can get one, too, I'm sure."

"What would I do with a thirty-two-year-old? She'd probably think the Great Depression is a hole in the ground and John L. Lewis is a rock group."

She laughed. It was pleasant, for a moment, to make a woman laugh.

"Your dress is pretty," he said. "You look real nice."

"Do I?" she said, seeming truly curious. "I never know anymore. I only knew what I saw in my husband's eyes."

He wanted to comfort her, to caress her soft, clean-smelling hair, to hold her closer. It was her size, probably, so like Linda's.

Suddenly it was painful holding her in his arms. He was forgetting why he had come here. He said, "Would you like to go someplace for coffee?"

She said, "All right. But I can't stay out very late. I have to go to work tomorrow."

"So do I."

"What do you work at?"

He hadn't prepared an answer. "Guess," he said.

"You're too big to be a midget in the circus and too small to be the jolly green giant. I give up."

He laughed. "You're cute," he said. And was astonished because he meant it. It wasn't only a dodge to keep from answering her. "I never met a librarian."

"I always hear that. I guess people still think a librarian is a little old lady sitting behind a desk, stamping out books."

"Well, I wouldn't expect her to be a dancing teacher." He took her raincoat from her to hold while she put it on. "You must meet nice people in a library."

"I hardly meet any people. I'm the cataloging librarian. I work in the office most of the time. I classify and catalog the books. That means I give them the number, and the subjects for the subject cards. I used to think we were a wonderful combination. A librarian and an accountant."

"Accountant?"

"George was an accountant."

"Who was George?"

"George?" she said, confused.

"You said George."

"I did?"

"Was George your husband?"

"Oh no. Simon was my husband. I don't know anybody named George." She looked bewildered. "I wonder why I said George."

Should he chance something? Would he scare her off? He couldn't figure her out. You couldn't arrest someone for having a yellow plastic umbrella. He wished he could see it, though. It had a broken shaft, he remembered. He said lightly, casually, "You must have heard the name on the news. A man named George was killed last night. They're making a big deal of it." But the name had not been released. Would she know that?

"I never listen to the news," she said.

"I know what you mean. It's depressing."

"No. It isn't that. What bothers me is that I know the news should depress me, but it doesn't. It doesn't matter. Nothing matters anymore. Except . . ." she stopped. "I'm sorry. I didn't mean to get so serious. I know men don't like it. It doesn't make you good company."

They reached her car in the parking lot and stood beside it.

"Except what?" he asked. "You were saying you don't feel anything except . . ."

"Sporadically. I feel sporadically."

"Everyone only feels happy sporadically."

"No. I'm never happy. What I feel sporadically is rage and fear and helplessness. Total despair. But mostly I feel nothing." She laughed. "I didn't mean to bore you. I guess I haven't talked to anyone, really, for a long time."

"Since the divorce from George?"

"Simon. My husband's name was Simon. No. It was before the divorce. He stopped wanting to listen. He had found some other voice he liked better. A new voice is better than an old loyalty. That's how it is nowadays. Well, you know . . . you left your wife."

"I did not!" he said heatedly. "She threw me out!"

"Because you were playing around?"

"No, I wasn't. Maybe I should have. You have a rotten view of men. Lots of women fool around, you know."

"Is that what your wife did?"

"No. At least, I don't think so. It was . . . I'm not sure what it was."

"I'm sorry. I wasn't prying. Maybe your separation is only temporary. Maybe your wife only needs a little time to be alone and think."

"I might do some thinking myself," he said angrily.

She touched his hand. "No, don't do that, Bernie.

157

You've both suffered, and it would be for nothing. You should never waste suffering." She smiled.

"Why not? Hell, you can always find more suffering."

"It's not the same. New suffering, unfamiliar suffering, is harder to cope with. And suffering that you suffer alone can be unbearable. It can drive you mad. . . ."

She was standing close to him. In the light from the parking lot, he could see her face. She was smiling, but there was no merriment in it. She had a wistful, shy smile. He felt very close to her; he wished he could comfort her.

He said, with surprise, "I haven't really talked to anyone for a long time either."

She cocked her head and looked up him. "Your wife doesn't understand you," she said.

He was startled. The gesture of her head reminded him so much of Linda, of the way she tilted her head and looked up at him, a gesture coy and mocking and very feminine. He had often caught her chin in his hand and bent his head to kiss her mouth when she did it. He caught himself moving close to her face and pulled himself back. Through the car window he saw the umbrella on the seat of her car, next to the driver's seat.

He said, "It might be complicated if we take two cars. I don't know the area here."

"You could follow me."

"Why don't we both go in your car. Then we can drive back here and I'll pick up my car."

"Wouldn't that make it kind of late? You still have to go back to Manhattan."

Wasn't this the place for him to say, "I could stay at your place or you could stay at mine?" The sentence was, "Your place or mine?" wasn't it? He didn't say it. He didn't know why. Was it because she hadn't said, "We could have coffee at my place . . . it's closer"? Was it because there was an air she had of resignation, of vulnerability? Did a flash of bitterness cross her face? Was it something else he didn't understand? Some feeling, or intuition? Was it merely because he didn't know how to say it? Good Jewish boy.

Anna smiled suddenly.

"Thanks," she said. "For not saying it."

"Saying what?"

"My place or yours."

"What made you think I might say it?"

"It was the right spot for it."

"Would you have said yes?"

She blushed. Even in the light from the outdoor lamp he could see it. "Yes," she said. "Nothing personal. It's expected nowadays."

"Why don't I call you tomorrow? We can have dinner. I'm not used to eating alone."

"I'm used to it," she said. "It's rotten." She reached over and pulled the name tag off his jacket, took a pen out of her purse and wrote her number on it. He put it in his pocket.

"Tomorrow," he said.

She was all he had to start with. He could go on from that. He said, "What's your favorite color?"

"I don't know. Blue, I suppose. Doesn't everyone love blue? What's yours?"

Linda loved green. Her eyes were green. Dark green, flecked with yellow. He said, "Yellow. I love yellow. It's so cheerful. Wear something yellow."

"If it rains. I have a yellow umbrella."

"Really?"

"It's in the car." She turned to the window and pointed. "There. Actually, it's not much good. It's broken."

"Where is it broken? Maybe I can fix it for you. Let me see it." He had to see it up close.

"It's really not fixable. I should throw it out."

"No, don't." He was trying hard not to sound frantic. "Maybe I can fix it for you tomorrow. I'm a very good fixer."

159

He took her hand.

"Good night," she said.

He held on to her hand. "Good night, Anna. See you tomorrow."

Impulsively, standing on her toes, she reached up and kissed his cheek. She opened her car door and got in. She hadn't locked her door.

"Do you always leave your car door open?"

She shrugged.

He waited until she started the car, and watched while she drove out of the parking lot. Then he got into his car immediately and drove after her. She didn't know his car. She would never pick it out if he followed her to where she would park. If she left her car door open and left the umbrella in the car, he might get to see it. It was worth a try. She had left the umbrella in the car before. She might do it again. Even if she locked her car door, what good cop didn't have a coat hanger in his car for opening locked car doors? He wanted to see that umbrella real bad. He couldn't arrest anyone for having a broken umbrella. He just wanted to see it.

He picked out her car easily on the road and followed from two cars back most of the time. She drove somewhat more sanely this time, but she wouldn't get any prizes for brilliant driving. A couple of times he wondered if she was trying to kill herself. A car was a favorite suicide weapon.

Her car was warm. Anna shrugged the raincoat off her shoulders. She caught a glimpse of the name on the shoulder of her dress. Allegra. She pulled it off carefully and dropped it into the rubbish on the floor of her car. The man, Bernie, had looked familiar. After a while all men looked alike.

He seemed like a nice person. Sensitive. She wondered what was wrong with him. Why would a man so attractive and warm be interested in her? A man like him

160

could get someone much better, much younger. Less damaged. No one like him had ever taken her number.

He was very masculine; she liked his voice. What was it he worked at? It wasn't accounting. She couldn't remember what he had said. He had nice hands, large and hard. Firm handshake. She remembered the nice way he had held her hand and said good night. "Good night, Anna."

He *had* said "Anna." She picked her name tag out of the rubbish holder. It said "Allegra." Had she told him Anna?

It didn't matter. He wouldn't call. Men like that never did. Still, why had he called her Anna?

She parked only a block from her house. He had seemed surprised that she hadn't locked the car. Not surprised, exactly. Curious. She took the umbrella and locked the car door.

It was strange how easily they had talked, how relaxed she felt with him. Forget it, Anna. Anna/Allegra.

There were no stars. The street was dark and empty, a street swept clean by rain. A street that seemed to be waiting . . .

Rubbish was piled neatly at the curb in covered metal cans and large black plastic bags. She dropped the umbrella onto one of the bags. It was broken, after all. Silly to keep a broken umbrella. Now that Emmy wasn't there to see everything, she would buy herself a new one. Maybe a pretty flowered yellow fabric, a good one that wouldn't break easily.

She didn't see the car that pulled up a few cars behind hers and cut its lights. She didn't see the man in the car watching her. A big man. He watched her drop the umbrella. He watched her go into the shrub-lined entrance to her building and up to the large, ornate glass-and-metal doors. He got out of his car and started toward the rubbish pile, walking silently, stealthily.

The sky was dark. There were no stars. The moon was locked up behind thick clouds. If it rained tomorrow, she would have no umbrella to go to work with. Maybe she couldn't get another yellow umbrella. She turned and ran back to the rubbish pile and picked up the umbrella.

She didn't spot the man who ducked down fast behind a parked car.

She held the umbrella close to her.

Maybe he would call.

She ran back to her building.

Chapter Twenty

Bernie locked the hotel room door and came into the room. He felt the presence of the fat girl; he smelled her, a sickening smell of dirty hair and cheap perfume. He turned and saw her, a look of terror on her face, edging toward the open door, trying to escape. He lunged for her. She wasn't there. There was only the door. Locked. He had locked it. Trembling, he put on the light. He put on all the lights . . . the overhead, the lamp beside the bed, the lamp on the dressing table, the light in the bathroom. He even looked in the closet. The room was empty. Even the smell was gone.

He couldn't stop trembling. He stood in the glare, in the middle of the room where he had almost killed a wretched whore whom he could more easily have allowed to run away, and felt as though he had suddenly been catapulted into a sordid, ugly world. Through most of his adult life, he had moved, impregnable, immune, like a god through that world. And now that world had touched him. Infected him. He was afraid. It was Linda's fault. No. It was his fault. He had somehow failed her.

Sweat broke out on his face; his body was drenched in it. He tore off his jacket and his shirt. He didn't know what to do with them. Where should he put the shirt? Linda always took care of his shirts, of all his clothes. He didn't know what she did with them. She decided when they were dirty and took them off somewhere, and she hung them up, clean and pressed and ready for him. His underwear and socks were always folded neatly in his drawers. She had been a good wife. She had taken care of him. Cooked and shopped and kept house and done all the bills. Their home was spotless. A cockroach could break a leg on her kitchen floor, Sean once said, laughing. Sean's wife was an indifferent housekeeper. With all those kids . . . Where was Linda tonight? How was she making out without him? Did she miss him?

He wanted to call her, to ask her if she was all right. Did she need anything? Need him? He should at least tell her where he was. There might be an emergency.

All of their life together had been an emergency. If she was in trouble, she could call Sean. She didn't want him. He had to face that. She hadn't wanted him for years. He had to learn to accept it. He wouldn't be here if she had wanted him.

Could this really be the way a marriage ended?

He had taken off all his clothes. They lay like a puddle at his feet. His body was damp and he was cold. He felt clammy and unclean. Take a shower. If he were in the shower, he couldn't call Linda.

It was a rotten shower. The spray was too light and couldn't be directed high enough. And the water wasn't hot enough. He came out quickly and dried himself and got under the bed covers. He saw his clothes on the floor and got out of bed and hung up the jacket and pants. He folded the rest neatly on the floor of the closet. He'd better start learning to take care of himself. He shut all the lights and got back into bed and lay there, wide-awake, staring into the dark, thinking: Linda. Seeing her still sleek legs, seeing her large dark green eyes that wouldn't look at him, that closed like shutters when he turned her face to his, seeing a lavender and green scarf knotted prettily, seeing bushy red hair like grotesque cotton candy lying faceless on a pillow, seeing a face like Theo's biting a pendulous, thick breast, biting off the nipple . . .

He heard a scream and bolted up, reaching for Linda, to protect Linda. She wasn't there. He was alone.

His head began to pound as though he had hit it against something hard. The scream pierced the silence again. It wasn't a scream. It was the phone. He reached for it and hit a lamp on the table beside the bed. Where had that come from? The room was unfamiliar.

He felt like a man coming up from deep waters, a drowning man. He couldn't breathe. His head was going to explode.

He dropped his legs over the side of the bed and recognized the hotel room, and when the scream came again, he knew where he was. When he picked up the phone, a woman's voice said, "This is the wake-up call you requested, sir. Six-thirty." He said thank you and lay back again and closed his eyes. He couldn't believe he had been sleeping. He tried to recapture the images that had been scattered by the phone. He couldn't focus on them. His mind clawed toward reality.

He would have to call Linda and get the rest of his things. But he had time for that. She had packed enough for three or four days at least. Maybe he ought to get a better place to live first. An apartment. He wasn't sure he knew how to start doing that. They had lived in the same apartment for twenty-seven years. She had selected all the furniture and everything else they had. Even his clothes. That was OK. He liked her taste. Classy. He thought she was classy.

It wouldn't hurt to call her. She might be worried about him.

He smiled. "Bernstein," he said aloud, "you are one tough guy. There is no evil in the heart or mind of man you haven't encountered or heard about in the thirty-one years you've been on the force. You've seen everything. Nothing fazes you. Nothing surprises you. Except the way you lie to yourself."

Work. That was the thing. He believed in work. It had never failed him.

His hand was on the phone. He wasn't totally aware of what he was doing until he heard her voice. Anna. That is, Allegra. She had told him Allegra. He'd better watch that. He'd better start thinking of her as Allegra.

Chapter Twenty-one

He said, "Hi. I hope I didn't wake you up. I know it's very early."

"It's all right. I wasn't sleeping. Sleeping isn't my best thing."

"What is?"

"Wife and mother, I used to think. I don't know anymore. Do you really want me to tell you all about myself at six-thirty in the morning?"

"Is it that early? I'm sorry."

"It's all right. Do you have the feeling we're repeating ourselves?"

He laughed. "Were you really up?"

"Yes."

"What were you thinking about?"

"If you'd call."

"I said I'd call."

She didn't answer. Finally she said, "Why are you up so early?"

"I don't know. A strange bed in a strange hotel, I guess. I've never been alone before."

"Your separation is very recent, isn't it?"

"Yes. Does it get easier?"

"Not noticeably. Did you ever know time to cure anything? It just makes things familiar."

"Isn't familiar easier?"

"No. Harder. It begins to mean no escape." She laughed suddenly, a fake laugh. "I haven't had coffee yet. I'm a terrible grump before coffee. Maybe you should talk to me later."

"OK. How about dinnertime. Tonight."

Again she didn't answer. She was silent for so long that he said, "Hello? Are you still there?"

"Yes," she said.

"Where would you like to have dinner?"

"Why me?" she said.

"I don't understand."

"I'm nothing special."

"He really did a number on you, didn't he?"

"Who?"

"Your husband. What's his name?"

"Simon."

"Right. Simon." Not George. "So what time do I come get you?"

"What I mean is . . . I could really . . . I mean, I could get to like you. And then what do I do when your wife takes you back?"

"What makes you think she'll do that?"

"When she sees what's out there in the jungle, she'll come get you."

"Seven o'clock all right?"

Again she didn't answer.

"I might decide I'm not an old shoe that she can throw out in the garbage and then take back in."

"I'm fifty," she said.

"Congratulations. A lot of people don't make it."

"How old are you?"

"Fifty-one. Are you going to offer me a thirty-year-old again?"

"They'll make the offers themselves."

"I didn't ask you to marry me. Only to have dinner. You have a rotten self-concept."

"It's called being realistic."

"A person can be too realistic. Have you always been so insecure?"

"When I was a child. I guess one reverts in bad times." She laughed. Even on the phone it sounded strained, and somehow distant.

"Allegra . . ."

She didn't answer. He felt she had drifted away from him. He was losing her.

He said sharply, "Allegra!"

"Yes?" She sounded startled, as though he had pulled her back from someplace faraway.

"I need someone to talk to. To be with. You're easy to talk to. Please."

"All right."

"What time?"

"It doesn't have to be dinner. You can come over and talk."

"You're doing it again."

"What?"

"Hanging out your rotten self-concept. I won't spend a lot of money on you. Will that make you feel better?"

She laughed. It seemed more real. "Seven is fine," she said. "If you have a pencil, I'll give you the address."

He almost said he had it. He caught himself just in time. He had to watch himself. Something about her threw him off guard. He went through the pretense of getting a pen and writing the address, repeating it, and taking directions.

169

"I'll see you at seven," he said.

He bounded out of bed, suddenly filled with energy, eager to get to his office, to find out if there was anything new on the case. He felt young. He could hardly wait to start the day.

Chapter Twenty-two

Feeley was on the phone in his office when Bernie opened the door. His elbows were on the desk and his head was bowed. His end of the conversation was mainly "Yes, dear." Bernie started out, but Feeley waved him in and pointed to a chair. He covered the mouthpiece and looked questioningly at Bernie.

"What've we got on the cock chomper?" Bernie asked, aware that he had said we, not you, including himself actively in the case.

Without a break in his *yes, dear's*, Feeley looked through a batch of folders on his desk, took one out, and handed it to Bernie, who read it thoughtfully.

As soon as Bernie looked up from his reading, Feeley said abruptly, "I have to go now, dear. The inspector is here." He listened a moment more. "*Hon* . . . I have a job. . . ." He hung up. Apologetically, he said, "She loves me. . . ."

"Don't knock it," Bernie said expressionlessly. He tapped the folder in front of him. "Let's add it up. What've we got?"

"Not much. Time of death between one and two A.M. Sunday. I guess the biggest thing is, we're pretty sure who the victim is, but we don't have a positive ID yet. Donlon is doing good work on it. He looked through the address book in the apartment and found the dentist. Victim had capped teeth. Dentist identified them. George Stone. He was the resident of the apartment. By the way, the renting agent has been calling endlessly to find out when he can clear out the place so he can rent it. Doesn't want to lose money, he says."

"Sentimental City," said Bernie. He wondered fleetingly if he should apply for the place. It looked pretty nice. How to get an apartment in New York City: Follow the hearse.

"Anybody have a line on the roommate?"

"No. The doormen are the only ones who admit to seeing him. They say he was very young. Chubby. Curly hair. Kept no regular hours day or night. One of them heard him call the victim George. He called up from the desk one time to find out if George was home."

"How young?"

"Sixteen, seventeen. Hard to say, they said. Tee shirt and jeans type, sneakers without socks. High a couple of times. They both came in stoned together one time. Doorman had to push their floor button for them."

"Did he see the victim on the night of the murder?"

"Doesn't remember. Doesn't think so. Over four hundred tenants in the building, he says, how can he remember every one every night?"

Bernie remembered one tenant. An old man. He grinned when he thought of him. The one with Anna . . . that is, Allegra.

"Sixteen, seventeen. Young enough to be a son maybe," Bernie said. "Anyone try talking to the ex-wife since Johnson and Ramirez?"

"Yeah. Not home. We tried last night. Although she said she hadn't seen her ex-husband for eight years."

"Keep trying. Divorced people like to keep tabs on each other; hatred is a pretty strong tie. The dentist know anything about him?"

"No. Only that he figured him to be a swinger. The one I'd like to get through to is the dame next door. Old dame. But she'd have to be stone-deaf not to have heard something. Postwar building. Thin walls."

"Bring her down here. Sometimes being in the precinct shakes them up. Makes it seem more official. Also, there's a man. An old guy. Tall. Thin. Loud voice. Has a long, dark-checked raincoat, kind of a cape, and reads the Sunday *Times*. Maybe gets it from the doorman. There were a bunch of those on his counter. I'd like him down here, too. I'd like to talk to that one myself."

Feeley looked like he was trying hard not to stare, but he didn't ask questions.

"Bring in everybody who lives on the ninth floor. Also the people in 8E and 10E. Space it so they aren't all here together."

Feeley said, "Right, Inspector." But his face said, *Why this case? Why are you so involved?* He proceeded, "We've got a couple of good leads on that other beauty from Saturday night. The torso without hands, feet, and head."

"Fine, fine," Bernie said. "Let me take that file, too. I'll look at it in my office."

Was Feeley looking at him peculiarly, or was he imagining it? Maybe you're looking at yourself peculiarly, Bernstein. He took the files and got up.

"Damnedest thing," Feeley said. "Years ago you could get a witness to a crime. Ten people would say they saw something or heard something. Nowadays nobody wants to get involved. Nobody cares. Nobody even cares for their own. People married thirty years splitting up, kids living together five years refusing to make a commitment, afraid of responsibility, not wanting kids."

Bernie said, "Out of the ten people that used to say they heard something or saw something, nine were making it up."

"I don't know; I don't know," said Feeley, "a woman screams for help in the street, people close their windows. A man is thrown out of a moving car, bleeding, and people walk right past. No one wants to get involved. I don't know. Sometimes I think it's this whole Women's Lib thing to blame."

"Never should have given them the vote," Bernie said, and went out fast, before Feeley got onto his really favorite topic: Women on the Force.

Alone in his office, Bernie read the file on Stone carefully. Donlon had done his work well. There were interviews with most of the tenants in the building and with everyone who had come in and out all day long. Nothing that told them anything. The woman living downstairs in 8E had heard the loud music. She hadn't complained. She had a teenage daughter with quadraphonic sound rock and roll. She was grateful when no one complained about her. She had also heard moving around and dancing and maybe some yelling. She thought it was a party. No, she didn't know the man upstairs. She didn't bother with men.

The couple in 10E had been away for the weekend. They hadn't come home until late Sunday night. The people in 9D had been out Saturday night. Young nonmarrieds. They hadn't come in until four A.M. They had sometimes heard loud music from 9E. What can you do, they said. It's an apartment building, not the suburbs with trees between the houses. They didn't complain. That's life. They didn't know the guy next door. They thought he was sort of an older guy. Forties or fifties or something. They didn't know if he lived with anyone. Did they ever see a woman there? One night, a year ago, maybe. A long-haired woman. Artist-looking type. They had only lived in the building a little over a year themselves.

But *someone* had called the police. *Someone* had reported finding the body. No one knew who.

The best bet was the Miller woman. 9F. She had been home all night. Bernie decided he would talk to her himself.

The doorman said Mrs. Miller was a quiet lady. Dignified. She always said good morning and good afternoon and she always tipped nice at Christmas. She didn't have much to do with anybody. He neither liked her nor disliked her. She wasn't a pain in the ass was all.

There were a lot of old ladies in the building, and old men, too. He knew right away the man the detective asked him about. Tall, thin, white-haired, all the time bitching about something. The world was only there for him to comment on. Mr. Russell. 15A. "He carries a brick in a paper bag all the time. He tells everyone about it."

Mr. Russell opened his door to Detective Donlon's ring and went through the whole let-me-see-your-ID bit. Christ, they all watched TV and got wised up. Before TV he would bet no one knew about asking to see an ID.

"Donlon," Mr. Russell said. "You're Irish?"

"Yes, sir."

"It wouldn't hurt to wear a tie if you're a detective. You ought to set an example. I always wear a tie, even if I'm home alone in my own apartment."

"Yes, sir." He was going to ask to be transferred to narcotics. Something easy like that. Something where he could deal with the Mafia. He couldn't take these old folks. "Mr. Russell, I suppose you know there's been a . . . problem in the building."

"Dozens of problems in the building. Half the time the hot water boiler is broken. But I don't believe that. I think the landlord is saving money on hot water. And burglaries! I saw a burglar myself the other day."

"You did?"

"Certainly. Yesterday. Saw him come right out of the elevator with a policeman. A very big man, he was. Bigger than you."

"When was this, Mr. Russell?"

"In the morning. Very early. Maybe five A.M. I went down to the lobby for my paper. Half the time that fool of a doorman doesn't even have it for me. He forgets. I never forget anything."

"You're sure it was a burglar?"

"Of course I'm sure. I know a burglar when I see one, don't you? I told that young woman he was a burglar, but she said he wasn't. Nice young woman. She said she would let me be in charge of the weather, if she could. But she said he wasn't a burglar. She was friendly. Some people get in the elevator and won't talk to you."

Donlon hadn't heard about a burglary in the building yesterday. He made a note to check it. "What I mean, sir, there seems to have been a murder in the building."

"Seems to have been? Aren't you sure? You ought to watch TV. It's been all over TV. Even showed the building, right there on the screen. And this morning's paper, too. I was at my daughter's house yesterday afternoon and evening. She kept going on at me, 'Papa, you have to move,' she said. 'You have to get out of that building. They're killing people in that building now.' What she wants, she wants me to go to one of those places for old people, those senior citizens' places, where they put things in the food. Saltpeter, to take away your sex drive."

Donlon cleared his throat. "Sir," he said, "we're asking everyone in the building to come down to the precinct to answer a few questions. If you don't mind, I could take you there now."

"Be happy to. I'll just get my coat and paper bag. I bet it was him that did it."

"Who, sir?"

"The burglar. I bet he did the murder."

"Could you identify him if you saw him?"

"Certainly," he said. "I have all my marbles. And I carry a brick in my paper bag."

Donlon sighed. He was going to resign. He was going to become a gym teacher. Or open a bar. "You might as well take an umbrella, too, sir. It's started to rain again."

Mr. Russell was clearly fascinated by the station house. He said right away, "This place needs a painting. It's a disgrace."

Sergeant Isabel Petersen, at the desk, said agreeably, "You're right, sir. We would be very grateful if you would write a letter to the mayor and tell him. That's Mayor Koch. K-O-C-H."

"I know who the mayor is," Mr. Russell snapped. "I can tell you all the mayors since LaGuardia: William O'Dwyer, Vincent Impellatiri, Robert Wagner, John V. Lindsay, Abraham Beame, Edward Koch. Crooks, all of them. Except Fiorello. The Little Flower. I write letters all the time. Mostly to *The New York Times*. They don't publish them. Those letters are all fakes. They're all written by one person. They all sound alike, even when they don't agree with each other."

"Yes, sir." Sergeant Petersen handed him a paper and pen.

"I used to be a schoolteacher. Retired fifteen years ago. If you think a person can live on that pension, you're crazy. I think I'll tell that to the mayor, too. Retired at sixty-five. I'm eighty years old."

"God bless you," said Sergeant Petersen. "You don't look it."

"Of course I do," said Mr. Russell impatiently. "Why

shouldn't I? It's no disgrace to look your age. But I'm thinking of dying my hair. White hair doesn't suit me."

Donlon came out of Feeley's office and signaled to Petersen who said, "We'd be happy if you got the mayor to paint this place."

"Ask for wallpaper while you're at it," Donlon muttered. "And fresh flowers every day."

Petersen indicated Feeley's door. "If you'll go into that office. Mr Russell . . ."

The old man started toward Feeley's office, when Bernie opened his door and came out, holding a folder, and heading toward Feeley's office, too. Mr. Russell stopped abruptly and said, very loud, "That's him!"

"Who, sir?"

"The burglar!" He pointed with his umbrella at Bernie, who stopped and looked at him, grinning, the way he had in the lobby. "That's him," Mr. Russell said firmly.

"That man?" Petersen looked confused.

"Yes."

"That's the commander of the precinct, sir. Inspector Bernstein."

"Nonsense. He's a burglar, I tell you. You're probably in on it with him."

Sergeant Petersen sighed. "Detective Feeley is waiting for you, sir."

Mr. Russell stalked past Bernie to the open office door. Bernie came in after him and closed the door.

Feeley stood up. "How do you do, Mr. Russell. I'm Detective Feeley. Sorry to get you out in the rain like this." He pointed to a chair. "Won't you sit down, please. This is Inspector Bernstein. We'd like to ask you a few questions about the murder in your building yesterday morning. We tried to reach you yesterday when we saw most of the residents in the building, but you weren't home. Do you know anything that might possibly help us find the murderer?"

"Ask him." The old man pointed toward Bernie, but he was also looking around the office with great curiosity.

Feeley looked confused.

Bernie pulled a chair up close to Mr. Russell and sat down. He crossed his long legs and smiled, looking friendly and relaxed, and handed the old man a black ID case.

"That's my ID, Mr. Russell. I'm sorry you think I'm a burglar."

Mr. Russell examined it carefully, lifting up his glasses to read it, taking his time, checking the photograph with Bernie's face, and handed it back to him.

"Am I clean?" Bernie smiled.

He glared at Bernie. "I don't know. I'm not sure."

Bernie got up with a broad sigh. "I guess we might as well get Mr. Russell back home, Feeley. He isn't going to help us."

Mr. Russell didn't move.

Feeley said, "I don't kow . . . maybe we ought to give him more of a chance. Mind if I smoke, Mr. Russell?"

"Of course I mind. You don't think I got to be eighty years old and in perfect health by hanging around smokers!"

"Really eighty years old? God bless you."

"What for? I didn't sneeze. Every time I say I'm eighty years old, somebody says, 'God bless you.'" He turned to Bernie. "What do you want to ask me?"

"Did you know the occupant of apartment 9E?"

"Is it true he was decapitated and lost his hands and feet?"

"No, sir. That's a different case."

"Oh, yes. This was the one . . ."

"Another part of the anatomy. Yes."

"He didn't deserve to have a penis if he couldn't take better care of it," Mr. Russell said.

"Did you know him?"

179

"No."

"Any idea who he was? Anything at all about him?"

"No."

"But you know some of his friends."

"What friends?"

"A woman. She was in the hall with you yesterday morning. A woman about five feet four inches. She was wearing a red raincoat."

"I don't know who you mean."

"You were talking to each other. She said I wasn't a burglar."

"I don't remember any woman saying that."

"Maybe you forgot."

"Never forget a thing. I can name all the capitals of all the states of the United States. Want to hear me?"

"Sure," said Bernie.

"Oh, Jesus," said Feeley.

"Alabama-Montgomery, Alaska-Juneau, Arizona-Phoenix, Arkansas-Little Rock . . ."

Bernie listened attentively while Mr. Russell rattled off all the capitals of all the states. All fifty of them.

"That's really great," he said, applauding. "Isn't it, Feeley?"

"Fantastic. You sure you mind *one* cigarette?"

"Absolutely."

"The woman has a yellow umbrella. Yellow plastic," said Bernie, and Feeley stopped fidgeting.

"One of those modern things? Bubble, they're called."

"Yes," said Bernie.

"They don't last," said Mr. Russell. "Trash. I have this same umbrella I've had for twenty years. Never lose anything."

"Do you know her?"

"Who?"

"Maybe you can tell us her name. Was she a good friend of the man in 9E?"

"I don't know. I don't know who you're talking about."

"She went up in the elevator with you yesterday."

"I don't remember anyone in the elevator with me."

"Do you remember what floor she got off?"

"There wasn't anyone in the elevator with me."

"All we want to do is ask her a few questions about Saturday night. She may have been a witness," said Bernie. "She had a nice smile. Blonde. Blue eyes. Slim. Red raincoat."

Mr. Russell pursed his lips and thought for a while. "No," he said finally. "I don't remember anyone like that."

Bernie sighed. He wrote his name and number on a piece of paper from Feeley's desk and gave it to Mr. Russell. "OK. If you happen to remember something, if you remember seeing her, call me. I'd like to talk about it. That's really great about the capitals of all the states. I don't know them."

"You would if I'd been your social studies teacher," he said. "And you wouldn't be a burglar."

"Right," said Bernie. "Nice talking to you, Mr. Russell. Don't lose my number."

"Never lost a thing in my life," he said. "I know all the presidents of the United States, Washington to Reagan, and all their vice presidents."

Feeley turned pale. He got up quickly and led the old man out of the door to the outer desk and hurried back to his office. Sergeant Petersen said, "Good afternoon, Mr. Russell. One of the patrolman will drive you home. He's waiting for you outside."

Mr. Russell nodded and went out. There was a large alley cat taking refuge from the rain on the top step of the station house that was protected by an overhang. "Wouldn't tell them a thing," he said to the cat. "That's not a real station house. It's some kind of a front. Probably a bookie joint. Maybe even a brothel. Why would they want to find that poor nice girl? Probably want to kill her to keep her from talking."

The cat arched its back, flicking its tail, and hissed at him. "Behave yourself," Mr. Russell said sharply, pointing his umbrella at it. The cat turned and slunk away down the stairs. Mr. Russell marched after it.

"They didn't even take my picture or my fingerprints," he said as he got into the waiting police car. "I know a burglar when I see one."

Chapter Twenty-three

Feeley came back into Bernie's office and sat down. "What do you think, Inspector?"

"Would I make a good second-story man?"

"You're too big. You'd get stuck in the window. Better stay with what you're doing. By the way, what is it you're doing, may I ask, sir?"

"What are you talking about?"

"There's nothing in the file on a woman in a red raincoat."

"No. And no umbrella, either," Bernie said.

"When did we start playing TV cops and robbers?"

Bernie was silent for a minute. "I've got nothing that would hold up in court," he said carefully. "I could be doing someone a lot of harm. Someone who doesn't need trouble." He stopped. Feeley waited.

Finally Feeley said, "That's it?"

"If it turns out to be something more, I'll hand it over. I'm not a vigilante, Feeley."

"You think that old man knows something?"

"He knows all the capitals of all the states and all the presidents from Washington to Reagan."

Feeley wasn't laughing.

"I bet he can do long division and fractions, too. Can you do fractions, Feeley?"

"Can the woman in the red raincoat with the yellow plastic umbrella do fractions, Inspector?"

"What woman, Feeley?"

"You're the one who knows, sir."

"I'll ask her if I find her. And then I'll tell you."

Feeley nodded and got up. At the door he stopped and turned. "Bernie," he said, "I'm going to step out of line. I mean . . . are you all right? I mean . . . the scratches on your face, the stitches in your forehead . . . I mean . . . You've been . . . you're not yourself . . ."

"If I'm not myself, who am I, Kevin?"

"Is everything all right? I mean . . . at home?"

This was one of those times Bernie wished he hadn't stopped smoking. He would be able to put a cigarette in his mouth and light it, covering the flame, and his face, with his hands. It would keep him busy. He fought hard not to let his body stiffen. He had known Kevin Feeley for thirty years. More. He had gone to Kevin's wedding, to the christenings of his four children, to his mother's funeral. But Bernie had never told Kevin about Theo. He had never told anyone. What was there to say? My son, the crazy?

"Josephine and me . . . I mean . . . we haven't seen anything of you and Linda for a long time."

"I'm sorry," Bernie said. "It's nothing personal. We don't see . . . anyone. . . ."

"I know," Feeley turned red. He was a big man, red hair, pink face, getting paunchy, getting soft. Comfortable. "I mean . . . well, you know . . . we see Sean and Kathy . . ."

"Yeah," Bernie said. Then Feeley knew about Theo.

What else did he know? Did he know something Bernie didn't know? "It's OK, Kevin." He brushed his hand over his face. "Dull razor. Thanks for asking." He picked up a folder from his desk and opened it.

Feeley hesitated. He was going to say something more. The phone rang on Bernie's desk. Bernie pounced on it.

"Inspector Bernstein."

The voice that answered was controlled, impersonal. "Bernie, this is Linda."

"Yes. Hello, Linda." His voice, he hoped, matched hers. "Just a minute, please." He put his hand over the mouthpiece. "Anything else, Kevin?"

"No, sir."

He went out quickly and closed the door. Bernie looked at the phone in his hand as though it would show her to him, as though he would be able to see her face. He took a deep breath and removed his hand from the mouthpiece.

"Sorry," he said. And then he didn't know what else to say. He was silent.

"Are you there?" she said.

"Yes."

"I'm sorry to call you at work." She might have been conducting a telephone survey. "I didn't know where else to reach you. You didn't let me know where you're staying."

"Did you want to know where I was staying?"

"Bernie, I hope we are going to be adult about this. We have to do what's best for Theo."

"And you think it's best for Theo not to have a father."

"That's ridiculous. You're still his father. In fact, I'm calling to remind you that this is Monday. You're supposed to pick up Theo at school and take him to the dentist."

"How will he get home?"

"You'll bring him, naturally."

"What's natural about it? You kicked me out. He must know that."

"I've explained it to him."

"Explain it to me."

"Bernie, you haven't been hearing me. Not for years. I've been telling you and telling you. Theo will be better off if you aren't in the house. He won't expect things from you if you aren't there, things you aren't able to give him."

"What things?"

"You don't love him."

"You told him that?"

"Of course not. But he knows it. He can feel it."

"Have I ever hurt him? You're the one who shouts at him and hits him and pressures him and makes demands."

"You don't make demands because you don't care about him."

"You told him that, too, I suppose."

"I haven't told him anything that will hurt him. I told him you will still be his father; you'll still see him and take him places . . . the park . . . the ball game . . ."

"He hates ball games. He's afraid of the park. He's afraid of birds and squirrels and worms."

"I told him you would take him to the beach this summer for a week on your vacation, and you would go fishing."

"He's afraid of the beach. He's afraid of sand. He's afraid it will get into his nose and suffocate him."

"He says he won't be afraid."

How many times had they had this same conversation? "He said that last year and the year before. And I wouldn't trust him with a fish hook."

"You see! You're negative about him! He'll be better off if you aren't there all the time to be negative about him!"

"Linda . . ." he took a breath, "will you be better off without me?"

"I've spoken to his doctor. We've talked about it many times."

"Will you, Linda? Will you be better off without me?"

"There's nothing between us anymore, Bernie. You have this exaggerated, obsessional idea of loyalty, of right and wrong. It's 'wrong' for a man to leave his wife and child. It has nothing to do with love."

"Maybe it's the love that's obsessional."

"It's only your background, your . . . cultural heritage."

"Right. I'm a Jew bastard."

"I never said that," she cried. "I never, never said that!"

"That's my cultural heritage. Jew bastard."

"You're too sensitive about it."

"I'm not sensitive about it at all. I'm proud of it."

"I know. Your people gave the world the Ten Commandments, and you became a policeman to make sure everybody keeps them."

"Why did Sean become a cop?"

"It's a job. That's all. Just a job. To you it's the Holy Grail."

"Aren't you mixing your metaphors?"

"I was hoping we wouldn't quarrel. That you would understand."

"Is that what you were hoping? Were you also hoping I was going to manage forever with three hundred dollars in the bank?"

"The money is for Theo."

"Theo still has a father, as you pointed out yourself. His father will support him. His father will also see a lawyer about the money."

"I didn't think you would be ugly and selfish about it."

"I didn't think I'd come home one night and find myself locked out of my home."

"It's better for everyone this way. For you, too."

"Thank you for thinking of me."

"There's nothing you can say that can make me change my mind."

"Linda," Bernie said, very slowly and clearly, "have you heard me asking you to change your mind?" The words startled him. He hadn't known he was going to say them, or even that they were in his head.

She seemed startled, too, he thought, because she was silent so long, and then she said coldly, "Theo expects you to be at his school to get him. Will you be there?"

"Naturally, as you said. Will you be home when I bring him there?"

"No. You know it's the day I take my course."

"I don't have the keys. Remember?"

"Theo has the keys."

"What if he loses them?"

"You always expect the worst."

"I expect the usual."

"Sean has the keys. He's off today."

"Do you really expect me to go to your brother to get the keys to my own home?"

"It isn't your home anymore."

"Bull's-eye, Linda. Right on target. I hope he doesn't lose the keys. If he does, I'll deliver him to you at your class."

"I pinned them to the inside pocket of his jacket," she said.

Should he remind her that she had done that before and Theo had lost them anyway? What would be the use? She knew it, or she would never know it. All of a sudden it didn't matter. He said, "I still have the mailbox key, unless you've changed that, too. Put the keys in an envelope in the mailbox."

She hesitated.

"I won't try to keep them, Linda."

"All right. You can take the rest of your things while you're there today," she said. "I packed them for you."

"I would appreciate your packing some money, too. I don't have any. Three hundred dollars, in case you don't realize it, isn't going to get me an apartment."

"Borrow," she said. "I can't touch any of the money. It's in irrevocable trust for Theo. He's your son, too, no matter how you feel about him. Will you see him this Sunday?"

"I'm working Sunday."

"You worked last Sunday, and yesterday."

"The hard life of Holy Grailniks. It gave you time to work out your little plans."

"When shall I tell him you'll see him?"

"I'll see him today."

"I mean, for the day."

"I'll work out visitation rights with the lawyers."

"You really hate him."

"No. I don't. He's my son, too, as you said. I don't even hate you, Linda."

He hung up.

Was that true, he wondered. Was it true he didn't hate her?

Chapter Twenty-four

Bernie sat in his car outside Theo's school for a few minutes. He had to pull his thoughts free from the file on his desk. And he had to steel himself for Theo.

Was this Theo's fourth or his fifth special school in as many years? Private schools. Schools for "exceptional" children. They were running out of them. He had been kicked out of public school in the second grade.

Some of the children were coming out of the building. It was time to go and get his son. Theo wasn't allowed to come out with the other children. Too often there was a fight when he did. He said the other children picked on him and called him names and pushed him. He had to defend himself, didn't he, Linda said.

Bernie wondered if Theo's behavior had been different today, with his father out of the house. Was he hoping the boy had been worse than usual, more belligerent and angry, acting out more?

Theo was at a table in the principal's office, drawing quietly. He looked up when his father came in and went right back to his drawing. For one searing moment,

Bernie imagined a tall, broad boy with an easy grin who said, "Hi, Dad." A boy he could put his arm around, throw a ball with, take fishing, maybe just horse around with, and talk. This boy made him uncomfortable. He was small and thin, with scrawny arms and legs, beautiful, dark, curly hair always too long because he was afraid of barbers, and large, dark, intense eyes. Bernie didn't know how to talk to him. For a crazy second he was tempted to tiptoe out of there. Run away. Where? Grown-ups don't run away, Bernstein.

He said, "Hi, Theo."

Theo didn't look up. "I can't get the dog's legs right."

"Do you want me to help you?"

"No."

"Mr. Bernstein, do you draw?" The principal had come into the room and was standing by the door, watching them. She put some papers and books on the table and looked up at Bernie, smiling. He noticed she wasn't wearing a wedding ring. All of a sudden he was noticing things like wedding rings.

"He isn't *Mr.* Bernstein," Theo said. "He's *Inspector* Bernstein. He draws real well. Mother says he could have been an artist."

"I can draw. That's about it. I'm not artistic. His mother is artistic."

"Theo is very talented," said Miss Farber. She was standing close to Bernie now, leaning against him slightly. "May we see what you have been working on, Theo?"

Theo flung down the crayons he was working with and snatching a thick black one he scribbled furiously all over his drawing, pressing so hard the crayon snapped. He hurled the broken pieces against the wall, and crumpling the paper in both hands, threw it after the broken crayon. His thin body was trembling violently.

"You s-stupid bitch!" he screamed at Miss Farber, and ran out of the room.

"I'm sorry," Bernie said. "Has he been difficult today? Unusually difficult?"

"Not that I know of," she said. "Has anything happened at home?"

"My wife hasn't spoken to you?"

"No."

"She should have. His teacher should be prepared in case he acts out. Mrs. Bernstein and I have . . . well, we've separated."

"I'm glad you told me. It's important for us to know. I'll talk to his teacher. I can call him at home if he's left school by now. If you like, you can call me at home this evening. I'll tell you how things went today." She wrote her name and number on a paper and handed it to him. She smiled. She was a pretty woman, tall and slim, about forty. Her lips were shiny and moist, as though her lipstick had been freshly applied. "Feel free to call tonight, or any time," she said.

He said, "Thank you. I wouldn't trouble you at home."

"It's no trouble. I don't have all that much to do since my husband died."

"Sorry . . ."

"It's been two years. I'll talk to Theo's teacher this afternoon."

"Thank you." He stuffed the paper into his pocket. "I'd better find my son."

Theo was waiting for him outside the office. "You're mad at me now," he said. "Now you really hate me."

"I don't hate you. I'm not mad at you. I only wish I knew why you behave like that, Theo."

"I wish I did, too." His lips trembled. Tears hung in his eyes.

"Is Miss Farber really a bitch, Theo?"

"No. She's nice."

"Do you think you could tell her that?"

"Can I do it tomorrow?"

"OK. We'd better go. We'll be late for the dentist."

"I don't want to go to the dentist."

Bernie's head suddenly began to throb. "Listen, Theo," he said fiercely, in a low voice. "I've had a rotten day. I'm still big enough to pick you up and carry you to the car and throw you in and then drag you out screaming to the dentist. We both hate that. Let's go without all that this time." He prayed that would work. Sometimes it did. He had told Linda a dozen times it was better to let Theo lose all his teeth than go through these scenes. The boy's teeth were congenitally bad and were probably made worse by his poor diet.

Theo seemed to be struggling. Bernie put his hand on his shoulder gently. He was so pathetically thin, it hurt Bernie to touch him. They walked together to the car.

"Mother changed the house a lot," Theo said.

Bernie didn't say anything. He didn't know what to say. When they had been driving for a while, Theo said, "When I get old enough, I'm going to kill you."

Bernie didn't answer.

"I didn't mean that, Dad. You know I didn't mean it."

"I know. The dentist isn't going to hurt you. He never does. He's going to put you to sleep and do his work and then you'll wake up. I'll be right there in the room with you the whole time. I promise."

"How do I know you stay there the whole time?"

"Have you ever awakened and found me gone?"

"But I don't know what you're doing when I'm asleep."

"I'm right beside you. I promise you. You're only asleep a short time."

How many times had they gone through this litany?

"I don't like to open my mouth like that."

"Nobody does. I don't like it either. We have to do it."

"There are so many things we have to do that we don't like to do."

"That's true. It's part of growing up."

"I'm never going to grow up! Never!"

He was beginning to get excited again. Bernie said, "OK, Theo. You're probably right at that."

Theo was sleepy on the way home, and leaned against his father quietly. Suddenly he asked, "Why did you have a rotten day, Dad?"

"That's how life is sometimes, Theo. Maybe tomorrow will be better."

"Mother changed the house a lot."

"So you said before," Bernie said. He didn't ask any questions. He didn't want to involve Theo by asking questions. Or was he afraid to hear the answers? He wasn't sure which. They passed MacDonald's and a Burger King and a kosher deli. Bernie wondered, as he did many times, what it must be like to take one's son for a hamburger and french fries and a shake or a corned beef sandwich. Maybe even a knish.

"Are you taking me home, Dad?"

"Yes, of course."

"Are you going to stay?"

"What did your mother tell you?"

"She said you were not going to live with us anymore."

"Well . . . we're trying that out. But I'm still your father."

"That's what she said, too. But why do you have to move away? Is it because of me, because I'm bad?"

"No, Theo. It's not because of you. And you're not bad."

"Mother changed the house a lot," he said again.

Theo had warned him. But the shock Bernie felt when he had come home and found the locks was as nothing compared to what he felt when he came into the apartment that had been his home for twenty-seven years. Linda had expunged him. It was as though he had never lived, never

195

been. His bed was gone from the bedroom. Their wedding picture, that picture of a happy couple smiling at each other, had been taken off the dresser. All his pictures, his diplomas, his citations for bravery, all gone. Every painting he had put up, all the drawings he had made in the early years of their marriage, his books; the picture of his parents at their own wedding . . . another happy, smiling couple . . . was gone.

His mind staggered. If he had died, there would be some sign of his having lived; she'd kept nothing. His desk had been removed from the study. In its place was her sewing machine and ironing board and the television from the living room.

A note on the kitchen table told him his clothes were in the suitcases in the hall closet. The rest of his things were in Sean's basement. He could get them whenever he wanted to. Sean, she wrote, had nothing to do with it. She had had them transported herself.

He looked around the apartment as though he were a visitor at his own funeral. He felt numb. She wanted to erase him from her life, as though she had never known him. The thought was unbearable.

Theo was tugging at his arm, shouting at him. He forced his attention back to his son; it was like pushing through fog. "I'm talking to you, Daddy. . . ." Theo was shouting. "You never listen to me. You never pay any attention. . . ."

"The house . . . it's all changed. . . ."

"I told you that," Theo cried petulantly. "I want some juice!"

Like a sleepwalker, Bernie got a can of juice and opened it for Theo. He poured it into Theo's glass, the only glass he would drink from.

"Are you upset by the changes, Theo?"

"Mother said it would be better this way. She said when you came to visit me, it would be to see me and not to do anything else. She said you would give me all your attention because that would be the purpose of your visit."

In the early years, before Theo, they had traveled to Ireland and England and Spain, Italy, France. They had brought things home for the house, things they had chosen together, argued and laughed about and treasured together. Belleek from Ireland, vases from Italy, china, paintings, wall hangings, glass, and leather. She had put them all away. She had turned him into a being without a history, without a past, without a place. A nonbeing. A man who had never loved and been loved.

She must have worked in a frenzy to have done so much so fast.

"Play with me."

"What?"

"Play chess with me."

"Theo, please . . . I can't right now. I really can't. I'm too upset. Can you try to understand? . . ."

"Mother said you would play with me!"

"I will. On Sunday. I'll see you Sunday."

"No! You won't! I don't believe you! I want to play now!" His face turned red. "I hate you! You're a shit! You're a big, stupid shit!" He flung the glass of grape juice at Bernie. It hit his face and the side of his shirt and ran down his neck. The boy grabbed the empty juice can and crushed it in his hands. Shocked by the cold liquid, Bernie roused himself. He saw the can in his son's hand. "Don't throw that!" he said furiously.

"I will! I will!" Theo brought his arm back. Bernie seized his wrist, twisting it, but Theo didn't let go of the can.

"Drop it!" Bernie growled.

"No!" Screaming, Theo kicked at his father's shinbone with all his strength. Pain shot through Bernie's leg. Without thinking, he swung his free hand and slapped Theo's face. The boy stopped struggling. The can fell out of his hand. A look of astonishment came over his face. He stared at his father. They stood staring at each other, both of them trembling, the skinny, undersized boy and the huge man. Bernie felt ashamed. The boy was so helpless. He had never struck him before. He had restrained him, picked him up and removed him from places, thrown him down roughly on a bed or in the car. But he had never struck him. He had been outraged at Linda for doing it.

The astonishment on Theo's face changed to hatred. "I'm glad you're not going to live here anymore," he screamed. "I hope I never see you again! I hope you die!" He bent to pick up the fallen can, but Bernie got it first. Bending for it, he was on eye level with Theo, who glared at him again and then spit. The purple spittle hit Bernie's eye. It ran down his face.

"I'm glad Mother threw you out," Theo raged. "We don't need you here!" He ran into his room and slammed the door. Bernie heard the lock click shut. He had heard that sound before.

He struggled for a moment. A part of him wanted to go after his son, try to talk to him.

Talk to whom? To what? How did one get into that violent brain and make it hear?

He opened the closet door and got the two large suitcases Linda had packed, and went out of the apartment without looking back. He forced himself to feel nothing. Numb. It was the safest way. Because men don't cry.

Chapter Twenty-five

Janet Stone didn't give her son time to grumble about the "power shortage." She had reserved two tickets for the early afternoon flight to Miami. Wasn't it lucky, she said, that he had called when he did. They could say hello to Grandma and Grandpa who were going to be at the airport to meet them and lend them their car to go to Disney World to stay for two weeks. Grandpa would surely have a nice present for Stevie; he always did, didn't he?

He had to talk to George first, Stevie said.

George wasn't home, she said. She had tried to reach him when she went out of the house to call about a ticket for Stevie, so he would know where Stevie was. "You can call him from the airport," she said. "But we'd better get going now, or we'll miss our plane."

Stevie moved slowly, reluctantly, not at all sure he wanted to go. His face felt hot, and he was sweating all over like he had a fever. But he had always wanted to see Disney World. And Grandpa always gave him a nice piece of bread. He could use some bread. George was broke a whole lot.

He ate a second piece of lasagne, mostly because she was in such a hurry, and then he had more string beans and more pie. "Most of my stuff is at George's. I'll have to go there and get it."

"We'll miss the plane." She was trying to keep her voice calm. Every car that passed, every footstep in the street, could be the police coming back.

"So we'll get another plane."

"It's not that easy. Flights are booked long in advance. I was very lucky to get a single ticket for you. You still have a few things here. You can get whatever you need in Florida. That should be fun. You can get a Disney World shirt."

Right there she ran into trouble. He said he wanted to wear his tee shirt. That disgusting thing.

"I didn't get a chance to wash it," she said. "Let's take it with us and we can wash it there and you can wear it in Disney World." Over her dead body.

"I don't give a shit if it's dirty. I want to wear it. George ain't all the time buggin' me about dirty and clean."

She reined in her anger. What difference did it make, after all, what he wore? "All right," she said. "But we'd better get going. Can you leave in about ten minutes? I'll finish doing the dishes."

But he was still angry. And he was feeling hot and tired, and his stomach hurt. But he fucking wasn't going to tell her. "I don't want to go. I want to stay with George."

She didn't know what to do. The social worker said, "Don't push him. You'll get his back up. Go slow. Nothing comes in a day." But she didn't even have a day.

"I'm leavin'," he said.

There was nothing more she could do. She had tried to protect him and she had failed.

"Do what you want," she said, defeated. She went out of the kitchen.

He called after her angrily, "You can just get your money back for my ticket!"

She didn't answer. She started up the stairs. She heard him come out of the kitchen into the front hallway. He shouted at her from the bottom of the stairs. "You don't want me! You don't give one flying fuck about me! You just don't want George to have me!"

She stopped and turned around. "That isn't true!" she cried. She bit her lip to keep from crying. "I love you very much. Your sisters always used to be jealous of you because they thought I loved you more than I loved them."

"They always teased me."

"What happened between us, Stevie? I never understood what happened between us. We always got along so well, you and I. We had fun together. We were friends. Then you got to be thirteen and everything changed."

"You're always on my ass," he said defiantly.

"It's only because I care about you."

"You want to run my life. You're always bossing me."

"I suppose I keep thinking of you as my baby."

"I'm not a baby!"

"I know. It's hard for me to realize you're grown-up."

"Well I am. And you're always on my ass. You want me to go back to school and study all that bullshit!"

"You used to like school."

"I never did. *You* like school."

"Maybe you're right. Maybe I wanted you to be something you really don't want to be."

"I fuckin' ain't gonna be no fuckin' doctor or dentist!"

"Do what you want, Stevie." She turned away wearily. "I'd better go out and call the airline and cancel your ticket."

"Wait a minute!" he said. "Why do you have to go rushing and doing things so fast? Why can't you ever fucking wait a minute. You make my head hurt. Maybe

I'll go with you to fucking Disney World. But I'm not going to come back here. I'm going to live with George."

"All right, Stevie," she said.

"And I'm gonna fucking wear what I want. I don't want you bugging me."

"All right, Stevie. I'll get the suitcases."

"I'll get the fucking suitcases," he said.

He didn't look right. She could see that. But she wasn't going to start asking him questions about that now. If she was lucky, the plane would take off right on time, and they would have only enough time to get on board with no time to spare for him to call George.

She had to get him away. She had no plan for after that. She would think of what to do later. For now, she only needed a little luck.

She didn't have it.

The plane was delayed. It would be thirty minutes late, they said.

Chapter Twenty-six

Something was going on. Stevie knew it. He didn't know what, but something. He wasn't dumb. He knew his own mother, for Chris' sake. If he didn't fucking know his own mother, what did he know? She was acting too agreeable. And what the fuck was he doing in this airport with her, and feeling so rotten.

He was always falling for that shit of hers. What-happened, we-used-to-be-friends, I-love-you shit. Well, he did want to see Disney World. And it would serve George right if he went away for a while. Him and his old cunts. Would George even notice he was gone? George didn't give a shit for him. But he was going to call George. He knew she was going to try to stop him. Not straight-out, but somehow she was going to try. She was tricky. She was all the time trying to fucking run his life some fucking tricky way.

Like the tee shirt. She washed all his other clothes and dried them in the dryer, but she didn't wash his tee shirt. Well, he would fucking wear it dirty. Even if he didn't really want to because it was sticky and damp and it smelled. He wouldn't wear a jacket over it, either, like she wanted, even though it was cold and like raining and he was freezing and his nose kept running. He was sick. He fucking felt like shit.

He could see she was fucking mad when they told her there would be a half-hour wait for the plane. He knew her. She was hoping she could hustle him onto the plane so he couldn't call George. Maybe she thought he was dumb, but he wasn't dumb.

As soon as they took the luggage at the desk, he said, "I'm going to call George."

"He isn't home. I told you. I called before."

"He could've come home, couldn't he?" he said belligerently. He noticed that she kept looking around her all the time, like she was looking for somebody. He thought she looked scared, too, like jumpy.

"Why don't we arrange for our seats first," she said. "Then we'll be all set."

She was making him tired. She always made him tired. Like she was watching to see what he was going to do wrong.

"You get the seats. I gotta go to the bathroom. I'll meet you at the gate."

Before she could say anything, he rushed away, and turning a corner, ducked into a men's room. Maybe there was a phone in there. Sometimes there was a phone in men's rooms. He heard her call after him, "Let's have ice cream first . . ." But he was on to her. He wasn't stupid. He ignored her.

But of course there wouldn't fucking be no phone. He wasn't going to rush out of there, anyway. Let her worry. He'd come out when he felt like it and then call George. Find some phone right where she could see him call.

He was standing at the urinal when he saw the man. He didn't see where he came from. A slick dude. Three-piece suit. Fifty-dollar haircut. Carrying an attaché case. He looked like the pictures of George the way he used to be, only he was a big, tall, strong-looking man, like a football player. The man stood at the next urinal. What the fuck was he doing that for? There were twenty empty urinals in a row. No one else was in the place. He wasn't even using it. The man turned to him and smiled.

"Nice shirt," he said.

Stevie looked at him suspiciously. Was the man making fun of him? But he kept smiling in a friendly way. He lit a cigarette and took a long, deep pull. Stevie watched him, feeling dizzy. Nobody fucking smoked cigarettes that way. It was a fucking joint. He could even smell it. He stared at the man. Shit, he could use one of those.

Still smiling, the man held out the joint. Stevie took it and dragged deep. He fucking sure didn't know when he'd get another chance, traveling with *her*, the way she kept her eyes on him like he was gonna fucking disappear or something. What was he going with her for, anyway? Greedily he watched the man suck in smoke.

"Who are you traveling with?"

He couldn't fucking say, "My mother," for Chris' sake, could he? He said, "Nobody. Why do I have to travel with somebody like some little kid or something!"

"You're by yourself?"

"Yeah. I'm going to Florida."

"Oh, yes. Lots of college kids going down there now, I hear."

Who gives a shit what he hears? Just pass the joint. "Yeah," Stevie said.

"I suppose you have a girl with you."

"No. I told you I'm alone."

"But you must have a girl waiting for you in Florida. A good-looking boy like you."

"No."

Why did he fucking talk so much. Why didn't he pass the joint? Couldn't he see he *needed* it.

Stevie watched the man breathe in. He was going to fucking finish the whole thing by himself. Stevie felt panic. It was down to where the man would be burning his fingers. Didn't he even fucking have a clip!

The man took one long, last swallow. Stevie felt he could see it going down, fanning out inside his body, making him feel warm and loose. Stevie felt so cold. Carelessly the man tore the last fragment of the cigarette paper and let the last tiny leaves drop into the urinal.

"No!" Stevie reached out as though to catch them. The man watched him.

"Whad ya fucking go and do that for?" Stevie asked.

The man smiled.

"You got any more of that?"

"You got any bread?" the man said, mocking.

Stevie didn't answer. He was thinking he could maybe go out and hit up his mother for five, maybe ten, bucks. But how? What could he say he needed it for? I wanna buy a nickel bag, right? She'd have a shit hemorrhage right in the airport.

Stevie knew the man was watching him. "Anyway, that's kid stuff," he said, smiling again. He tapped the attaché case. "What I have in here . . . that's real."

"I got no bread," Stevie said. He was feeling terribly cold. His teeth were chattering. Fucking air-conditioning. Maybe he would put on his jacket when he got out of here. Do his mother a favor.

"You're cold, poor boy," the man said, like he cared. "Poor, handsome boy. You are handsome, you know."

"Fuck off," said Stevie.

The man shrugged. "I could do something for you."

"Like what?"

"We could do something for each other." He was smiling, all the time smiling. He put his hand on Stevie's shoulder and his neck, and down his back.

"Someone is coming," he said suddenly. "Come

on . . ." He grabbed Stevie's hand and pulled him into the last stall with him and shut the door.

Stevie saw a man's feet and heard someone pissing and the urinal flush and then some other feet and more pissing and more flushing. The man whispered, "Ever use the real thing? Ever use horse?"

He never had. He always figured he fucking would sometime, but he hadn't yet.

"That's the way to good. Real good. . . ."

"I don't want to miss my plane," said Stevie.

"You have plenty of time. I'm on the same plane. You'll feel fantastic in a minute. Warm . . ."

"I got no bread."

"You have something better, dear boy, darling boy. . . ."

He wanted to feel good. He really needed it. Everybody always tearing at him all the time, like they was going to pull pieces off him.

She must be wondering where he was. Good. Let her wonder. She didn't care about him. George with that skinny broad, with all his broads; George didn't care how he felt. And that fucking Shelley, she didn't care about him, either. Fuck them. Fuck all of them.

He was so tired and so cold.

The man had the attaché case open. Stevie watched him take a short length of rubber and a needle. He measured some white powder into a spoon. "Hold that, darling boy." With his cigarette lighter he heated the white powder, sucked it into the syringe. "You'll feel wonderful. You've never felt anything like it. You're not afraid, are you, handsome boy?"

Stevie was afraid. He'd seen some of his friends shooting up. He didn't know why he hadn't done it. He just fucking hadn't.

The man tied the rubber tight, high on Stevie's arm, caressing the flesh on his inner arm to raise a vein.

"I don't know," Stevie said doubtfully. He started to pull away, but the man plunged the needle into the vein, then quickly loosened the rubber and pulled out the needle and threw all of it into the attaché case and clicked it shut.

Stevie said, "No! I gotta go. I don't like you and your three-piece suit. . . ."

"All right," the man whispered nervously. "Sh . . . I'll just make myself a small fix, and then we'll both go out, together. I don't want any trouble. OK?"

The man was whispering, so Stevie whispered back. "OK." He was beginning to feel drowsy. Warm. It felt nice.

The man heated up some more powder. "I want to see if the rubber is still good," he said. Stevie watched him as though from a great distance. Very fast, he tied the rubber around Stevie's arm again and jabbed the needle into a vein.

"Feel better? You're not going to give me trouble now, are you?" Stevie nodded, his eyes half-closed, watching the man open his fly. If he was going to piss, why didn't he face the toilet bowl? What was that greasy stuff he was smoothing all over his prick? Stevie could hardly keep his eyes open.

"I like you," the man said. "You're a lovely boy. Do you like me?"

Stevie tried to say, "Yeah . . . yeah, man . . ." like George, but his lips felt numb. He tried to smile. The man's hands were under Stevie's shirt and he was rubbing the soft flesh on his belly. "Darling boy," he whispered. "Let me do something nice to you. Would you like that?"

Stevie nodded, smiling. He had trouble standing up, but he felt nice, warm, floaty. He wanted to sleep.

The man's lips were close to his ear. "But I wouldn't want you to make any noise, darling boy. I love you so. Oh, I love you. Let's play a game. . . ." Stevie heard a short, tearing sound, and felt something being put over his mouth. "This is fun, isn't it?" His breath blew in Stevie's ear. "We're playing a game."

Stevie nodded. The man opened Stevie's pants and took them all the way off, lifting Stevie's legs one at a time, and slipped his hands into Stevie's underpants.

"Nice," he whispered. "Lovely, wonderful boy. . . ."

Stevie lifted a weak, limp arm to the tape on his mouth, but the man moved it down. "Mustn't be naughty, lovely boy. Mustn't spoil the game." He bent Stevie's body forward, supporting him with one hand and holding his genitals with the other. Prick's getting hard, Stevie thought, feeling a powerful rush, and a warmth and the nice feeling of his prick getting hard and then he was only feeling. Feeling good. The man was messing around his asshole with his hands, but Stevie was feeling warm and light, floating. It was like coming and coming without an end. He felt something hard go into his asshole. It hurt. He would have screamed, but there was something over his mouth, and the thing went in and out, in and out, smoothly. Someone was holding his prick and squeezing it and kissing his neck and rubbing his belly. It hurt and it felt good. Someone was whispering over and over in his ear, "Darling boy, lovely boy . . ."

Then suddenly the thing came out of his ass and he was sitting on the toilet seat, feeling drowsy, feeling sweet, like after a good fuck. Dimly he saw the man close his fly and fix his clothes.

Then Stevie began to feel like he was going to faint. He wanted to vomit. He wanted to sleep. He felt the thing over his mouth ripped off.

"Are you all right, dear boy?" someone whispered.

It was the last thing he ever heard.

Chapter Twenty-seven

BERNIE. Anna was grateful to him. Because for a day, for one whole day, as soon as the name Simon crept out of some crack in her brain, Anna brandished BERNIE, like a cross before evil spirits, and Simon vanished . . . not forever, not even for long, but he vanished, slipped back into the secret place where he lurked.

She didn't use the magic name against Emily. She let herself worry about Emily. Had she gotten a job; how was she making out with her new friends, her apartment; when would she call?

Her job was no help in the fight against evil spirits. Her job was neither pleasant nor unpleasant, difficult or easy. She neither liked nor disliked it. It was a job. It gave her money. That was all it had ever been. She had never wanted more from it. Yet she thought how odd it was that she spent eight hours of her day on her job cataloging and classifying books; checking them in; examining *Library Journal, Hornbook, Booklist, Publishers' Weekly*, the book reviews; buying; checking bills, paying bills; charging books in and out. Eight hours of the eighteen she was awake, and it impinged so little on her life. She had never looked for satisfaction in work. She had looked for it in her family.

She had worked in this library for fifteen years. She did her job competently, often excellently, and when she walked out of the place, the job fell away from her consciousness, like a coat slipped off her shoulders and hung away in a closet. For those fifteen years she had worked with Miss Lucy Haines, the Librarian-in-Charge. Lucy, now over sixty, had taken to wearing space shoes and her glasses on a chain that bounced on her boney chest. For fifteen years she and Lucy had exchanged Christmas cards, Easter cards, and birthday cards. She had attended Lucy's mother's funeral. Lucy had called on Anna when her mother had died. They maintained pleasant relations on the job. Anna called her Miss Haines. She called Anna Mrs. Welles. Anna never mentioned her divorce. She didn't know if Miss Haines knew about it.

There was also John Saxe. The Reference Librarian. He wore heavy black-rimmed glasses and his toes pointed out when he walked. He was gentle and had a soft voice and he was always tired because he had two other jobs. He had a wife and eight children.

When there had been Simon, Anna hadn't wanted a more demanding job. She saved her energy for him. And now? Demanding jobs were not for a person who suddenly found tears running out of her eyes. Not for a person whose head might at any moment be possessed by one paralyzing thought: *What did I do wrong?*

BERNIE. Today she clung resolutely to her thoughts about him. She didn't know enough about him to think concretely. She held on to his voice. Baritone. Pleasant. Very masculine. His grace on the dance floor, the urgency of his interest.

But something else kept stealing in, the uneasy feeling that his interest in her had nothing to do with her. Maybe he was simply lonely. Feeling lost. Newly-separated was often frightened. Newly-separated often made mistakes. "Meaning I am a mistake?" Was this only her self-concept talking? The part of her that said if Simon didn't want her, if she had somehow spoiled their connection, if she had done something so wrong, so terrible, who else would want her?

The shrink's voice said again and again, "You didn't do anything wrong. Like . . . in a business . . . there are good partners and bad partners." Anna heard the words. She heard them and heard them, pounding at her head like a battering ram, trying to break through to the inside. Failing.

BERNIE. Finally the hour arrived when Lucy Haines said, "Closing Time," and "Good night, Mrs. Welles. Good night, Mr. Saxe. Have a good evening."

Anna closed her *Sears Subject Index* and her *Dewey Tables* and put them on her shelf and said, "Thank you. You, too, Miss Haines."

In her car, she realized she had been vaguely uncomfortable all day. Something was gnawing at her, something she needed to do, or remember. And she had this awful taste in her mouth all day. Maybe she ought to see a dentist. Dentists were expensive.

She forced her attention completely to Bernie. There was a part of her that was hoping he wouldn't show up. She didn't know why. Maybe because there was something about him she couldn't explain. When he was with her, he suddenly seemed to slip away, to move out of reach. Or was it she who slipped away from him?

She stopped to buy Brie and Jarlsberg and ricotta insalata. Did he like cheese? Did he drink? She didn't think he had been holding a drink last night. She bought white wine and scotch. It all came to a lot more than she expected it to. Didn't everything? Well, there was always spaghetti later.

She hadn't left herself much time to get ready, and she had to hurry. She showered quickly and dried her hair, wishing she had left herself time to color it. The gray was beginning to show at her temples. "What are you getting so excited about? It's a date, that's all." Yes, but it was a date she liked, for a change.

Still in her ancient, faded blue robe, worn through at the elbows, a robe she couldn't bring herself to part with, she applied her makeup carefully. There was something in her that rebelled at painting her face; the something that said, "I'm fifty. This is what I look like at fifty. Why do I have to try to cover it up?" But the realistic in her had to win.

She had put on the last finishing touches when her doorbell rang. It was six-thirty. She had half an hour to dress and put out the cheese. Plenty of time. If she had been faster, she might even have had time to color her hair, after all. The doorbell rang again, more urgently.

She opened the door.

It was Bernie.

"Don't you ask who it is before you open the door?"

"I didn't expect you so early."

"All the more reason to ask who it is."

"I always forget. It doesn't matter. How did you get in downstairs without buzzing?"

"It does matter. It's not safe. Someone was coming in and held the door for me. People are always polite when they shouldn't be and cruel when they shouldn't be. It's the nature of the beast. I should have buzzed, I know. Listen, if this is inconvenient, I can go out and take a walk and come back later. It isn't raining hard."

"Oh no, I'm sorry. Come in. I wasn't thinking . . ." Yes, she was. She was thinking, but she couldn't hold on to what she was thinking about. Something about Bernie. His face or his voice. Or the size of him in a doorway. There was some nagging thought.

She opened the door wide for him. "Come in."

He looked at her and laughed. "That's a real chic outfit."

She blushed. "I can't bring myself to throw it out. It's so comfortable. I have a new robe."

"I had one like it, before I was married. I guess it's kind of a security blanket."

"Probably." She had led him into the softly lit living room. Peripherally she noted he was carrying a paper bag. "I'll be with you in a minute." She started out to the kitchen. He followed her. "I'm going to put out some cheese," she said. "Would you like a drink? Wine? Scotch?"

"Don't bother."

"It's no bother. Besides, I bought it, so you'd better have some."

He watched her putting the cheese on a board, arranging crackers in a basket. He leaned against the door frame and his eyes followed her, watching her hands.

"You don't wear nail polish," he said.

"No. Should I? I don't like it. It always chips."

"My wife never liked it, either."

"What's her name?"

"Linda."

"It's a pretty name," she said.

"She's a pretty woman. You look like her."

"You miss her."

He looked startled. "I don't know." He thought a minute. "I miss . . . a wife . . ." he said. "A woman to come home to. I'm not sure if it's Linda in particular. How about you? Do you miss your husband?"

The pain of the question was terrible. It seemed to bring Simon's presence into the room . . . his smell, the taste of his lips. She turned her back to Bernie, busying herself with the cheese.

"Wine or scotch?" she asked cheerily, surprised that she could talk at all.

"Wine."

215

She handed him the bottle and a corkscrew, hoping he didn't notice the trembling of her hands. He took it. Their hands touched. He put one hand under her chin and turned her face up to him.

"I'm sorry," he said. "Dumb question."

"You're observant."

"Sure. After I trample the flowers, I notice."

She patted his hand. "You're a nice man," she said. She carried the cheese and the wine into the living room and he followed her with the glasses, his package still under his arm. She wondered what it was. "I'll be out soon. It won't take me long to dress."

"Don't go yet. Join me."

"In this?" She held out the robe and turned, modeling it.

"Why not? It's nice. Comfortable."

"All right. For one drink." She held out the glasses and he poured for them both. His jacket was buttoned. She wanted to tell him to take it off, make himself more comfortable, but was afraid of how it might sound. He held up his glass. "A toast." She raised hers.

"To life," he said.

"Or death," she said. "Whichever comes first."

He put his glass down. "Don't drink to that. You must respect life."

"Why? Has yours been so wonderful?"

"Maybe it was my fault if it hasn't been wonderful. But life is all there is. It's all we know of God."

She was surprised. She didn't know why. "Do you believe in God?"

"I don't know. But I believe in life. I respect it. Don't you?"

"I don't know. Not my own, certainly. I'd give it away if I could." She laughed. "Do you know anyone who wants a life, partly used, somewhat battered, in need of repair. Free."

"You mustn't joke about life."

Was I joking, she wondered. "Do you think God will hear me and punish me?"

"Do *you* believe in God?"

"I? No. I used to, long ago. In some other life. People invented God. It's their last defense against death."

"You aren't afraid of death?" he asked.

"No."

He said carefully, "They say that a person who isn't afraid of death, who doesn't respect life, could take someone else's life."

What would I want with someone else's life? I don't want my own, she thought. She put some Brie on a cracker and handed it to him. He turned it round and round in his hand.

"Do you believe that . . . what you just said?" she asked.

"I don't know. Do you?"

She was suddenly dizzy. It must be the wine on an empty stomach. She hadn't eaten anything since her yogurt-and-coffee lunch. She put down her wineglass and cut herself some cheese. She felt a pulsing in the room. A waiting. She felt he was watching her. She smiled. Her smile was her protection.

"I think . . . anyone could kill," she said lightly, smiling still. "Don't you?"

Before yesterday he would have said no. A fat girl with bushy red hair flashed before his eyes. His face flamed.

"Accidentally, maybe. Or in a moment of grief or despair or madness." He refilled their glasses. He seemed far away from her. The room was suddenly very still. She licked her lips. They were sticky with wine. "Do you think you could kill?" he asked. She had known he was going to ask her that. "Do you think you could kill?" he said it again. He seemed to be sitting very close to her.

"You haven't had any cheese," she said. "Don't you like

217

Brie? That one is Jarlsberg and that's ricotta insalata. It's sheep's milk cheese. Quite nice."

She handed him some and he ate it. "Delicious," he said. He smiled. "No, I'd guess you couldn't kill anyone. You're too gentle."

"Do you think I'm gentle?"

"Yes. Aren't you?"

"Weak, I think. Ineffectual. It's often mistaken for gentleness."

"And vice versa," he said. "People who can't fight, who are gentle, are called weak."

"They are weak. People should strike back when they're wounded. At the right time and the right place," she heard herself say.

"Who can truly judge that?" he said. "Only the law."

Her head was suddenly pounding terribly. Her mouth felt terrible again. She would have to put some mouth-wash into her purse when they went out.

He said quietly, "I suppose, in the end, it isn't God who controls us. Or the law. Ultimately, it's ourselves. Guilt. Conscience. Don't you agree?"

She had run out of words. Her head turned off. Or had it turned off before? Was it she who had spoken? She didn't recognize herself. It must be the wine.

He was sitting very close to her. Leaning toward her. She stood up. "This is a strange date. We're so serious. I'd better get dressed. Make yourself comfortable. Take off your jacket. Have some cheese. I won't be long." She went out quickly.

He was alone in the room. He was sweating. He wiped his face with his handkerchief and opened his jacket. The ugly purple stain was all over his shirt. He had kept his jacket closed to hide it. He looked around the room. It was a pleasant room, comfortable, with charming artistic touches. The drapes were incongruous. Too elegant.

Probably came from her house. He got up and looked at the books on the shelves. Classics, mostly. A whole bunch of poetry. And a book on gardening. What were you looking for, Inspector Bernstein? Murder mysteries? There was a stereo and a tape recorder. Not new. Nothing in the room was new. She had left the recorder on. She must have been using it. The unit felt very hot.

"Hi. I'm back."

"That was quick. And you look lovely. You left your tape recorder on."

"I did? I couldn't have. It's Emmy's. She hasn't been here since yesterday."

"Your daughter?"

"Yes." Anna came closer to look at it. "Who could have been using it? I wonder if she was home this afternoon while I was at work. I wonder if she left me a message on it. But she's never done that before."

"It's set on record. You could try it and see."

"I suppose so. But there would be some other sign of her having been here." She pushed the button for rewind and glanced at him. "Your shirt! Did you spill the wine? It should be washed immediately. If you put salt on it and then club soda . . ." She shut the recorder. "You have to wash it while it's fresh. Let me have it . . ."

He shook his head. "That's very kind of you. No. It's not the wine. It was . . . an accident. In fact, I have a clean shirt." He pointed to the bag on the couch. "If you don't mind, I'd like to change."

"Of course. Why didn't you tell me?"

"I meant to. Actually, it's the reason I'm early. I was kind of stuck. I had a choice: go to the hotel and change, and I would have been late, or come here directly, and I would be early. I opted for pulling a shirt out of my suitcase in the car and coming straight here. Early. I hope you don't mind."

"No, of course not. Let me have the shirt. It has to be

washed immediately or it will stain. It's all over the collar, too. I didn't notice it before. It looks as if it might still be damp."

"No, you're all dressed. You'll get yourself dirty."

"I'll be careful."

"No. Thanks, anyway. You're very nice." He picked up the clean shirt. "You are, you know. Very nice. And I'm going to get changed even quicker than you did. Since this is your neck of the woods, you pick the restaurant."

She covered the cheese and left it on the kitchen counter with the wine. They might want it if they came back here. Then she went back to the tape recorder and brought it to the couch. She had her hand on the rewind button again when he came out of the bathroom in his clean shirt.

"That was quick. And you look lovely," she said.

He laughed. "I washed my face, too, while I was making myself lovely." He had also taken some of the hair from her comb in the bathroom; it was wrapped in tissue in his pocket. He noticed she had the tape recorder. "If you want to listen to that . . ."

"No, it's silly. There would be some sign if Emmy had been here. She would have left a note. Are you sure you don't want me to soak the shirt, at least?"

"No. I'll wear it the next time I visit Theo, so if he throws his juice at me again, it won't matter."

"Theo?"

"My son. He's twelve. He's brain-damaged." He stood still and stared at her. "That's the first time I've ever said that out loud to anyone except my wife. Ever."

"It didn't sound hard to say."

"You know, it wasn't. It just . . . said itself, by itself." He moved closer to her. "It felt good to say it. My wife . . . Linda . . . won't talk about it."

"It's not your fault he's brain-damaged. Not like a divorce."

"I doubt that was your fault, either." He held her chin in

his hand again and smiled at her. "Whatever the reason, it's his loss." He took his hand away too quickly. "I'm starving. Let's go. It's raining again. Better take your unbrella."

"If it's raining, we could stay here. I make wonderful omelets."

"I bet you do. Some other time. I'm parked two blocks away, so you'll really need your umbrella."

She got it and her coat. "It's not much good. I told you."

"Let me see. Maybe I can fix it."

He took it from her and looked at it carefully. His hands were trembling. "The shaft is broken," he said, trying to control the excitement in his voice. This was it. He was sure. Absolutely. *The* umbrella. It was something. A beginning. He was on his way. He opened it.

"Oh . . . oh, no . . ." she said, upset. "You shouldn't have done that. It's unlucky to open an unbrella indoors."

"You don't really believe that?"

"It's silly, I suppose. I thought we might be lucky for each other."

She was standing in the foyer, her eyes downcast, in her soft lilac dress, her arms at her sides, the red coat in her hand dragging on the floor. She looked so lonely and so frightened. Fragile. Almost childlike. What was he doing? No one else had seen the unbrella. Had he invented it? Was he mad? Why didn't he forget the whole thing?

Then she looked up at him and smiled. She had a lovely, wistful smile. She had been standing beside the old man . . . Russell . . . and she had smiled her lovely, wistful smile. . . .

There would be no point in talking to Russell again. His testimony wouldn't be worth two cents in court.

"Do you like Italian?" she was saying.

"Italian?"

"Italian food. Chinese, Spanish, Indian, Korean, American? Or maybe fish? They're all nearby."

"You're the boss." He closed the umbrella and carried it out with them. He was depressed. He should have felt exhilarated, excited.

"I know," she said, looking suddenly delighted, "if you don't mind driving, there's a place not far where the food isn't bad and there's dancing."

He felt himself drawn closer by her smile. Her smile made him want to protect her, to reassure her. It was so rueful, so tentative, reaching out, yet afraid. He started to put his arm around her, then stopped himself and reached instead for the elevator button she had already pressed. Sternly he told himself, "You are a cop on a case, Bernstein, not some middle-aged swinger. A cop on a case."

She seemed to feel his sudden withdrawal. Her smile disappeared. She stared straight ahead at the elevator door without speaking.

Chapter Twenty-eight

Feeley was on his way out of the office when the phone rang. He hesitated and then went back for it. He was annoyed when he heard Jake Harris's voice.

"Feeley, did you happen to see the afternoon papers? The *New York Post*, excuse the expression?"

"I work for a living. I don't sit around reading the papers. What's up?"

"Teenager ODs in Kennedy Airport, in a men's room. Also was sodomized."

"You know how many teenagers overdosed in this city last night? It's a damn epidemic. Besides, the airport is Queens. Not my precinct."

"Kid's name is Stone. Steven Stone." Feeley sat down and opened his coat. "His mother is hysterical. They were on their way to a Florida vacation. Keeps saying it's his father's fault. They're divorced."

"The father's name is George Stone?"

"Yeah. You should hear the names she's calling him. It would embarrass a drunken marine."

"Thanks, Jake."

"She hasn't mentioned yet that he's dead. You think maybe she doesn't know?"

"She knows."

"I can't sit on it any longer, Feeley. You understand. That's why I called you."

"Yeah, OK, Jake."

Feeley called his wife and told her he would be late, and listened impatiently while she told him what she thought of his job, the department, the damned rotten city, and him. Also his mother. She didn't like his mother, either.

Then he said, "Love you, baby," and hung up.

He dialed Bernie's home.

The kid answered. When Feeley asked for the inspector, the kid said, "He doesn't live here anymore," and hung up.

Kevin was stunned. He stared at the instrument in his hand for a full minute, and then remembered the kid was nuts. Sean had mentioned it a couple of times, but he hadn't gone into it much. It was Sean's sister's kid, too, after all. He dialed again, and when the kid answered, Feeley tried to change his voice and asked for Mrs. Bernstein. The kid said, "Why didn't you say so the first time you called," and went away, and then Linda got on the phone. Feeley said, "Hello, Linda, how are you? This is Kevin Feeley."

"Fine, Kevin. How are you? How is Josephine?"

"Fine. Fine, thank you."

"And the boys?"

"OK. Driving us nuts, as usual."

"Say hello for me."

It went exactly like that every time he had to talk to her. At that point she always got her husband. This time he had to ask, "Could I talk to the Inspector?"

She hesitated. He could hear it. "He isn't here, Kevin."

"It's kind of important, I think. If you hear from him, would you ask him to call me?"

"If I hear from him."

"Do you happen to know where I might try to reach him?"

"No. I don't."

He heard a crash in the background, and she must have covered the mouthpiece because he heard no sound at all, and then she said quickly, "Good-bye," and hung up.

He looked at the phone in his hand again, thoughtfully, and then put it down. Some damn thing was going on with Bernstein. The kid said he wasn't living there anymore, and Linda said, "*If* I hear from him."

Had Bernie left his wife?

Bernie?

Never. He had never looked at another woman. He never even made jokes about women. He never stopped at a bar on the way home. Never hung around late for some poker. Was something happening to him?

Maybe Linda had kicked him out. It couldn't be easy living with Mr. Clean.

He picked up the phone again and dialed the Queens precinct. He wanted to talk to the Stone woman. The case was warming up, getting interesting. He really wanted to talk about it to Bernie. Bernie had been one hell of a detective. Kevin wondered what Bernie knew and wasn't talking about. That wasn't like him, either, to keep back information, even if it was only speculation. He'd hang anyone who did that. It wasn't good police work. Bernstein had always been a good cop.

Kevin hoped everything was OK. The thing was, he liked the guy. Admired him. They had worked together a lot of years. He was a little tight-ass, maybe, but an OK guy. No chicken shit.

And more than that, Kevin owed him.

Chapter Twenty-nine

Outside, Bernie held the umbrella for her against the rain, which was not much more than a heavy mist. The silence had become uncomfortable. Some essential part of her had withdrawn. He needed to recapture it.

As soon as they got into the car, he said cheerfully, "OK, navigate."

She smiled, too, then, too brightly, the smile she probably put on for singles' dances. "Are you sure? I mean, do you want to dance?"

He smiled back, suspecting his smile was the same as hers. He knew that wasn't going to get him anywhere. "I'm sure. Where to?"

"It might be more expensive than the places across the street."

"That's OK. Let's celebrate."

"Celebrate what?"

"Anything. Everything. Our meeting. The rain."

She laughed. It was almost real. She was coming back, but cautiously. "The rain?"

"Why not? It makes the flowers grow." He suddenly

remembered the roses he had bought for Linda, dead now, probably, in the trunk of his car. He wished he had brought roses to Anna.

She told him where the restaurant was, about fifteen minutes away, on Long Island, and rested her head back, half with him again, and half hiding. He started the car.

"OK," he said, "we're going to have a ball." Keep it light, Bernstein. Light. A game. "Relax. Close your eyes. Empty your head. No thoughts."

"Ummm."

Was she back with him? "Now, answer the first thing that comes into your head. Tell me about yourself."

"I'm divorced," she said.

"Is that your ID?" he said angrily. "There must be more to you than that!"

She didn't answer. He was afraid he had lost her again. He said, "You must be very angry at him."

"No," she said dully. "I'm angry at myself. I failed."

"What did you do wrong?"

"I don't know. That's what makes it so hard."

"So you weren't the perfect wife. Was he the perfect husband?"

"I loved him. I wasn't looking for perfection. He was my husband for twenty-eight years. I just loved him."

"You *must* be very angry at him."

"I'm not! I'm not!" she said furiously.

"You sound angry."

"He didn't have to be so cruel at the end. He didn't have to hurt me and humiliate me. The shrink said it was because he was feeling guilty."

"More likely, he was trying to get you so mad you'd leave him. He'd do better in the courts if you left him."

"He did well enough anyhow."

"Probably because you didn't fight him."

"I didn't really believe I would have to."

"You had lost your spirit. I can understand that."

"You didn't think you were worthy," said the shrink. *"You accepted his judgment of you. . . ."*

"I couldn't bring myself to believe he could want to hurt me. After all the years together. And we had a child. I never hurt him on purpose. I may have failed him, somehow, but I never tried to hurt him."

She sat up suddenly. "Would you like a piece of gum?" she said, too cheerily. She unwrapped it for him, and a piece for herself. "I didn't mean to bore you."

"I'm not bored."

"Tell me about you," she said.

"Shall I relax and close my eyes?"

"If you like," she said, still cheerily.

"Then you won't be able to go to any more of Louise King's parties."

"It's a deal," she said, laughing. "Have you ever been to her parties?"

"No. She had one Saturday night, didn't she?"

"Yes. It was dull." She closed her eyes again and leaned back, frowning. He glanced at her. She looked like she was trying to remember something. She said, as if to herself, "It was a very dull party. Louise asked me to wait for her to take her home . . . I think."

"Why would she ask you?"

"We used to live in the same town. On the same street."

"Did you take her home?"

"I don't think so," she said slowly.

"Don't you remember?"

"I didn't take her home."

"I suppose you went to a better party afterward."

"Do you think so?"

"At George's," he said casually.

"George? I don't know any George."

"On Amsterdam Avenue. Noisy party. Jazz. Pot."

She laughed and sat up. "I never had pot in my life. I

suppose that's ridiculous. A person my age should have tried it at least. I never have. Have you?"

"Tried it? Sure. Couple of times. Didn't do a damn thing for me."

He glanced at her again. She had retreated once more, inside herself.

Let it rest, Bernstein. He turned on a music station. They rode for a while in silence. It wasn't uncomfortable.

"Is that the restaurant, across the street?"

She roused herself. "Yes. You have to go to the corner and make a left into the street and then make a U-turn and come back."

"Why can't I turn left here?"

"There's a double yellow line. It's illegal," she said.

"There are no cops around."

"But it's illegal," she said earnestly.

He smiled. He didn't know he was smiling. She saw the smile and said, "Did I say something wrong?"

He patted her hand reassuringly. "No, not at all." Her fingers, under his, were taut. "Hey, relax. . . ." he said. He stroked her fingers and felt them flutter and then lie quietly under his, like a fragile bird.

He remembered his first night with Linda. He remembered her little gasping cries of anguished pleasure. And afterwards, how she came to rest in his arms, like a trusting bird, fragile and soft.

She said, "Dollar for your thoughts."

"It used to be a penny."

"Inflation," she said.

He pulled into the parking lot and stopped. He sat for a moment and looked around. There was a motel across the road, advertising water beds, color TV, and adult movies in the room. The light from its flickering red neon sign illuminated her face like a blush. The thought came to him that she might have ended a dinner date with some other man by going to that motel. The thought made him uncomfortable, even angry. The motel was flanked by a Burger King and a Chinese restaurant. Her fingers stirred. He realized he was still holding her hand. He wondered what would happen if he were to say casually, lightly, "Did you read about that murder? It's in all the papers. Gruesome thing. The man's penis was bitten off."

It wasn't the right time; she had one hand on the door.

"Allow me . . ." he said, smiling, and getting out of the car, he went around to her side to open the door and help her out.

"Chivalry is not dead," she said.

"It's like truth," he said. "It will never die, but it lives a miserable life."

"I didn't know you were cynical."

"Neither did I." He laughed. "I suppose we really don't know what we are. Or we are different things at different times." He laughed again. "Right now, I'm hungry."

And also you're a cop, he told himself sternly, again. A cop on a case. Don't forget it.

He said it to himself again at dinner. He was enjoying the dinner. Maybe it was her awareness of him. He was missing a fork and she quietly gave him hers, and she listened to him when he talked; she looked at him as if she really saw him. He had forgotten how nice that felt. Maybe it was her attention, or the white cloth and silver and the ruby water goblets and the candle in its ruby holder and the fresh rose in a vase on the table. Maybe it was simply having a dinner without Theo. He couldn't remember when he and Linda had gone out alone, to dinner. He was aware that he was having a good time. He was gratified when she said her meal was delicious. It made him feel good. She looked delighted when he said his fish was great. He liked her choice of restaurant. They must come back again, he said, and realized he meant it. He wanted to come back. With her.

When the band went out on their break, he held her

231

hand leading her off the dance floor. He ordered more wine and they sipped it slowly. And then he was telling her about Theo. Twelve years worth. He didn't know how it happened. He was telling her the way it was, how he felt. She was listening. Caring. He was still holding her hand when the band came back half an hour later, and he led her back on the dance floor because he wanted to hold her close.

She said, "You're a very good dancer."

"I'm rusty," he said.

She shook her head and moved closer to him. Her head rested on his shoulder. He felt that she was dancing with her eyes closed. He held her firmly, protectively, moving smoothly so she wouldn't trip.

So he liked it. He was having a good time. What was wrong with that? What harm was there in it?

So, Inspector Bernstein, what harm was there in it when the cops fucked the whores before they brought them in? It doesn't happen in my precinct. Not Bernstein's precinct. Not if they wanted their jobs. Is that so, Bernstein?

What the hell was he doing?

He said, "I hate to break up the party. Work tomorrow."

She sighed and nodded and then said impulsively, "Do you think they would play a waltz for us if you asked them. A last dance . . ."

There was something childlike and appealing in her eagerness. He couldn't refuse her. And he wanted a waltz, too.

The band played the waltz for them. It was one hell of a nice waltz, he thought.

She laughed when they stopped, breathless and flushed. Her pleasure was infectious. She said, "Thank you," and hugged him impulsively and kissed his cheek and then hurried, flustered, back to the table.

In the car, going back, she sat closer to him. She looked

relaxed, happy. That made him feel good, too. It was so long since a woman had been happy being with him, so long since he had felt he could make a woman happy. He wanted to touch her. He put his hand on hers.

She said, "Will you come up for a nightcap?"

He couldn't say no. He couldn't hurt her, could he? "If it's not too late for you," he said.

"It's not too late."

She looked pleased. Walking from the car to her building, she put her arm through his, and their fingers touched. He took her hand and held it lightly. It seemed to come to rest in his. They were walking close.

And then they passed the incinerator room on the way to her apartment. Someone had put a bundle of newspapers outside. The paper on top was that day's *New York Post*. The three-inch headline screamed: TEENAGER OD'S AT AIRPORT. In slightly smaller print it continued. "Sixteen-year-old Steven Stone . . ."

Stone!

He lifted the paper off the bundle and read rapidly. Janet Stone!

Anna was waiting for him at the open door of her apartment. She looked at him questioningly.

"I just remembered something. I have to do something . . . about . . . Theo. . . . Listen, it's been great. Really great. But I have to go now. I'll call you tomorrow. . . ."

She looked stunned, and then hurt. And then her face closed up again and he couldn't read it. He couldn't leave it like that. He couldn't. He came close to her.

"Good night," he said.

"Good night."

He stood awkwardly, impatient and torn. She turned to go in. He grabbed her arm. "Good night," he said again. "I don't remember the last time I enjoyed an evening so much."

233

She didn't answer.

"I'll call you. I can't explain."

She nodded, not speaking. He was holding her arm, hard. He pulled her toward him. He didn't know it was going to happen; he meant to kiss her cheek, to be friendly, to keep the contact. He kissed her mouth. He held her, and kissed her mouth hard. Then he turned and walked quickly down the hall to the stairs.

What are you doing, Bernstein? What the hell are you doing? His heart was pounding. He raced down the stairs to his car and drove, very fast, to the Queens precinct mentioned in the paper.

The chief of detectives there, Joe Scanlon, was a former partner of his.

Chapter Thirty

Through a one-way mirror in the Queens precinct, Bernie and Detective Feeley watched Detective Scanlon talking to Janet Stone. Her eyes were swollen from crying, but the tears had stopped. A young policeman came into the room and offered her a cup of coffee. She shook her head.

"Could we go over it again, Mrs. Stone?" Scanlon said gently. "You say you were at home on Saturday night, playing mah-jongg with some women?"

"Bridge. I said we were playing bridge." Her voice was strung tight.

"Sorry. Bridge. They left about eleven-thirty. What happened after they left?"

"We've been all over that. Over and over!" She was suddenly shouting, or trying to. Her voice was hoarse and strained. "I've told you and told you. They left my house at about eleven-thirty. I don't know the exact time. I didn't have them punch a time clock. I tidied up and went to bed." Her voice cracked and she started to cough. The detective offered her the coffee again. She waved it away, then changed her mind and took it. She had a sip and then put it down on the table. Wearily, her voice hardly more than a croaking whisper, she said, "If you think I killed the son of a bitch, charge me, but let me alone. . . ."

"You hated him."

"I did. I do. But I didn't kill him. Maybe I should have killed him long ago. I'm sorry I didn't. But I didn't. Now charge me or let me go home."

"It's nothing like that, Mrs. Stone." Scanlon smiled, very friendly. He had a broad, freckled, open face. "We need your help."

"Too heavy," Bernie muttered. "He's coming on too heavy."

"They ought to lay off until they get the report on her bite from her dentist," said Feeley.

Bernie shook his head. "No. She might be able to tell us something now, when she's too upset to hide it."

Scanlon was trying now for a jocular tone. "Mrs. Stone, you've watched TV. You know if we thought you did it, we'd be reading you your rights."

"Do that," she said. "Read me my rights. All of them. The rights of a middle-aged woman whose husband suddenly joins the Now generation. I had three young children. Tell me about their rights in a mindless, drug-infested, narcissistic world. Who helps a woman alone with her children? Who helps the children? What would have happened if I had decided to take off too?" She was crying again. "You think I didn't think a thousand times of saying to hell with it all and running away. . . ."

"Plenty of Now generation women around," the young policeman said, with obvious bitterness.

Scanlon glared at him. But Mrs. Stone didn't notice either of them. She was crying, out of control. "Why don't you read Stevie his rights, too. What was he entitled to expect from a father?"

"Did they get along, Stevie and his father?"

"Of course. Stevie loved him. Why not? I was the bad guy. I was the one left to say no to him."

"Was he with his father any time Saturday night?"

"You keep asking me that. How would I know?"

"Didn't he tell you where he had been?"

"No. Of course not. He never told me anything. I didn't ask him. The social worker said don't ask him questions. Don't bug him."

"He called you at five o'clock in the morning and you picked him up in a street corner phone booth and you didn't ask him any questions?" Scanlon sounded incredulous.

"You think you would have asked questions?"

"You're damn right," said Scanlon.

"Wrong tack, wrong tack," Bernie muttered. "She needs sympathy, not criticism."

"It's tough for a woman alone," said Feeley. "Today's teenagers . . . I don't think Josie could make it alone."

Bernie didn't answer. Feeley flushed. Bernie saw the color in his face and looked away, embarrassed. For himself? For Feeley? For Linda? He didn't know. But he understood Feeley must have called his home . . . his former home. So he knew.

Janet Stone was saying, "Stevie didn't kill him, either. He loved him. He went looking for a phone to call him, to say good-bye because we were going on vacation."

"Stevie might have known what person or persons were with his father Saturday night. He might have told you. Didn't he say anything? Was there a party? Who was there? He must have let something slip. Try to think. It could help us find out what happened to Stevie. Anything could help. Anything could be a start."

"He told me nothing."

"I can understand you really don't care who killed your husband . . ."

"I care. If you find him, let me know. I'll congratulate him."

"Will you congratulate the person who killed your son, too? It could be the same person, or it may be connected."

"If it is, it's George's fault. All George's fault."

"Don't you want us to find out who it is?"

"Will it bring Stevie back to dig up all kinds of filth?"

"What kind of filth, Mrs. Stone?"

"I don't know! I don't know! I don't know anything! Let me alone!" She was crying uncontrollably.

Scanlon turned away, starting to the door. With his hand on the knob, he looked back and said casually, "By the way, Mrs. Stone, what happened to your umbrella?"

Out of the corner of his eye, Bernie saw that Feeley had turned to look at him. He kept his face blank. Scanlon repeated his question to Mrs. Stone, who looked at him without comprehension.

"Umbrella?" she asked.

"Yellow plastic with a broken shaft?" The detective shot a brief, involuntary glance toward the one-way mirror. Bernie stared intently at the woman. After all, lots of people could have umbrellas like that; and cheap umbrellas, their shafts often broke. Mrs. Stone looked totally bewildered.

"Did Stevie have such an umbrella?"

"Stevie would never use an umbrella."

Bernie was aware of a sense of disappointment. And he became aware of how intensely he had been hoping that this woman, too, might have had such an umbrella, that the one he had seen in Stone's apartment might have been hers. Or at least, not Anna's.

Scanlon was saying, "At no time on Saturday night were you at the apartment of your ex-husband?"

"No. Certainly not. I had nothing to do with him."

"You didn't know any of his friends? Men? Women?"

"No."

"And you don't know if your son was there?"

"No."

"Or where he was?"

"No."

"Despite the lateness of the hour you asked him no questions?"

"No! No! No! Let me alone!" She buried her face in her hands, crying hysterically.

Scanlon watched her for a moment. "Mrs. Stone, if you happen to remember something . . . anything that might help us . . . help you . . . help some other kid . . . will you call us?"

She nodded, crying.

"And of course, don't leave town. Just in case we need you." He glanced again involuntarily toward Bernie and left the room. Bernie stared at Mrs. Stone. A middle-aged woman with the thick body of middle age, sagging breasts, short black hair turning gray, not stylishly cut. Not stylishly dressed.

There was something familiar about her grieving figure. Head bent into her hands, she reminded him of his mother. She must be about the same age that his mother had been when his father had died. His death had destroyed his mother. She had never recovered from it. His mother was what came to him when he thought of women alone. Had he loved her? Why was he asking himself that now? He hadn't asked himself questions when his father died. He had quit college, taken a job, become the man of the house, father to his two young sisters, making the decisions his father would have made, trying to make them the way his father would have made them. Even now, he felt good thinking about his father. He had been a man of middle height, chunky, balding, eyeglasses, quick to anger, quicker to forget, impulsive, emotional.

239

He had worked twelve hours a day, six days a week, in his tailoring shop. On Saturdays he took his son fishing, or all the family to a park. He had adored children, hugging and kissing them all, even his son. Bernie smiled, remembering how he had to bend down so his father could kiss him; his father had loved that.

He had loved his father. He had wanted to be a father just like him.

"Crazy world," Feeley said suddenly. "Where are we all going? Where does it all end? What ever happened to love . . . like till death do us part, even if warts suddenly grow on her nose. . . ."

Bernie laughed. "Where have all the flowers gone?"

Scanlon came in and slumped into a chair. "What do you think, Bern?"

"About what?"

"Life on Mars. What the hell do you think I mean?" He took out a pack of cigarettes and offered them around. Bernie shook his head. "What's so important about this case it brings down the commanding officer and the chief of detectives of a precinct?"

"I happened to be passing and I answered the 1010. I got interested."

"And so's your Aunt Tillie," said Scanlon. "How's Linda?"

"Same. How's Sarah?"

"Worse. Here I am, the pride of the Irish, led through the nose these many years by a Jewish American princess. Could I interest you in a trade, maybe?"

"It does seem the way, doesn't it, dropping spouses. Kevin here doesn't like it."

"Kevin here has a wife that could call in her Mafia cousins if he gets funny," said Scanlon.

"Didn't you ever hear that not all Italians are Mafia?"

"Better luck next time," Scanlon laughed, pounding Feeley's arm. "So come on, Bern, what's with this case?

You think there's a connection between the two homicides?"

"I don't know. There's no record on either of the
victims. We'll just have to stick with it. We should keep
each other posted. Thanks for your cooperation, Scan."

"Thanks for yours."

Bernie nodded. "Yeah. Well . . . we'll be in touch. So
long." He nodded at Feeley and went out.

Kevin watched him go. Bernie seemed to him, suddenly, a lonely man.

Scanlon mashed his cigarette in an ashtray. "What's up
his ass, Kevin?"

"What makes you think anything is?"

"Come on, Feeley. I've known the guy for twenty
years."

"I've known him for thirty. He was my partner for eight
years," said Feeley.

"Saved your life once, didn't he?"

"More than once. He took a slug for me when we were
both rookies."

"He's the best," said Scanlon. "A little tight-ass, maybe."

"Tight-ass! He'd give his own mother a parking ticket."

"He don't have a mother. Never did. He only had the
Ten Commandments," Scanlon laughed, and lit another
cigarette.

"I think maybe he and Linda split up."

"He should have left her long ago. Now *there's* a tight
ass."

"They have this kind of . . . crazy kid. . . . By the
way, what was that umbrella bit?"

"You tell me. Bern asked me to get that in. What's it
about?"

"I wish I knew. I wish I knew what was going on in his
head, what he's doing." He looked determined suddenly.

Glancing around the room, he pointed to a hat on a rack.
"That your cap, Scan?"

"Yeah."

"Can I borrow it? It's raining. I have a cold."

"You don't sound like you have a cold."

"I do. Can I borrow it? I'll return it Wednesday, at
bowling."

"What do I wear in the rain?"

"A plastic bag, pulled low. Come on, Scan . . ."

"You buy all my beers at bowling for a month?"

"Bastard. OK. If we also switch cars. And no questions."

"You got it." He tossed his car keys to Feeley.

Feeley caught them and dropped his own keys on
Scanlon's desk, grabbed his cap, and ran out.

"Be careful, you dumb mick. He's still smarter than you
are," Scanlon yelled after him.

"He's not God," Feeley yelled back.

"Nobody's God," Scanlon muttered to himself. "Not
even God."

Chapter Thirty-one

The rain had stopped falling, but it hung in the air, cold and wet. Bernie pushed through it to his car. He sat at the wheel, trying to put his head together. He was tired but not sleepy. He knew if he went back to the hotel, he wouldn't be able to sleep. The thought of the hotel depressed him. He ought to begin doing something about moving out of there. Lots of things he ought to be doing something about. He couldn't think about them. The face of Anna/Allegra, looking surprised and hurt and finally closed up tight, blocked out his thought.

He ought to call her. It was too early in the morning. It was too early to go to his office. In the rearview mirror he saw Feeley coming quickly down the steps of the station house. He didn't want to talk to Feeley. Or anyone. He started the car and drove off.

He was surprised when he found he had driven to Anna's house. He pulled around the corner to the side of the building and parked. In the silent, empty street, a cat leaped on the garbage cans, arching its back, its tail flicking angrily, and then darted away. What would she do, Anna/Allegra, if he called her now? Or rang her bell? Stupid idea. He slid onto the passenger seat. He saw her face again, and her tentative, wistful smile. He closed his eyes. His body felt painfully cramped. He always felt cramped, staking out in a car. He was so big, he was always uncomfortable in cars.

It took days in a steamroom and hot shower and pool to ease the pain of a stakeout.

Interrogating Committee: Stakeout? Is this a stakeout, Inspector Bernstein? And you around the corner from the building's entrance.

Inspector Bernstein: Not exactly a stakeout. I guess I must have been confused. I haven't been sleeping well.

I.C. (with mock sympathy): Ah . . . it's sorry we are to be hearing that. And what could be the trouble, laddie boy?

Bernie: Or maybe I didn't want to go back to that hotel.

I.C.: Or maybe it's how to be a good policeman you're after forgetting.

Bernie: Maybe I'm after forgetting about Linda and Theo.

I.C.: Liar! When was the last time they came into your head?

Bernie: It was she kicked me out! I never would have left her.

I.C.: And maybe it was you drove her to it. Maybe you disappointed her the way you used to be telling her you were going back to college to become a lawyer and all, before you got her to marry you, and then you stayed on in the force.

Bernie: Bullshit! She was so busy trying to have a baby with her tests and her doctors and her taking her temperature every damn morning and crying every month like she had nothing in the world to live for, she didn't know or care what I was doing, so long as I kept trying to plant a baby in her. She never paid any attention to me. I didn't exist except as a baby-making machine.

I.C.: She was probably right. You never really wanted a baby. You didn't want Theo. You never loved him.
Bernie: I don't need this, you know! I could retire. Leave town. Make a life for myself. There are a lot of women out there. I could find one who would love me, appreciate me. We could go away together, to some warm, sunny place.
I.C.: What women, Bernstein. What *woman*?

His eyes flew open. He sat up, suddenly awake, and felt for the gun in his leg holster, peering out cautiously through the foggy window. The street was still quiet. There was only an occasional person, and a few cars, moving in the dirty gray dawn. In the cold car, his body was wet, his face dripping sweat. His legs were asleep. He rubbed them, then got out shakily and stamped his feet to get the circulation going and stretched his back. The dream lingered, disturbing him still.

He looked at his watch. He must have been asleep about two hours. He wasn't tired at all. He got back into the car and started the motor. There was still time to go back to the hotel and shower, shave, and change before going to work. He wanted to talk to the doorman again. And that woman who lived next door to Stone. The old woman. Mrs. Miller.

On the other side of the street, a few cars down, another car started. Detective Feeley, at the wheel, with Scanlon's cap pulled down low over his face, followed his CO's car, keeping careful distance. If anyone had asked him why, he wouldn't have been able to answer. Except maybe to another detective. Maybe to Bernie himself. Another detective would understand: It was a feeling he had, a sense of trouble.

Chapter Thirty-two

Anna wanted desperately to sleep, but sleep wouldn't come. She couldn't turn off her head. Finally she got up and wrapped herself in her old robe and a blanket and went into the living room. Now you have two rooms to stay awake in instead of one. Thanks to Emmy.

She curled up on the couch. "All right, Head," she said, "you want to keep working. Work."

Since when do I need your permission? I'll work if I feel like it.

Don't expect any help from me. I want to sleep.

What's so great about sleeping? Someday you'll sleep forever.

Promises, promises.

You want to forget; that's what you want. Sleep doesn't always work.

If you could concentrate on one thing, Head. If we could get one thing at a time settled and packed away . . . but you hop from one thing to another.

You give me too many things to work on. It's too much for me.

You never were much good, Head.

I was! I was! But there's too much now. Too much to think about, too much to remember. Too much to forget. And I have to admit there's something gnawing at me.

What is it?

I don't know.

All right, crybaby. What happened last night with Bernie?

You tell me.

Silence from the Head department. It had turned itself off.

"A lot of help you are," Anna said.

In that case, forget about me. Stick with feelings.

That was worse. That hurt like hell. So what happened, Head? Everything was going so well. I thought he liked me. I thought we were having a good time. And then I turned my back for a second to open the door . . .

That was your first mistake. Never turn your back on a man.

You're no help. You and your wisecracks. What did I do wrong?

There you go again. Why is it always *you* did something wrong. Maybe it's his fault.

Head, you've become contaminated by my shrink.

Maybe Bernie has some problem. Guilt. Fear of sex. Maybe he has a rash on his balls. Maybe he really did have something he remembered to do with his son.

Maybe he only used me to tell his troubles to, and he realized he doesn't like me.

Why don't you stick with feelings! Leave me out of it entirely. Then the two of you can have a good cry. The two of you have been trying to drown me for years.

What will I do if he calls?

What makes you think he'll call?

He said he would. Do you think he will?

Do you want him to call?

He probably won't. I can't figure out what happened. He seemed to like me.

You liked him.

Yes, I liked him. He seemed so comfortable.

You were comfortable.

He was, too. He seemed . . . *it* seemed . . . so natural.

He kept holding you off a lot of the time.

I was holding him off, too. I was afraid. Maybe he felt me holding back.

Blaming yourself again.

He's a sensitive person. A decent man.

By that you mean old-fashioned.

All right. Old-fashioned.

Like you. You hate the way you've been living.

What's to like?

You could give up. Come home every night and read and watch TV, maybe learn needlepoint, do volunteer work twice a week with retarded children, and masturbate a lot.

Bug off.

Her head became a vacuum.

The silence began to creep in.

I'm cold. I'm terribly cold. Why is the silence always so cold?

Let's get back to Bernie. You let go his arm and turned your back to him to open the door and he mumbled something about having to go, and ran off with his newspaper.

What newspaper?

He was holding a newspaper when he left. I'm sure of it.

Where did he get a newspaper?

From the garbage outside the incinerator, probably. There are always newspapers there. Maybe something he saw in the newspaper made him run away.

Maybe maybe maybe. Maybe I have halitosis. My

mouth feels awful. What made Simon stop loving me? Maybe I can find that in the newspapers, too.

She pushed her legs out angrily, to get up. Her foot hit something hard. It was the tape recorder. She and Bernie had thought of playing it. She stared at it in the sick, pre-dawn light. She ought to play it. Emmy might have been home and left a message. Maybe she should have stayed home last night. Emmy might have called. Emmy might need her.

My dear Anna, face facts. Emmy doesn't need you. No one needs you. What you need is sleep.

I could get some if you would turn off and quit bugging me.

You never pay attention to me. You and your feelings are thick as thieves.

I'm tired of both of you. I'm tired of everything.

She got up and gathered her blanket around her. She had to go to work in the morning. She had to sleep. She picked up the tape recorder and carried it into the bedroom. Maybe she should record something. Her life story. Dear Tape Recorder: Help. Stop me before I do it again.

Do what again?

That's a joke, stupid Head.

The subconscious doesn't tell jokes. It's too introverted.

We're going to sleep. All of us.

Chapter Thirty-three

Bernie read the file on the Stone case and reread it and then read it again. The key, he decided, the key had to be the old lady next door. Mrs. Miller. She would have to be deaf not to have heard something. But he couldn't get a line on her. He couldn't figure what might open her up.

The professional killers, underworld witnesses, in a way, were easier to reach. You knew what might get to them: money or the need for power or revenge. Or you might promise to take care of them or their families. But there was no hook to this old lady. A widow. She lived alone, no one to worry about or to worry about her. Living in genteel poverty, but proud. An old egghead-type. Good citizen. He would have to feel his way.

Detective Donlon had been competent but not brilliant. Donlon was thorough, cautious, unimaginative.

Bernie sent Johnson and Ramirez to bring Mrs. Miller to the precinct. She would be uncomfortable, maybe even frightened. Probably she had never been inside a station house before. It could weaken her defenses. He might be able to get more out of her.

Of course, she could refuse to come, or demand that she bring a lawyer. He didn't expect that. She hadn't that degree of sophistication about the law. And lawyers cost money. Probably she didn't know any lawyers, certainly not criminal lawyers. Very solitary, the doorman said. Seemed to be all alone now that her husband was dead. The doorman didn't know of any friends who had ever come to visit her. He had never seen her with anyone but her husband. He had never known her to say anything more than good morning or good evening to anyone.

Bernie drank coffee and paced his office, waiting for her to arrive.

He was aware that he should be tired. He hadn't slept more than two or three hours last night. But he wasn't tired. He was, in fact, acutely awake. All his nerve endings seemed to be open and alert, almost tingling. He seemed to be breathing pure oxygen, his head was so clear and so light. His whole body was filled with anticipation, with excitement. And something else. Something he couldn't recognize. He tried to sort out his feelings and he couldn't. Something eluded him. A feeling. . . .

He needed to do something with his hands. He should go back to smoking.

"Got a cigarette, Feeley?"

"You don't smoke anymore."

"Linda didn't like it. She made me quit. You want my whole life story for one lousy cigarette?"

Feeley shook out the pack for him and then struck a match. "Why do I have the feeling I'm corrupting you?"

"I'm incorruptible. Haven't you heard," Bernie said. It sounded bitter. The nicotine bit his tongue. He sucked the smoke in deep. Anna didn't smoke. He remembered her earnest protest about making an illegal turn. It made him smile again. He became aware of Feeley watching him, not in a direct and open stare, but surreptitiously.

"Anything new in Queens on the Stevie homicide?"

"Not since the last time you asked, Inspector. Except that the teeth on the bite didn't belong to Mrs. Stone or to the boy."

"They checked the son's bite for *that*?"

"It's a crazy world, Inspector."

Bernie mashed the cigarette against the side of his metal waste can and dropped it inside. "Dirty habit," he growled. He attacked the stack of papers on his desk. Feeley watched him openly. Bernie didn't look up. Feeley leaned toward him.

There was a knock on the door, and Bernie shot up and pulled it open.

"Mrs. Miller?" he said briskly to the dignified woman standing outside with Johnson and Ramirez.

"Yes."

He opened the door wider, but he didn't smile. "Come in."

Hesitantly, obviously frightened, and showing no curiosity, she moved into the room. He watched her move. She seemed tired. He pulled out a chair for her courteously, still unsmiling.

"I am Inspector Bernstein. This is Chief of Detectives Feeley."

"How do you do," she said.

"You live next door to a Mr. George Stone, Mrs. Miller?"

"I live in Apartment 9D." Her voice was firm and clear.

He looked her over. Tall, thin, sparse white hair carefully arranged to border a well-used small black hat, a neat black coat that might have been stylish ten years ago. She sat up very straight, but it was clearly an effort.

"The man in the apartment next to yours appears to have been murdered. Brutally murdered."

"I know nothing about it."

"You didn't know the man?"

"No."

He sat down close to her, on the edge of his desk. She looked away, as though to escape. He knew his size must be overpowering.

"You have lived in your apartment"—he picked up some papers and consulted them—"twenty-six years."

"Yes."

"And Mr. Stone lived there six years. You never saw him?"

"I saw him very seldom. We didn't keep the same hours."

"How do you know what hours he kept?"

"I don't know. I assumed, since I seldom saw him come or go."

"And you never heard him?"

"No."

"These new buildings, a person could hear a fly's wings."

"I am not as young as I used to be. I don't hear well."

"In six years you never borrowed a cup of sugar from each other . . . so to speak?"

"Certainly not!"

"He wasn't your cup of tea?"

"No."

"How did you know?"

"At my age, young man, I should be able to spot who is and who is not my 'cup of tea,' as you say."

"Was it because of the music he played?"

"I don't know anything about that. I took a sleeping pill early and fell asleep."

"Every night?"

"Saturday night."

"There must have been other nights you heard him. Other people did. He wasn't a very considerate neighbor."

She didn't answer.

Feeley said, "Would you like a cup of tea or some coffee, Mrs. Miller?"

"No, thank you."

"This may be a very important case, Mrs. Miller," Bernie said. "You may have heard that Mr. Stone's son was a victim of homicide too."

"I heard it on the radio this morning."

"You didn't tell Detective Donlon the young man was his son."

"I had no way of knowing that. The young man called him George. I already said that. They didn't look at all alike. And Mr. Stone didn't look like anyone's father. He looked like . . . I believe it's called a swinger."

"Was he a swinger, Mrs. Miller?"

"I'm sure I don't know."

"Did he have many parties?"

"I don't know."

"Surely you would have heard people coming in and out. Music. Noise. Dancing. The door opening and closing. You might have seen someone coming in and out. Men. Women."

"No," she said. "I mind my own business."

"We don't know what's at the bottom of the case. It may be drugs. The boy seems to have been killed by an overdose."

"I wouldn't be surprised. He looked like that kind of person, with his obscene shirt."

"You aren't afraid to tell us what you know, are you? It would be held in the strictest confidence. You would be in absolutely no danger."

"I know nothing."

"Anything would help us. If you know even one fact, saw even one person. The color of someone's hair. The color of a coat. An umbrella."

She shook her head.

"It would be your duty as a citizen to help us. I know you are a good citizen."

"Yes, I'm a good citizen. Morris wouldn't so much as

drop a scrap of paper on the street. A lot of good it's done me. A lot society is doing for me! They even want to reduce my Social Security payments. What's going to happen to me? How will I pay my rent?" She stopped herself. "I don't know anything," she said more calmly.

"Do you ever remember, at any time, any man or woman who came or went from that apartment?"

"I don't spy on my neighbors."

"Even if you don't like them?"

He could see she was getting tired, losing control. It was harder for her to keep her back straight. And her answers were getting longer.

"Of course, we'll know more when the reports come in from the lab on footprints and fingerprints."

"Footprints?"

"Yes. We'll know more about who had been in that apartment."

"What would that prove?"

"Who was in the apartment. Were you ever in his apartment, Mrs. Miller?"

"What would I be doing in the apartment of a person like him?"

Was it real indignation, or was it fear?

"You might have gone in to complain about the music, to ask them to lower it. He might have laughed at you, become abusive. You might even have become angry and killed him."

"I'm an old woman, Inspector!"

"People like him are no respecters of age or decency. Allowing their children to run around wearing shirts like that."

She looked down at her hands clenched in her lap. Don't let her think too much. "This could be the opening we need. It could be the right catalyst for a big cleanup. This city is getting tired of filth. We have so little to go on now. A few fingerprints, soon some footprints. You could do a very important thing. Think. Think! Did you see anyone, hear anything, at any time, day or night? Anyone in the apartment, at the door, in the hall, at the elevator? Mrs. Miller, please . . . you could help make your city safe again. . . ."

She looked at him. There was a battle going on behind her face. She took a deep breath and closed her eyes and sighed. She opened her mouth as if to speak and closed it again, struggling. . . .

Almost . . . almost. . . . He almost had her. He could feel it. Careful now. He had to say the right thing. "Mrs. Miller, if your husband were here, I'm sure he would tell you to help us. He would want you to tell us what you know, whatever it is."

"Morris," she said. Her eyes flew open. "Morris . . ." She sat up very straight again. "My husband and I, we always minded our own business. We never got involved. I always mind my own business. I don't know anything. I took a sleeping pill and went to sleep."

"We'll work on her some more," said Feeley.

Bernie nodded. He knew it wouldn't do any good.

"She might know something. Right now, anything would help," Feeley said.

"Yeah."

"You nearly had her. I was sure you had her."

"Nearly isn't enough."

"I wonder what pulled her back?"

Bernie knew. He had made a mistake. He had said the wrong thing. He should have known it was wrong. He had read the record and reread it. A couple. Childless. No friends. Living alone. Mr. Miller would not have told his wife to talk to the police. To interfere. To get involved.

He should have known it. Knowing things like that had made him an inspector.

Why had he made a mistake?

257

He felt drained. The tingling anticipation, the excitement, were gone. And also that other feeling . . . that was gone too. He knew what the feeling was. It was fear. He even knew what he had been afraid of.

He would have to do something to redeem himself to himself.

He dialed her number. Anna/Allegra.

There was no answer.

Chapter Thirty-four

"Louise King?"

"Yes."

The young man thrust an envelope at her and ran down the stairs of her house. Louise stared stupidly at it. Then she opened it. It was a summons.

"Damn bitches," she said. "Damn, mean, rotten bitches."

She wanted to run out into the street dressed as she was, in her red flowered mou-mou, and scream at them all, her neighbors, her former friends on the street, the still-marrieds, "Wait, it'll happen to you. You'll be alone and broke with your kids to raise, and then you'll beg me to let you come to one of my parties!"

They had actually done this to her. They were taking her to court to prevent her from having a party this Saturday night in her own home. They claimed her parties were a business, and the neighborhood was not zoned for business, only for one family residences. They claimed that the cars blocked their driveways, which was bullshit, and all the traffic was a public danger. They had been threatening to do it if she advertised another party.

What the devil was she going to do now? Over forty people had called about the party. Maybe thirty of them would show. There was no way to notify them not to come. She didn't take addresses or phone numbers. She ought to put an ad in the papers saying, "Party cancelled because of neighborhood rats."

She would have to try to get someone else in some other neighborhood to let her use a house again, but then she would have to split the take. It was probably Rae next door who had organized the whole campaign against her. She was probably afraid someone would step on her driveway twice and then it could be considered public property. They used to play mah-jongg together, she and Rae and the other bitches. So much for neighbors and friends.

Louise had gotten the house in the divorce, and nothing else. Not a dime to maintain it or the two kids. Her neighbors would all have been delighted if she had sold her house and come back every Thursday to play mah-jongg and regale them with sad or funny stories of the singles' world. It wasn't a world at all. It was a marketplace.

She caught sight of herself in the gilt-framed door mirror in the front hall. "Fat Louise." If only a woman could be sold by the pound, she'd be a millionairess. "Fat Louise." That's what they all said. She has a real pretty face, if only she weren't so fat. If she hadn't been so fat, she wouldn't have lost her husband. It didn't matter that Frank made her look like Twiggy by comparison. It was OK for a man to be fat. And bald. And stupid. And even sickly. Her latest best friend, Dotty, was about to be married to a man ten years older than she was, who also had a pacemaker. And was bald and overweight besides. "He reads," Dotty said. "He actually reads books and goes to the theater and the ballet and loves good music. The only man I've met like that in eight years."

"You've met hundreds of women like that. You've met me. I read. I go to the theater and ballet when I have the money, and I adore classical music."

"But you can't make love to me," said Dotty.

"Can he? At his age?"

"It works about half the time," Dotty said.

Which was a better average than her own ex, Frank, had. She really had no right to complain now. She had wanted the divorce. No one believed her because Frank was so rich. That was all he cared about, being rich and getting richer. It never occurred to her that after the divorce a man so rich would leave the state and not send money for his kids. He was out west somewhere, with a new wife, probably getting richer. She could try to track him down, and then what? Try to get him to send money? The law said he didn't have to if he lived in another state unless the state had reciprocity with New York. She could fight it. She could spend her whole life fighting it, and maybe even win and get him thrown into jail for non-support. By then her kids would be senior citizens. Besides, it wasn't the way she wanted to spend the rest of her life. She really was awfully damn glad to be rid of him. She was still young, still pretty. She had lovely, thick black hair and she took care of her face. No one ever caught her without makeup, no matter how early in the morning.

The trouble was, she had a lot of talents, all suited to being a rich man's wife. Her best talent was giving parties. She was trying to use it to earn a living for herself and her two children. Now the damn bitches did this to her! And the damn cops who helped them and gave out tickets to people parked in the street who came to her parties. It was one of those private streets where no one was allowed to park except in the driveways without prior arrangement with the police.

To hell with them all! What she needed was a big piece of homemade chocolate cake. If anyone was ever going to love her, he would have to love her fat.

She went into the kitchen.

When the bell rang again, she brought the piece of cake to the front door with her. The man standing in the doorway was very big. Tall and broad-shouldered, with thinning dark hair and dark eyes and a great smile. She thought he looked delicious.

"Hi," she said.

He held out his ID. "Inspector Bernstein."

"I already got the summons," she said.

"You did?"

"Yes. Is this another one?"

"No. Not at all. I need your help. But check the ID first."

"I did. You take a rotten picture."

"I do?" He looked at the picture. "You think I'm better-looking than that?"

"Much."

"Thanks."

"What can I do for you? Are you collecting for the PBA? They don't send inspectors for that, do they?"

"Not usually. I only want to ask you a couple of questions."

"Ask away."

"Aren't you going to invite me in? Your neighbors are watching."

"How do you know?"

"I'm a maven on such things. I can see a curtain move a quarter of an inch from across a street."

"You're right. They are watching. They want to make sure I'm not running a party. A singles' party. They think there's something declassé about it. Something that demeans the neighborhood and lowers property values."

"Is that what the summons is about?"

"Yes. Come in. Would you like a piece of chocolate cake? Homemade."

"Why not?" He followed her into the kitchen. Her dress billowed out like a huge red sail. She cut him a tremendous piece of cake. "Coffee?"

"If it's no trouble."

"Food is never any trouble for me," she said.

"By the way, I should tell you that you don't have to talk to me at all at the moment. I'm a New York City cop. I have no jurisdiction here."

"But you could get it."

"Something could be worked out. I didn't take the time. Do you want me to?"

"No. At least, not yet." She bent to pour the coffee; the loose dress fell away from her body. She wasn't wearing any underwear. For a second, he was afraid her huge breasts would slip out and land on the table. It seemed to him she had to bend over a long time to pour one cup of coffee. "It's about my parties, I suppose."

"In a way. You ran a party on Saturday night, in Manhattan."

"I run a party every Saturday night. And Wednesday nights. It's how I make a living. I fill a need. What's wrong with it?"

"Nothing. I'm interested in the one last Saturday night."

"You should be interested in the one this Saturday night."

"Why?"

"Because you could come to that one."

"Thanks very much. I'm married."

She shrugged. "The good ones are always taken."

"How do you know I'm a good one?"

"I'm a maven in such things," she said. She leaned over to refill his cup and he looked alarmed again. He said quickly, "I'm interested in a woman who was at the party. Anna Welles."

"What does she have that I haven't got?"

"A yellow plastic umbrella," he mumbled.

"What?"

"I said, 'Do you know her?'"

"Not very well. She used to live on this block, but she wasn't in my group. She didn't play mah-jongg."

"Whose group was she in?"

"I don't really know. None, probably. She was a homebody type. It's not one of the friendliest blocks in the world. No one seeks anyone out. I think she may not be particularly assertive. Her husband left her for a younger woman. It kind of destroyed her."

"How do you know that?"

"The bitches gossip a lot. About everyone. They gossip about me, too, but I don't give a damn."

"Are you divorced?"

"Yes. But I was the one who wanted it. I said to Frank one night, 'Frank, I want a divorce.' He said, 'Huh?' It was the most conversation we had had for a year. The most intercourse of any kind, in fact. More coffee?"

"No, no. Thanks." He held his hand up. "Wonderful cake. Anna was at your party on Saturday."

"It's possible. I run so many parties, I can't remember who was where when."

"I believe you asked her to drive you home. Is that correct?"

"It's possible. My car has been on the fritz. I usually ask a few people, in case one backs out."

"Did she drive you home?"

She thought a minute. "Saturday was in Manhattan. . . . No. Someone more interesting came along rather late. I got a ride with him. There are fringe benefits to my parties."

"Did Anna leave alone?"

"I don't know. Look, I set up a party. People pay their admission and go in. What they do after that is their business. I don't keep tabs on them. They're all adults."

"Hey . . . I thought we were friends. What are you getting so mad about?"

"I'm not mad. I'm just . . . animated. I'm sorry. There's been so much flak about the parties. Summonses and threats and nasty comments. I guess the world is controlled by married people, and they all feel threatened lately. I don't know what they imagine goes on at the parties. Group sex in the bathtub, I suppose. Listen, you go to a party and you pay your admission and maybe a guy asks you out for a cup of coffee when you leave. You split a sandwich with him and ask him all about himself and he tells you, at length, and then maybe he takes your phone number and maybe he'll call you and maybe he won't."

"Maybe he'll ask you to his apartment for coffee."

"Maybe," she said, looking at him directly, "and maybe you'll go and maybe you won't, depending on how lonely you are or how desperate you are or how hard it is that night for you to go back to your empty nest."

"Or whether or not you like him or not. As a person?"

She shrugged. "Maybe. That may or may not be a factor. It may only be for sex. Women need it as much as men, you know. You wouldn't understand. You're married. Probably getting laid regular."

He felt himself flush. She was sitting across from him, her large soft breasts with their protruding nipples outlined clearly under the thin, red-flowered fabric. Her posture was an invitation.

She laughed. "OK, Inspector, we're friends. Can you fix that summons for me?"

"No," he said.

She laughed again, waving her hand. It knocked a spoon to the floor. They both bent down to pick it up. Her dress opened again. He felt as though he had fallen into the billowing white breasts. He got the spoon first and straightened up and handed it to her. He thought she was laughing at him. Or was he laughing at himself? Bernie Bernstein, Good Jewish Boy.

He said, "You don't remember noticing if Anna left alone?" Louise closed her eyes and thought. She was one of those women who can eat chocolate cake and not eat the lipstick off her lips. They were bright red and shiny.

"Come to think of it, I do remember. She left alone. She got her umbrella. I was standing in the hallway talking to a couple of guys, and I saw her get her umbrella. I noticed because there were people waiting for the elevator and she didn't wait with them. She went down the stairs."

"Why did she do that?"

"Maybe she doesn't like elevators. People who get used to living in a house often can't get used to elevators. Maybe she didn't like the people who were waiting. I don't know."

"Maybe someone was waiting for her downstairs and she was in a hurry."

Louise shrugged.

"Did anyone else notice her?"

"I wouldn't know. We didn't talk about everyone who left. It wasn't a suburban bridge party."

"Did you notice if anyone followed her, or if she followed anyone else down the stairs?"

"She was alone. What's this all about? Is she in some kind of trouble?"

"I hope not. By the way, it would be better for everyone if you didn't mention any of this to her."

"Why would I mention it to her?"

"I don't know. Loyalty of the Sisterhood, maybe."

"I don't read *Ms.* Magazine, Inspector. I never see Anna, except at my parties."

"Did you happen to notice the umbrella? What color was it?"

"I didn't pay attention. I noticed her coat, though. It's the same coat she's worn for the past two years. A raincoat. Red. She could use a new one. She really got a screwing in the courts from that S.O.B. ex of hers if she can't get herself a new coat in two years."

He got up. "One more thing. I'd like a guest list of the people at the party."

"Are you kidding? What list? Who'd sign a list? Some of those people are married. You look surprised, Inspector Bernstein. Faithful, devoted, married Inspector Bernstein."

"I've been a cop too long to be surprised by anything," he said.

"Really?" She leaned against him and put her arm on his shoulder, smiling. Her lips were very red and shiny. Moist.

He smiled back.

"I like big men," she said.

He didn't move away. "Do you know a lot of the people who come to the parties? How long have you been doing it?"

"About two years. I know some. The regulars. And sometimes someone interesting comes in. Those don't get to be regulars."

"Know a man named Stone? George Stone? Was he at the party Saturday night?"

She moved back from him, but not by much. "The guy in the papers? The one who was killed?"

"The same."

"Gays don't come to my parties."

"Who said he was gay?"

"The papers."

"Papers, shmapers," he said. "They have to sell their merchandise. There's no proof of anything like that."

"If he was there, I didn't see him."

"I suppose if it got out that he was there, it could hurt your parties. Especially if he left with someone who later killed him. Is that what you're thinking?"

"It crossed my mind," she said.

"Who'd tell anyone? I'm not even officially here. I'm only getting information for myself. You could deny you ever told me anything, or even saw me. You can trust me."

She laughed, a very clear who-can-trust-a-cop laugh. "You could be taping this whole conversation."

"Search me."

"Don't tempt me. You're not thinking Anna Welles did it?"

"I never said that."

"She's a gentle soul."

"Anyone can kill, you know that."

Louise smiled. "She should have killed the son-of-a-bitch husband who walked out on her the way he did. And hung his body upside down in the village green as an example and a warning to other aged adolescents."

"Like men a lot, don't you?"

"They're all right for a roll in the hay. Sometimes."

"Was George Stone at the party?"

"If he was, I didn't meet him. I really don't know if he was there. I'd like to say he wasn't, but I really don't know. He might have come with a friend who would remember him. My parties are clean. They're meant to be a pleasant way for single people to meet. I have no real way of checking who comes and who doesn't."

"You never have problems?"

"Sure, once in a while someone gets drunk and stupid. Or a jerk comes in with some pot. Generally uses it in the bathroom. It isn't usual. These are middle-aged people."

"Stone had quite a lot of pot around, among other things."

"I read that. I didn't recognize the picture of him in the paper."

"That was an old picture. At least eight years old. A man can change in eight years. For one thing, he was much thinner now. And as you say, you aren't responsible for who comes to your parties."

"I don't know him." She moved closer to him again. Her shiny lips were very close. She had a pretty mouth. A pretty face. Smooth, bright skin and intelligent dark eyes and thick, lustrous hair. He felt her breasts move against his chest. "Of course, there could be something lodged in my subconscious. You could try to shake it loose."

"Would it work?"

"It would be fun to try."

He laughed. And then he stopped laughing. Faithful, devoted. Married. To whom? To a wife who had thrown him out?

"No one is asking you to desert your wife and family, Inspector."

"Will it prove to you we're not being taped?" He put his arms around her shoulders. He wouldn't have made it around her waist. He saw himself as though there were a mirror facing him. What was he doing? What was happening to him? He had never done anything like this before. He watched himself curiously, as though he were watching a stranger. A stranger he didn't understand. Or like.

"You aren't expected to carry me upstairs," she said. "I can walk." Her mouth was close to his. He brought it closer.

Louise knew spectacular things to do with her pretty mouth. She exhausted him. And finally she lay back and smiled at him and said, "I knew you would be good."

It was nice to hear.

"You do OK yourself," he said.

"What's also nice about you, you never said I'd be the most beautiful woman in the world if I lost fifty pounds."

More like seventy-five. "Are you planning to do that?"

"Hell, no. Not even for someone like you. Love me, love my fat."

"Did your subconscious shake up anything?"

"About Stone? No. I don't know the man. But you can come around anytime you want and question me. To hell with jurisdiction."

Before he left, he said, "Of course, you understand that if it turns out you're lying, and you do know that Stone was at your party, and you know who he left with, you'll find yourself with bigger problems than a summons."

"So what's up your ass, Bernstein," he said to the steering wheel in his car. "What's wrong with you?" He had had more sex in the last three days than he had had in the last three years. He should be feeling great. Relaxed. He didn't. What was he feeling so rotten about? Two consenting adults. And why did he have to be nasty to Louise at the end?

Other policemen did this kind of thing, even if he never had before. Women liked the macho cop image.

Could anyone say he was unfaithful to Linda?

It wasn't Linda he was thinking of. It was Anna/Allegra. He kept seeing her delicate, sad face.

So get back to the case, Inspector. What have we got? Possible witnesses:

Old man Russell:	Scratch that one.
Louise King:	Not much help there.
Mrs. Miller:	Maybe. But it would take a long time. And they would have to get tough.
Stevie:	Dead.

There was really only one way. Anna/Allegra. Herself. He would have to work on her.

But he had known that all along. Why had he been avoiding it?

Louise rested in her bath in a mountain of perfumed suds. Christ, how she hated men. They knew what to say to bring her down. She reached a plump, sudsy hand out to a plate on a table beside the tub and took a large bite out of a piece of lemon cake. That bastard cop, he didn't have to threaten her when he left. It was probably because he felt guilty. She really didn't remember anything more than she had told him. She finished the cake. He could have left her feeling good. He was great in the sack. A little mechanical, maybe, but that was to be expected. It was the first time, and he didn't know her. Probably the first time he cheated on his wife. He'd probably confess to her. Get it off his chest, and onto hers.

Why did he have to spoil it? She hated him. Him and all men. Pricks. All they were good for was a fuck, if they were good for anything.

She wished there were some way to get even. She was no Anna Welles. That poor trusting idiot had been screwed to the wall. What did they want to do to her now? They'd probably try to pin that lousy murder on her because they couldn't find the real criminal. Anna could no more kill anyone than she could fly without wings.

Louise smiled suddenly. She hoisted herself out of the tub—the water was getting cold, anyway—and pulled on a terry robe. "I'm going to call her. Tell her to be careful. Watch out for herself."

She looked up Anna's number in the Queens directory and dialed.

Chapter Thirty-five

There were some messages on his desk. He went through them quickly. Sean had called. And Linda, twice. And of course, the newspapers and TV. He'd have Feeley handle them. Feeley always seemed to be coming in and out right after him. And there were protests from Gay Rights groups. And also the landlord wanted to know when Mr. Stone's apartment was going to be released by the police. He thought again about going after it himself. And there were a good number of confessions and catch-me-before-I-do-it-agains. They all had to be checked out.

He dialed Anna's number. There was still no answer. He wondered what time she got home from work.

Maybe she wouldn't come straight home. She might go out after work and come home late. Then he wouldn't be able to see her. Damn.

She was a librarian. In Queens. There couldn't be a whole lot of libraries in Queens. He went to the outer office for a Queens directory. He waved to Feeley, who was sitting out there, and went back into his office.

I, ANNA

There were fifty-eight branches of the Queens Borough Public Library. He hoped he wouldn't have to call all fifty-eight to find out which one she worked in.

Chapter Thirty-six

Anna heard the alarm. It seemed to come from a great distance. She lay still, gathering the strength to move her hand through the surrounding silence. Mornings were the hardest time. Or was it nights? No reason to get up. No reason to go to bed. There were some species which died the instant they had outlived their usefulness, or at least, their function. A bee. A bee stung and it died. You're not even as intelligent as a bee, Anna.

There was something she was trying to remember, or was it forget? Was it a dream still hovering on the rim of consciousness? She couldn't remember, and it wouldn't let her rest. Had she been dreaming? Had she been asleep? When? Last night? Last week? Last year? When was the last time she had slept, really slept, relinquishing all consciousness? Total oblivion.

The ringing went on. She mustered all her strength and directed it to her arm. It moved slowly through the thick, soundless void around her and reached the alarm and pushed the button. The ringing stopped.

Gratefully, she closed her eyes.

Another ringing began.

That had to be the phone. To hell with it. The phone would have to fend for itself. She couldn't move her arm to shut it. She didn't listen to it. She wasn't aware when it had stopped. She only felt the silence drawing closer, like a blanket. She waited for it to cover her.

The ringing came again, shattering the stillness, scattering the pieces.

Who was calling her? They didn't care about her. No one cared about her. They didn't want her to sleep. They didn't care if she lived. They just didn't want to let her die. She should be allowed to die if she wanted to. There was an aborigine tribe in Australia whose members could will themselves to die. She had seen a movie about it. She had gone home after the movie and lain down and tried to will herself to die. But the damn phone rang. That was the trouble. That tribe in Australia didn't have any phones. That's what was destroying our power over ourselves. Our control over ourselves was draining out through the telephone wires. It was making us impotent. Telephones and television and the new morality. The fucking new morality. That's what the new morality consisted of: Fucking. Except for you, Anna/Allegra, the ex-Mrs. Welles. You have the telephone and the television, but for the rest, he ran away. Saw someone he liked better. Someone young, pretty; someone who wasn't sad. Men don't like sad women; they call them bitter. They like women who are cheerful and lively and pleasant and don't have troubles or dependents and don't talk about themselves because that interfered with their listening to the men. Why had he run away like that? Had she done something? Said something? Had she been too available? She was trying to fix a face in her mind. Simon? Bernie? Someone else?

The phone was ringing again. It kept interrupting her. Maybe it was Emmy.

Emmy didn't need her. Emmy was starting a whole new life. In the tribe in Australia, when a young man came of age, he set out alone to make his way somewhere. He went out without food or water, with only a loincloth. Not even a pair of designer jeans. Emmy had the jeans, at least.

And an old person, a useless person, could lie down someplace under a tree and call on death to come and get her. If you did that Anna, the birds in the trees would rain their droppings on you.

I have outlived my self.

Be still, be still, damn phone!

She leaped up and grabbed the phone wire and ripped it out of the wall. It made a terrible, fierce grunt. The sound chased away the silence.

The effort exhausted her. She sat panting on the bed, gasping for breath, holding the telephone cord in her hand.

All the same, she should call Miss Haines and tell her she was going to be late. Poor Miss Haines. Anna suspected she was a worrier; discreetly, quietly, a worrier. She had probably devoted her whole life to worrying. She worried about her mother, her cat, the library, the frightening increase in the theft of books and magazines. Worrying was all she had. John once said, when Miss Haines had annoyed him, "What she needs is a man."

"Everyone can use love," Anna had said.

"Love?" John had laughed. "What she needs is a good fuck."

That was supposed to cure everything. All the world's problems. It was the grandiose illusion of the male ego. The Invincible Prick. Or was it only a cure for women? It used to be that women weren't supposed to like it. Now it was supposed to be the thing they needed most.

And when did you become a man-hater, Anna?

"I'm not! I'm not!"

What about Miss Beige Spaghetti Straps? Doesn't she have some responsibility?

There is no responsibility anymore. And no more guilt. They are out, like the bustle and spats.

She had this terrible taste in her mouth again. She had better brush her teeth. She never used to have such a terrible taste in her mouth.

She ought to have some coffee, too. And music, to chase away the silence that was stealing back. She wasn't hungry. She was only tired. Even after she brushed her teeth and washed her face, she still wasn't hungry. But she went into the kitchen and found a bag of rolls in the freezer and a scissors to cut the bag open, and turned on the radio. ". . . Detective Feeley said, this morning, the police were following new leads in the brutal murder of . . ." She shut the radio. Well, what did you expect to hear on the radio?

Oh, something lovely. Something . . . "It was announced today on the news that love is back in style. Old-fashioned love: Until death do us part, and they lived happily ever after and their children really cared about them . . ." You won't say that, will you, Radio? Who needs you!

She put down the bag of rolls, picked up the radio wire and cut it with the scissors. "There," she said. "What you need now is a good fuck. That will fix you."

She went into the living room to the TV and cut that wire, too. "That goes for you, also," she said.

She went back into the bedroom and got into bed and covered her head with the blanket and tried to sleep, tried to blot out the man's face: Simon or Bernie or someone else. The nameless ones she always tried to forget.

Why hadn't he stayed? It would have been nice if he had stayed. It would have been warm, a live person holding her.

She should get up and go to work. She needed to keep busy.

"What you need, Anna, is a good fuck," she giggled. And tried again to sleep.

Chapter Thirty-seven

Bernie lost count. Somewhere along the list of calls, he got the answer he wanted. "Yes, there is a librarian here named Mrs. Welles."

"May I speak with her?"

"Is this Mr. Welles?"

"Why do you ask?"

"I'm sorry. I didn't mean to . . . It's only that Mrs. Welles hasn't come to work today. In fact, we are worried about her. She hasn't called to say she wasn't coming. She hasn't ever done anything like that. Never. In fact, Mrs. Welles's daughter also called, asking for her mother. She said she'd been calling all morning. The phone appears to be out of order. Her daughter is worried . . ."

He hung up and reached for his coat.

The phone rang. Impatiently he seized it and growled, "Inspector Bernstein."

"Bernie, this is Paul Thompson."

The mayor's office. He sat down.

"You white folks cuttin' up on each other real bad lately," Thompson drawled.

"You got no monopoly on cuttin', boy."

Thompson laughed. He said, in his Harvard-trained accent, "You'd never know it to hear the white folks talk. This is an official call, Bernie. The mayor wants you to catch the bad guys in a hurry. All this crime in the city is bad for business."

"You can assure the mayor we're working on it. We're doing our best."

"Your best is always good enough for me, Inspector. But the mayor wants you to hustle yo' ass."

"Yes, sir. We'll do that. You can give him my assurance."

"Catch somebody for something, for Chris' sake, man," Thompson said, and Bernie laughed, hearing the exact tone and voice and manner of the mayor. Shiny brown, beautifully groomed and handsome, Thompson should have been an actor.

Bernie said, "Yes, sir." He could have argued and protested and told Thompson everything the department was doing in every area. But he had stopped doing that long ago. Nobody ever listened; nobody really wanted an answer. Thompson went on talking. That was his job, to talk to people for the mayor. The mayor himself talked to the newspapers. That was his style. Thompson's voice droned out of reach of Bernie's consciousness. His mind drifted. How many mayors had he survived, all of them saying the same thing, each in his own style? There was the grandstander who marched into police precincts, declaring war on crime, with his retinue of reporters and photographers; that one swore he would clean up the city, or at least, Times Square. And there was the great liberal mayor who declared war on poverty and marched in the streets with the muggers and pimps he imagined he could use for his own purposes; and the one who looked like a little storekeeper and was never known to utter an obscenity in public or private. He should call up old Mr.

Russell. Russell would remember them all. But he said he
didn't remember Anna.

". . . bad stuff going down in the city," Thompson
was saying. "Too many muggers and murders and prosti-
tutes . . ."

"And singles' dances," said Bernie.

"What?"

"Nothing."

"You boys have got to get cracking. Crack down. Start
in the precincts. You have to clean up your house."

"I don't do windows," said Bernie.

Thompson paused. "Are you all right, Bernie?"

"Yes, Paul. Just kind of busy chasing the bad guys.
Could you get to the punch line? I'd like to get back on the
job."

"The public wants the police to earn their keep." He was
irritated. "Catch a crook, for Chris' sake. They want to
read about it in three inch headlines. Catch somebody.
Catch the S.O.B. who chewed up the prick. That'll make
good reading."

Right. If you let me get off the phone.

When Thompson finally finished talking, there was a
delegation of business men waiting outside to see him.
They refused to speak to anyone but the commanding
officer of the precinct. They stomped into his office
belligerently. They were very unhappy about crime in the
neighborhood: prostitution, murders, muggings, burglaries, double-parking. Bernie agreed it was bad. He sym-
pathized. He told them his troubles: too few police
officers, too little money, too many throttling rules and
regulations. But the police were doing their best. He cited
statistics. If the community set up a committee, his
community relations officer would meet with them and
they could work on the problems together. He ushered
them outside and introduced them to his community

relations officer, Sergeant Wilson, and rushed back to his office for his coat.

His phone was ringing again. He let it ring. He was reaching for the door, when it opened from the outside. Feeley was there.

"Your wife is on the phone," he said. "She's been trying to get through to you, and finally asked for me. I told her you had this delegation and I had her hold, and told the switchboard to put her through as soon as you were available."

Bernie hesitated. He couldn't embarrass Linda by walking away now. He strode back to his desk and picked up the phone. "Thank you, Feeley," he said.

Feeley nodded and went out.

Blandly, Bernie said, "Hello, Linda," and was surprised that he felt nothing.

"I've been trying to reach you all day," Linda said furiously. "I left a dozen messages."

"Two," said Bernie. "I've been trying to reach you for years."

"What's that supposed to mean?"

"What did you call about, Linda?"

"I don't know where you're staying."

"I haven't decided yet."

"You're staying someplace. I have to be able to call you. We have to talk."

"I don't have much time. I was on my way out."

"Do you think you could ever forget your job long enough to remember you have a son?"

"What do you want me to say, Linda? You locked me out."

"When are you going to see him again?"

"I don't know. You said he would be better off without me."

"I didn't mean for you never to see him."

"What's never? I saw him yesterday."

"You upset him terribly yesterday. I've never seen him so upset. You have to see him today. Try to make him understand."

"Understand what? What can I make him understand?"

"You HIT him!"

"You hit him all the time."

"But you never did before. You *hit* him. You *hurt* him. He feels terrible."

Bernie didn't answer.

"You don't love him. . . ." Suddenly she was crying. "You're hard and mean and callous. You're nothing but a cop! And Sean is no better than you are. He doesn't care, either. You're both the same."

"I'm sorry, Linda. I'm sorry if I've disappointed you."

"You've changed," she said bitterly. "I suppose you've found someone else. That's where you're staying. It didn't take you long. Well, you'll disappoint her, too."

"That won't be any concern of yours, will it, Linda?" he said coldly, and hung up.

He grabbed his coat again, and ran, before anything else could keep him from Anna. Peripherally, out of the corner of his eye, he thought he saw Feeley leaving right behind him.

Chapter Thirty-eight

A person is supposed to get out of bed. A person is supposed to brush her teeth and her hair, not with the same brush, of course, and shower and dress and eat breakfast and do the dishes and . . .

What the hell for?

Don't be a pain in the ass, Anna. Do what you are supposed to do.

That's what I did all my life. At least I tried to. Look where it's got me.

Get out of bed.

First I have to sleep.

You're never going to sleep and you know it. You've been trying all night. And all day. Get out of bed. You ought to eat something.

I'm not hungry.

You have to eat. You're beginning to look like a dried-out old prune. Concentrate on coffee. On the smell of it. There's nothing in this world like the smell of fresh-brewed coffee.

You see, I haven't become totally demoralized. I maintain standards. Coffee standards. I never drink instant coffee. I still grind fresh coffee beans and brew real coffee.

So get up and do it. Do it!

Someone pulled out the telephone wire.

You know perfectly well who pulled out the telephone wire. Don't be a wiseass.

But why? Why?

Was she mad? Is this what madness is? Do crazy people know they are crazy and are helpless to do anything about it?

How is it going to help you, Anna, to be deserted and alone and a dried-out prune and be crazy besides? How will it help you to be crazy? Especially if you know it.

How will it help Emmy?

Fend for yourself, Emmy. Have 'em, love 'em, and leave 'em be. She'd read that somewhere. She used to read a lot. She used to do a lot of things. The old gray mare, she ain't what she used to be. If you start to sing, Anna, with that voice of yours, I'll kill myself.

Think about the smell of coffee. Get up and follow the smell of coffee. . . .

There was a bag of rolls on the table. Damn lunatic thing to do, to cut the radio wire. Maybe it was a joke. She always had this silly sense of humor. How would she explain it to Emmy? Emmy didn't live here anymore. She didn't have to explain anything. To anyone.

Maybe she cut the telephone wire so she wouldn't have to explain why no one called her. They *couldn't* call, you see, because the telephone wire was cut. Or maybe that's why she couldn't call anyone. It wasn't that there weren't people who loved her. She *couldn't* call them if the wire was cut.

There is nothing to entertain me at home. No radio. No television. I will not go back to bed. I will drink my fresh-brewed coffee and eat my roll, breaking it into small pieces and buttering it, and spreading it carefully with marmalade, and I will even have a piece of that lovely, expensive cheese I splurged on last night. And I will color my hair. And I will go out. If there isn't a party or a dance or a rap, there is always a bar. A singles' bar. Why not? She had never tried a bar yet.

She had to go back into her bedroom to get to the bathroom. Could she get by the bed without crawling back in?

The tape recorder was on the night table. Sometimes Emmy recorded music from the radio on her tape recorder. Maybe if she played it now, it would help her. It would be a sound in the silence. She started toward it.

Stop! It's only an excuse to get close to the bed, to sit on it while you fiddle with the tape recorder, to lean back, lie down. . . . You want sound? You want music? You want the comfort of a live body? Go out. Get out of the house!

Maybe I can rest a while, first. I haven't slept. . . .

Am I crazy? Am I really crazy? I know my name. Allegra. No. Anna. Anna Welles. I know the day of the week. Tuesday.

I know the multiplication tables through 12×12 is 144.

But do you know right from wrong?

Which right and wrong? Right and wrong have changed.

Truth has changed.

Everything changes.

I must change, too.

Thank you, Simon. You have brought me up to date, into the new, changed world.

Maybe there is no longer right and wrong.

Maybe truth doesn't exist.

Maybe I don't exist.

There is only change.

If no one knows you are alive, if no one cares, do you exist?

If you don't know about anyone else, are you dead?

If I die here, alone, and no one knows, did I die? Did I ever live?

If I go crazy here, alone, and no one knows, am I crazy?

If a man do evil, and no one knows, was it evil?

But you would know, Anna.

She was trembling. She didn't know why, all of a sudden, she was shaking. Her mouth felt terrible. It was nauseating. She had to brush her teeth again, and rinse her mouth.

Something was happening to her, maybe had already happened. She had to get away. Terrified, she ran into the bathroom and slammed the door behind her, as though someone were chasing her.

Chapter Thirty-nine

The problem was, she couldn't decide what to wear. She thought about it all the time she was doing her hair and showering and putting on her makeup. And then she stood, in her old blue robe, in front of the closet and stared into it. Nothing was pretty. Nothing was new.

Maybe it was pointless to go out, after all. She had nothing nice to wear. All the other women always looked so attractive.

When the doorbell rang, she stopped and listened. It was the first sound she had heard for hours that she hadn't made herself. It confused her. She couldn't move. It rang again. It was only on the third ring that she was able to rouse herself and go to the door.

The big man was holding a bouquet of flowers. He looked excited. "Hi. Remember me?"

"You're the runaway," she said.

He laughed. "I'll explain if you'll let me in."

She didn't move.

He thrust the flowers at her. "Peace offering."

Slowly, in a reflex action, she put out her hand for the flowers. "Thank you," she said, also a reflex.

"I've been trying to reach you all day. Your phone is out of order. So I just came."

"I was getting ready to go out."

"Oh . . ." His voice showed his disappointment. "I'm sorry. I mean, I'm sorry for me. I'm glad for you if you have a date."

"It's not a date. I'm going out." She smiled that wistful smile that tugged at him. "Hunting, you might say."

She turned back into the apartment. He followed her. She went into the kitchen and opened a closet. There was a vase on a top shelf. He reached up and got it for her and filled it with water.

"The water isn't too cold, is it?" she asked. "Flowers shouldn't be put into very cold water."

He pushed up the sleeve of her robe and scooped up some water with his fingers and sprinkled it on her inner arm, as though he were testing it for a baby's bath.

"It's just right," she said, and smiled again. He pushed the sleeve down and held her wrist for a moment. His hands brought her wrist to his lips and he kissed it. They both flushed. When he let go, she put the flowers into the vase and fussed with them.

"They're lovely," she said. "Thank you." She carried them into the living room.

"You always seem to see me in this old rag."

"I like it. It's homey."

She shook her head and kept walking into the bedroom. Without thinking, he followed her. She didn't appear to notice him. She took off the robe and stood in her bra and underpants. It seemed a natural thing to do, uncalculated. She put on a white body suit and a pair of fitted black slacks. "I lost the safety pin. I ought to fix the hook," she said to herself. "It doesn't matter. The belt will cover it."

Somewhere he had seen a safety pin. It was on a dusty black glass table. Where was it?

She put on a silver stretch belt and high-heeled black sandals and started back to the living room, passing close to him. He said, "You've done something nice to your hair."

She became aware of him again, as if for the first time. She stopped. She was standing very close to him. "You're very observant. Why would a woman be unhappy with a man so observant?"

"Maybe I stopped being observant. Maybe I assumed she knew how I felt. She was my wife. I loved her."

"Maybe you ought to try again. Now you've learned something, you'll do better with her."

"The opiate of middle age," he said angrily. "The Dream of the Second Chance. Resurrection without death."

She started away. He seized her hand. "Is that what you're after? Is that what you're hoping for? A second chance?"

She smiled again, a smile like tears. "No. I don't know what I'd do with a second chance. I haven't learned anything from the first chance. I don't know what I did wrong with it."

"Then what do you want? What are you after?" he said harshly. "Revenge?"

Tears overflowed out of her eyes, as though they had been stockpiled there. She turned away.

"Why are you crying, Anna? What do you want?"

"I want," she said in a voice mocking and bitter, "I want you to hold me. Pick me up and lie with me and hold me. Nothing more. Only hold me. As though I mattered to you. As though you had known me for twenty-eight years and we had suffered together and laughed together and I were important to you." She smiled ruefully. Tears streamed down her face.

His large, strong hand caressed her cheek. "You are important to me, Anna," he said.

He lifted her easily and held her for a moment, close to his chest, without moving. She pressed her face against his shoulder. He kissed her hair and moved to the bed. He put her down gently and took off his shoes and his jacket and lay beside her. He held her, as he had so often held his Linda when she wept, month after month, when the blood began to flow; as he had held Theo when he was a small boy and he had cried and cried from some overwhelming, mysterious misery.

"I'm sorry," she said, trying to stop crying.

He held her closer, caressing her neck and her hair. "It's all right," he said tenderly, "It's all right. . . ."

She abandoned herself to her tears, trusting him not to violate her grief or offer empty comforting words.

She was crying the tears he couldn't cry.

He felt closer to her than he had ever felt to anyone in his whole life. He felt strong. Protective. It was a feeling like love. It warmed him. He was happy.

They must have slept. He felt her stir and opened his eyes. She lay pressed against him, holding him, her face on his neck.

"Thank you," she said.

His hand moved over her shoulder and her back. An image came to him of a bird with a broken wing. Her body relaxed against him.

"You're a kind man."

The room was warm and dim. It was as though it were suspended in space, removed from any other place, and they were alone together, safe, untouched by the world. They dozed and woke, drifting together. Obscurely, he thought she got up and then came back to him.

"You like taking care of people," she said softly.

"I suppose." He hadn't ever thought about it. All of his

adult life he had taken care of people: his mother, his sisters, his wife, his son. Even his job had been taking care of people . . . the whole city. "I suppose I did. I don't know if I do anymore."

"Do people ever change?"

"Sometimes a change is forced on you, and it forces you to change yourself."

"Only temporarily. For one instant, we are free; some powerful emotion releases us from ourselves; we can do something we would never have done. And then it passes and we are ourselves again."

"Maybe. I don't know." He kissed her. "All I know right now is that I'm starving. I've hardly eaten anything all day."

"Me, too. But it's so comfortable."

"Get up, lazy. We'll go out and get something to eat."

"Do we have to go out? We can have cheese omelets."

"I don't want you to fuss in the kitchen. Besides, don't you want to go someplace to dance?"

"I want to fuss. And we can dance here."

She moved to get up and he pulled her back and kissed her and then let her go. She got up and turned on the lamp beside the bed. He looked at her and burst out laughing. Before she could become offended, he pulled her back to him and kissed her again and then said, "Your mascara . . ."

She rushed to the mirror. Her tears had made the mascara run down in smudgy black lines along her cheeks and on her upper lids, giving her the ludicrous funny-sad look of a clown. The image startled her, adding surprise to her face. He laughed again.

Laughing too, she picked up a pillow and threw it at him and ran into the bathroom. He watched her scrubbing her face. She looked happy. Really happy. He was grateful to her. It was a long time since he had made a woman happy.

He put on his shoes. His jacket was hanging neatly on a chair. She must have put it there when he was sleeping. He had dropped it on the floor.

"Where's your radio?"

"It's broken," she called over the sound of the water running.

"Then how are we going to do all this dancing you were telling me about?"

She was patting her scrubbed face dry with a towel. In the soft light, without any makeup, she looked very young. Innocent.

"I'm sure Emmy left some cassettes with music. She was always taping things from the radio. There might even be something in the recorder now. Or you could sing for us."

He laughed. "My voice may be the reason Linda dumped me." He kissed her on her damp forehead and trotted over to the night table. He turned on the play button of the tape recorder. On the undershelf of the night table, folded neatly, was a sheet. It had a wild geometric pattern in black and brown. It struck a vague chord in his memory. Then the loud beat of hard rock invaded the room. It came from the tape recorder. Bernie started to laugh. "Hey, hey . . ." he called, gyrating and flailing his arms.

She came out of the bathroom with her towel, laughing too. He grabbed her arm and pulled her to him, snapping his fingers and grunting like the male voice on the cassette. She joined him, waving the towel like a burlesque queen's prop, and they gyrated together, bumping and laughing. And suddenly Anna's voice on the recorder broke through the music.

"There is something I'm trying to remember. It keeps slipping away, gliding in and out of my consciousness, like the moon tantalizing the clouds. . . ."

They stopped, frozen in their grotesque motions. The voice on the recorder was lifeless, without emotion.

"I want someone to understand," the voice said. *"I don't ask for forgiveness. I don't forgive myself. But I would like someone to understand. . . ."*

"Shut it," he whispered.

She didn't move.

"Shut the fucking thing!" he shouted.

She sank onto the bed, her head between her hands. "I can't. Can you?"

He saw the horrible, mangled creature on the ugly black and brown sheet that was hideously splattered with blood. He remembered where he had seen that dusty black glass table, with a safety pin. He sat beside her on the bed. He didn't touch her.

"It looked like rain all day. The sky was dark. In the rain the apartment closes in on me. . . ." The voice went on relentlessly. . . .

". . . I can't afford to keep losing umbrellas."

The faint whirr of the recorder continued into the silence and then clicked shut. The silence enclosed them both.

Bernie said miserably. "I'm a cop, Anna."

"I know," she said. "I think I've always known."

"Anna . . ."

"I never told you my name was Anna."

"No one has heard the tape but us. No one knows."

"Your ID fell out of your jacket when you dropped it on the floor."

"I can't turn you in," he said.

She didn't answer.

"He was slime. Filth. He deserved to die."

"You're a cop, not a judge."

"I love you," he said.

"You loved your wife once."

He shook his head. "We were healthy, beautiful young animals. One has to have suffered to love, really love."

297

"You don't know me."

"I know you. I know you better than I ever knew Linda. There are things one just knows. Just feels."

"People saw me."

"No one. No one remembers," he said.

"They might later."

He stood up and pointed at the tape recorder. He didn't go near it. "That's the only evidence there is."

She moved toward it slowly and shut it. It clicked. The room was terribly still. She turned toward him. He stood motionless, his arms at his sides.

"You could have made up that whole stupid thing. People do, you know. You should hear the lunatic confessions we get."

She moved to him silently over the carpet. "I'll go and put on some makeup. I won't be long." She put her arms around him and raised her lips to his. He hesitated. She felt him hesitate. She started away. He seized her and kissed her savagely, desperately, clinging to her.

Shaken, he let her go. She smiled at him, her old wistful smile. "Thank you," she said. She walked away from him into the bathroom and closed the door, and locked it. He heard the lock click.

He knew. When he heard the door lock, he knew. He rushed to his jacket. The gun was gone from his pocket. He dashed to the bathroom door and battered at it. "Anna . . ." he screamed. "Anna! Allegra! No . . . No! Wait!"

The gunshot boomed like a cannon in his ears. He heard himself screaming her name as he crashed through the door.

She had shot herself in the head.

There was pounding on the outside door. Someone was ringing the bell and banging on the door. He didn't know how, but he got to the door and opened it. He wasn't surprised to see Feeley.

"Are you OK, Inspector?"

He nodded.

"What happened?"

Bernie pointed toward the bedroom and followed Feeley in. While Feeley was in the bathroom, Bernie slipped the cassette out of the player and put it in his pocket.

Feeley came out looking pale. "Christ," he said. "How did she get the gun?"

"I had taken it out of my leg holster and put it in my jacket pocket. She took it."

"Is she . . . the one?"

"What one?"

"Did she kill George Stone?"

"Why would you think that, Feeley?"

"The umbrella." He pointed to an umbrella stand in a corner of the bathroom. It held one umbrella. Yellow. Plastic. Bernie hadn't even noticed it.

"What umbrella, Feeley?" he said. His voice sounded distant, as though it were coming from far away. "Why?"

"Inspector?"

Why had he listened to the tape? Why hadn't he destroyed it immediately? Why hadn't he gone to her at once, taken her in his arms?

"Are you sure you're all right, sir?"

"I'm a cop," said Bernie.

Feeley looked at him, at his CO standing like a statue. Then he saw a young, lithe Bernie leap out of a car, gun drawn, yelling, drawing fire to himself that would have gone into his careless partner's back. He saw him again, his own leg bleeding, crawl, under a storm of bullets, to pull his wounded and unconscious partner out of a building under siege.

He went back into the bathroom and uncurled Anna's fingers from off Bernie's gun. He wiped it clean with his handkerchief, then wiped the doorknob. With his gloves on, he pulled out drawers and emptied them on the floor and scattered the contents over the room. He found Anna's purse and took out the wallet and removed the bills and threw the rest on the floor. Then he got Bernie's jacket and tossed it to him. Bernie was standing like stone beside the bed. The jacket fell to the floor. Feeley went over and picked it up. "Put it on," he said firmly.

Bernie didn't move.

"You looking for some kind of official investigation, Inspector?"

"I destroyed her."

"I would guess someone else started it."

Bernie started toward the bathroom. Feeley blocked him. "A cop is only required to be a cop. He isn't required to be a saint. Also, I owe you." He put Bernie's jacket around his shoulders. "Let's go."

He turned Bernie around and moved him toward the door. In the living room, he stopped to throw some pillows and books around on the floor. He opened the outer door cautiously, with his gloved hand, and peered out. There was no one in the hall. He got his arm under Bernie's elbow and hustled him out and down the stairs and into Scanlon's car, and drove off, fast.

Bernie stared straight ahead, seeing nothing. "How am I different from a common criminal, Kevin?" he said dully.

"You're not. You're imperfect, like they are. Like we all are. I always figured you didn't know that."

Bernie didn't answer.

"They got the man who killed Stevie. Caught him trying it with another kid. In the bus depot." He was silent a moment. "You want to talk, Bern?"

"No."

Kevin nodded.

Alone, in his hotel room that night, Bernie cried. It was the first time since the death of his father that he had cried.

Chapter Forty

The early edition of *The New York Times* carried a brief story of a Queens woman, Anna Welles, who had been murdered in an apparent burglary. Police believed that she had been in the bathroom at the time of the burglary, or had attempted to escape there since the door had been broken in. Mrs. Welles had been shot in the head. Her wallet had been emptied of all cash, and drawers and shelves had been ransacked. There were no clues as to who had commited the crime. Since there was no sign of forced entry, it was presumed that the woman, who lived alone, had let the perpetrator in herself, or that she had not locked her door. Police again warned area residents to keep their doors locked and not to open them without first ascertaining who was there.

The late edition did not carry the story. The space was taken by a story about an attempted mugging of an elderly couple outside a Manhattan bank.